R O M A N

MEN OF THE FALLS BOOK 2

NEW YORK TIMES AND USA TODAY BESTSELLING AUTHOR

MELANIE MORELAND

ROMAN -Book 2 Men Of The Falls
by Melanie Moreland
Copyright © 2024 Moreland Books Inc.
Copyright #1210684
ISBN Ebook 978-1-990803-75-8
Paperback 978-1-99-0803-72-7
All rights reserved

MORELAND
BOOKS INC.

Edited by Lisa Hollett of Silently Correcting Your Grammar
Proofreading by Sisters Get Lit.erary Services
Cover design by Feed Your Dreams Designs

Readers with concerns about content or subjects depicted can check out the content advisory on my website: https://melaniemoreland.com/extras/fan-suggestions/content-advisory/

Roman Costas

Powerful. Intensely private.

Cold. Dangerous.

When he unwittingly puts an innocent woman in danger, he does something he

never planned.

Becomes involved.

He didn't anticipate the feelings Effie Warner brought out in him.

He didn't expect the woman he rescued to become his world.

All he knows is that he'll burn down the city to keep her safe.

No matter the consequences.

DEDICATION

Sometimes you write a book for yourself.
This is it.
I hope you enjoy.

DEDICATION

CHAPTER 1
ROMAN

I pulled my glasses off my face, dropping them onto the stack of paperwork in front of me.

God, I hated paperwork. I rubbed my eyes and stood, walking to the large windows in front of me. Niagara Falls in all its glory met my gaze. Its never-ending rage mesmerized me. So much power from something as simple as water. A flowing stream, peaceful and calm, belied what danger lurked beneath it at the end.

Much like me.

That odd thought made me laugh, and I shook my head at my wayward thoughts, strolling to the bar and pouring a finger of scotch. I tossed it back, the liquid gold coating my throat and helping to ease the tension in my shoulders. I set down the glass before I was tempted to have another. It was only eleven in the morning, and although I could handle my liquor, I didn't want to be drinking this early in the day by myself. If my right hand were here, he'd be happy to sip some scotch and talk shit for a while, but the bastard was away on his honeymoon, leaving me short my most trusted employee, which was beginning to cause issues.

I glanced at my desk and the necessary evil that waited for me. Despite hating the paperwork, I liked what it showed me. Our bottom line was strong. Ironclad. It grew monthly. Our holdings were vast and diversified. Aside from the money we laundered through the casinos, the businesses themselves made my brother and me very wealthy.

I sat down, almost grateful for the knock at the door that interrupted me.

"In," I called.

The door opened, and Franco stepped inside. I tamped down my impatience. "What?"

He came closer, his face and neck damp, showing his fear. He should be scared—I was still pissed over the situation he had come to talk about.

"You better have good news."

"We found her, boss."

"Fucking hallelujah. She should never have got away."

"I know Tony feels bad—"

I cut him off. "I hope her pussy was fucking heaven and makes up for the hell he's in now."

Fresh sweat beaded on his forehead. "You want me to bring her in?"

"No. Downstairs. I don't want her in here."

"Okay, boss. I have her there already. I thought so." He lifted his eyebrows as if expecting praise. He was lucky I didn't cut his balls off. He was almost as much to blame for this as Tony.

"Someone better be watching her."

"I got two men on it."

I indicated the door with a tilt of my chin. "I'll be down shortly. She better not have fucking touched anything on my desk. Or I'll be touching you—with my fist. You understand me?"

"On it."

He scurried off, and I turned to my bank of monitors. The entire far wall was covered with them. I could see and hear any part of the casino with a tap of my finger. I entered a code that showed me parts the public never saw. I zoomed into the lower office. It wasn't like this space at all. Up here, I had a view, an opulent office, and a set of private quarters, including a luxurious en suite. The office downstairs had cement walls, a simple desk, and a sofa. A couple of visitor chairs. Filing cabinets. Windows that looked onto the street—the view uninspiring. It looked like an office. I met with people there when I wanted total privacy. Especially when I wanted to make them uneasy.

Like the woman sitting in the visitor's chair, attempting to look bored and unaffected. I tapped the zoom, getting a closer look.

Tall, blond, slender, with big tits. A pretty enough face. She was relaxed back on the chair, pretending not to be uncomfortable. But I knew she was. Those chairs were designed to be that way. If you were sitting in them, I didn't want you there for long. She crossed her legs, swinging one foot impatiently. Four-inch heels adorned her feet, her toes a bright red. The polish matched the lipstick on her mouth.

She was the sort of woman I might gravitate to. Pick up at the casino or bar and take upstairs to fuck. Then walk away from and forget about.

But she didn't interest me in the slightest. Except for one thing.

She owed me money. A lot of it.

I stood and buttoned my jacket, adjusting my tie so it was straight. I stopped in front of the mirror and made sure my hair was in place. Image, after all, was everything.

Then I went down the private elevator to collect what she owed me.

She turned her head as I walked in, shutting the door behind myself, the lock slipping into place with a loud click. She watched me stride to my desk and sit down. We regarded each other silently. This close, she wasn't as attractive as she appeared on camera. She looked hard, the lines on her face cleverly hidden with makeup. Her hair wasn't naturally blond, and I would bet my last buck her tits weren't real either. Her lips were too full, her dress too revealing, and her makeup applied with a heavy hand. Her eyes were a dark brown. Flat. Cold.

She no doubt saw the same lack of emotion reflected in mine.

"You've been busy, Miss Warner."

"Ms."

I inclined my head. "*Ms.* Warner. Marianne, right?"

She tossed her hair, showing a fringe of dark on the top. Not a blond at all. I had a feeling nothing about her was real.

"So, Marianne. You must be good."

"I beg your pardon?"

"Not only did you convince my floor manager to extend your credit far beyond what it is allowed, you somehow walked out of here without securing your debt. You wasted my time, my patience, more of your own money, and you cost me the wages of two men to hunt you down." I drummed my fingers on the wooden desktop. "I am not a man who takes kindly to my time and money being wasted."

I got another hair toss. "Not my fault your people fucked up."

I leaned forward. "I would be careful what you say next. Where is the sixty grand you owe me?"

She frowned. "Fifty."

I shook my head. "Interest, Marianne. And it grows daily. As does my anger."

"That's robbery!"

"You want to call the cops?" I asked. "Be my guest. Be sure you mention who you owe the money to." I pushed the phone her way. "I think you'll find yourself without much support."

She changed her attitude. Her skin paled under the fake tan she wore. It was a little orange in this light, reminding me of a pumpkin. For some reason, that made me smile, and I had to bite my lip to stop from doing so.

"Listen, I'll pay."

"Today. You will pay *today*."

"I can get it in a couple of days. I'm trying. I really am. Fucking Effie is proving to be difficult."

"Fucking Effie?"

"My damn sister. She has the money. I just have to get it."

"Your sister is your account manager?" I asked, for some reason. I didn't care where she got the money, just that she got it.

She huffed out a breath, pumping her leg in vexation. "No. Our mom died and left us money. I spent mine. Goody-Two-Shoes that she is invested it and opened a stupid little breakfast place. I just need her to loan me some of her cash. I'll pay her back. I just need one good night at the tables."

I sat back, weary. She was a typical addicted gambler. Always looking for the quick win. The right angle. The tip. Always in denial. Blaming everyone else for their losses. Unable to admit they were the problem.

"Perhaps your sister is right not to give you the money."

Anger flashed in her eyes, and she sneered. The carefully crafted veneer cracked, and I saw her true colors. "Righteous little bitch. Always lecturing me.

Marianne, you should do this. Not do that. Ha," she snapped. "Always staying in the safe lane. Leading her boring little life, living over her precious Bagels and Bites shop, working herself to the bone." She crossed her arms. "She'll give me the fifty thousand."

"By the time you get it to me, it'll be seventy."

She opened her mouth then shut it. A gleam appeared in her eyes. She leaned forward, her voice low, as if telling me a secret. "We could make a deal."

I lifted an eyebrow in question.

"I could work off the interest," she said coyly, pulling on a lock of her hair and leaning forward suggestively, making sure her tits were on display. "I bet I could relax those tense shoulders of yours." She fluttered her eyelashes.

I barked out a laugh. "Not even remotely interested, sweetheart. You may have used your magic pussy on my manager, but that shit doesn't work on me."

She sat up, annoyed. She swung one leg in aggravation, thinking hard. I could almost hear the cogs of her brain working.

"My sister. You could have my sister. I'll get the fifty, and you can have her for the rest."

Her words caught me off guard, which was a rare thing. "I beg your pardon?"

Her voice dropped more. "She's a virgin. I bet that's something in your world, right? You could have her for fun or sell her to someone for a night or something. Forever, I don't care. But that would probably make you more than the interest, am I—"

She didn't have a chance to finish. I was across the desk, my hand wrapped tight around her throat before she completed the sentence. "You're offering to *sell* me your sister? A human being? You would let her have sex with a stranger, or even a group of strangers, to erase a debt that you owe?"

She clawed at my hand, and I let go. "You are despicable," I spat.

"I thought your kind went for that sort of thing," she gasped, her voice rough.

"My kind?" I sneered.

"Mafia men."

"You have confused me with the Santinis. Go peddle your offer to them. I run a legitimate business here."

"With extortion on the side."

"You signed the agreement. You could have walked. I want my money, or you pay the forfeit."

"Oh, murder is legal here too?"

I crashed my hand on the desk. "Twenty-four hours, Marianne Warner. You have twenty-four hours to get me the total amount of money you owe me. Or pay the consequences. Your choice." I headed to the door, calling over my shoulder, "And my men will be watching you, so trying to disappear will do you no good."

I slammed the door shut behind me. "If you lose her, you're dead," I snapped at the two men standing outside and kept walking. I didn't have to look at them to know they took my words seriously.

In the elevator, I let my head fall back with a groan.

Tony was going to have to suffer for this one.

CHAPTER 2
ROMAN

Back in my office, I shook out my shoulders. Smacking Tony around hadn't done much to ease the tension I was feeling. He was still suffering from what I had done to him the other night to be of much use to me.

I grabbed the bottle of scotch and sat at my desk, pouring out a finger and swallowing it down. I did it again then leaned back into the rich leather of my chair.

Her words kept playing in my head. *My sister. Virgin. Have her for fun or sell her. For a night. Forever. I don't care.*

The callous tone she used and the uncaring attitude shocked me. In my world, family was important. Big or small. You protected those you loved, using whatever means necessary. You didn't offer to sell them to the highest bidder as if they were a piece of unwanted art. And somehow, a woman doing it to her sister seemed even worse. Men were notoriously bastards. To deal with a woman that coldhearted was unusual. Not the first for me, but she seemed viler than I expected.

I turned in my chair, staring at the rushing water again. It was almost one now, and I knew below me, the gaming rooms would start to fill soon. Locals, tourists, people visiting from Toronto or the States for the day would begin spending their money. Most had a budget, and for so many, it was simply a fun day. For some, it was a career, based on calculated risk. Others, like Marianne, it was an addiction. They all fed my bottom line. I stood and went to the window, sipping my scotch. I had built this casino from the ground up. As soon as the laws changed and the casinos could be privately run, I had put my plans into action. I owned two casinos. One here in Niagara Falls, one in Toronto. Plus now, I had another one currently under construction in Ottawa. They made money. All were the perfect front for laundering the dirty money for the family.

I sighed as I thought of the family. There was only me and my brother, Luca. My father had run our family with an iron fist. Weakness was punished. Strength rewarded. We were molded in his image. Pitted against each other constantly.

We should have hated each other, but instead, it forged a silent but strong bond between us we never let him see. My father's methods were old, violent. His ways of seeing things outdated. When he became ill and died, Luca and I changed things. Began to legitimize what we did and how we did it. Luca fronted me extra money, and I followed my dream of running real, profitable businesses. He carried on with overseeing the cities in our territory, but in a different way. Fear was still high. Intimidation ruled. But many of my father's methods had disappeared. The ways we made money changed. Hard drugs were out. We no longer handled weapons. Art, smuggling, legalized drugs, other ways of making millions were where Luca excelled. Others of our generation learned newer ways of operating within the syndicate. New territories were mapped out, more respect shown. A few elders were still around and in control, and until they were gone, some things stayed the same. Many of them scoffed at us. Called us soft.

We were anything but.

Luca's world crossed into mine far more often than I liked, but it was necessary. You didn't mess with the Costas brothers. As much as I disliked the business, I enjoyed the perks. The fear. The power. The violence. At least, I used to.

But lately, I had grown tired of it all. I still exercised my rights to it, but I was weary.

Yet, this was my life.

I leaned my head on the glass, the colors of the water mixing and swirling. Hypnotic. Enthralling. Calming somehow.

My phone rang, and I tossed back the last of my scotch and answered it. "Luca."

"Roman. How are things?"

"Good. Business is good."

"We need a meeting."

"When?"

"Tonight."

"Fine. I'll come to you. My table will be waiting."

"See you at seven."

I hung up without replying.

I looked out the window of my SUV, watching as the city went by. Leaving the busy tourist section where the casino was, I frowned at the area we were in.

"Why are you taking this route?"

"Roadwork, boss. We'll be back on the highway in a few moments," Ralph, my driver, assured me. "I put cold water in the fridge for you."

"Thanks."

I stared at the scenery. It was hard to recall at times there was an entire bustling town that lived and thrived far from the spectacle of the Falls. That away from the tourists and bright lights, families worked and existed, having little to do with the remarkable Falls.

Ralph cursed. "One more detour, boss. Right into the neighborhood, and then we'll be done." He turned and drove down some streets, the area pretty and well-kept. He stopped at a light, and I turned my head, frowning at the sign I spotted.

Bagels and Bites.

The vehicle started forward. "Stop!" I commanded.

The SUV came to a jarring halt. "Boss?"

"Pull over."

Ralph did as I asked. I had no idea why I did so. I climbed from the SUV, telling him and my security guy, Carlo, to stay in the vehicle. Carlo wasn't too happy about that, but he didn't argue.

I opened the door of the small restaurant, inhaling the fragrance of fresh-baked bread. Savory and rich.

Yeasty and warm. My stomach growled, and I decided to get something to eat.

I approached the counter where a woman was filling a basket. She looked up as I cleared my throat. She was young—maybe eighteen, with blond hair. Pretty.

Was this the sister?

"May I help you?" she asked.

I scanned the menu. "Toasted bagel, light cream cheese, no butter."

"What kind?"

"Whole wheat."

"Boring," she mumbled. "Anything else?"

"Black coffee."

She turned and grabbed a bagel, cutting it and popping it into the toaster efficiently. She peered into a container, then stuck her head in the doorway. "Effie! I need more light cream cheese!"

For some reason, I tensed.

Nothing prepared me for the woman who walked out the kitchen door.

Tiny. Curvy. Maybe twenty-five. Her hair was so dark it resembled a raven's wing and hung down her back in a thick braid. She had a heart-shaped face with rounded cheeks and full lips that begged to be kissed. And her eyes. I had never seen eyes like them.

Wide, under arched eyebrows and long, dark lashes were a pair of the most unique blue-violet eyes. Her irises were rimmed in black, the combination so stunning, it caught me off guard. So did her expression. Her mouth curved naturally, a sweet smile gracing her face.

Innocence dripped from every tiny, delicate inch of her body. She was incredibly beautiful. Even in a simple apron and jeans, she was stunning.

And unknowingly sexy.

And her sister wanted to sell her for a night. Or forever.

"Effie?" I questioned without thinking, rage beginning to build in me at the thought of the callousness shown by her sibling.

She looked startled, meeting my intense gaze. "Yes. How may I help you?"

"You're Effie Warner?" I repeated, thinking how the name suited her. It was soft and fluid, much the way she appeared. The urge to reach out and touch her cheek was so powerful, I had to clench my hands into fists. The sensation was disconcerting, to say the least.

"Yes, I am. I'm sorry, do I know you?"

"I met your sister."

A shadow crossed her face, and her pretty lips frowned. "Well, I'm sure that was pleasurable for both of you. I'll repeat my question. How may I help you?"

"Has she been here? Today?"

"No." She crossed her arms. "Look, Mister——"

"Roman," I interrupted her.

"Look, Mr. Roman, whatever your beef is with her, I can't help you."

I tried not to smile at her salutation. It was rather adorable.

I hated adorable.

"How do you know it's a beef?" I asked.

"I highly doubt you came in here to sing her praises. If she ran over your dog or stole from your liquor store, you have my deepest apologies. But I can't fix it."

I had to tamp down the urge to laugh.

Liquor store?

"That'll be four fifty," the blond girl said, handing me a cup and a bag.

Effie pushed the food my way. "On the house. I'd appreciate it if you would leave."

I didn't take exception to her words. In fact, I was proud of her. She recognized me as dangerous. Wanted nothing to do with me. I could respect that.

I pulled out my wallet and took out a fifty. I pushed it into the tip jar on the counter.

"If your sister comes to you, say no," I instructed Effie.

She frowned. "What?"

"Just say no," I repeated.

"I have no idea what you're talking about, but if you've met her, then you know that rarely helps with Marianne," she said dryly.

"Do it anyway."

I picked up my food, and I left before I could say anything else.

My bagel was tasty and the coffee hot and strong. The surprise was the small, wrapped cookie in the bag. I hadn't ordered a cookie—in fact, I never ate sweets. I looked at it, noticing it was shaped like a sunflower and decorated perfectly. I ate and sipped as the car sped along the highway toward Toronto. I gave in to temptation and had the cookie. It was decadent, tasting buttery and rich, the icing adding to the flavor. Why I consumed it, I had no idea.

I watched the skyline appear, the downtown core almost invisible with all the growth the past few years. My building sat among the skyscrapers, a place of play for people in the city and its visitors.

I couldn't get Effie out of my mind. Those eyes. The lips that smiled naturally. The sweetness of her expression. The sheer unworldliness that surrounded her. I forced down the rage that continued to rise up. The image of the innocent woman Marianne Warner was so eager to use to help settle her debts kept reappearing in my head. I shuddered, thinking what some men would do to Effie. How quickly that innocence would be replaced by pain. How fast her life would be destroyed.

Something in your world, Marianne had said.

Effie Warner wasn't my type. Nor did I pay for women and sex.

But many did. And they wouldn't care anything about her. Her life before or after wouldn't matter a thing to them.

The casino, Maple II, came into view, and I admired the building. Different from the Maple in Niagara Falls, which followed the flow of the land around it, this building was tall and thin, but still eye-catching and formidable.

My phone buzzed with a text from the men I had trailing Marianne to tell me they still had her in their sights. She was sitting in a bar, drinking and talking to someone on the phone.

I rolled my eyes. Running up a tab she would skip out on, no doubt.

I pushed the thoughts of Marianne and Effie from my mind. I had a meeting to concentrate on. Carlo opened my door, I stepped out of the SUV, the doormen and staff immediately jumping to attention. I strode through the large doors, stopping at the front desk, bypassing the line waiting.

"Mr. Costas. How good to see you," the manager greeted me. "What can I do for you?"

"My suite and my table at seven."

"Your suite is ready as always, and I'll make sure your private booth is cleared and waiting."

"Send up some scotch."

"Immediately."

I headed to the private elevator, ignoring the looks and the obvious attempts to get close by a few women. I wasn't in the mood for company. I dismissed Carlo, knowing I was safe in this building. He would stay close, but out of my way.

I was in the mood for physical release, but not of a sexual nature. I didn't want a stranger around me right now, and I never kept anyone on "retainer," so to speak. I texted the trainer at the gym located downstairs. When he replied he was there and up for some sparring, I smiled.

Since sex was off the table, then punching someone would have to do.

I hoped he was ready.

CHAPTER 3
ROMAN

I looked around the restaurant, pleased. Booked solid as always, it was bustling. It was an elegant but comfortable place to dine. My table was in the corner, shielded from view and always available to me or my brother. I stood as Luca appeared, and we greeted each other with a hard hug before sitting down. I had a scotch waiting for him, and we clinked glasses and then each took a sip.

He undid his jacket, running his hand down his tie. "How are you, Roman?"

"Good. You?"

"Busy. Exhausted. Happy. All of it."

"How is Justine?"

A real smile played on his mouth. "My bride is amazing."

I chuckled. Luca and Justine had met, hated each other, and fallen in love in a matter of days. Once they did, there was no stopping him, and they were married quickly in Vegas. They'd had another wedding that had been held at the Maple in Niagara Falls, the room packed full of people, some of whom had no idea that over half the guests were dangerous. Justine was the daughter of a powerful man, but she had lived a life away from the business, so her friends were clueless.

But it had been a joyous day, and I had to admit I had never seen my brother look so happy. I had sent them on a monthlong honeymoon to Europe, stepping in and running both sides of our business while he was gone. I was relieved when he returned, happy to turn back over his side of the business. It gave me a headache.

"You need to bring her to dinner at the Maple. The new chef is incredible. I stole him from the top restaurant in Italy."

He grinned. "I'll do that."

We discussed casino business for a while, never bringing up anything else. That would happen behind closed doors where there was no chance of being overheard. He waited until we had eaten the main course and coffee was in front of us, and he cleared his throat.

"What is it?" I asked. "You asked me here for a reason, and you've been edgy all dinner. Do we have a problem?"

He wiped his mouth. "In a manner of speaking."

"What is it?"

"Nonna."

I frowned, putting down my cup. "What? Is something wrong? I saw her two days ago, and she looked fine. Her doctor keeps me up-to-date with everything, and he hasn't—"

He held up his hand, silencing me. "She's fine, Roman."

I relaxed back into my chair. "What, then?"

"I had dinner with her last night. She's worried."

"About?"

"You."

I blinked. "Me? I'm healthy as a horse."

"Not your physical self, Roman." He toyed with his napkin. "I can't believe I'm saying this to you." He took in a deep breath. "She is worried you are lonely, and she wants to see you married. She asked me to talk to you about settling down."

For a moment, all I could do was stare. Then I began to laugh. He looked at me, smiling, lifting one shoulder in defeat. I understood. When Nonna asked you to do something, you did it.

Our mother died in a car accident when we were young, and her mother, our nonna, came to live with us. To the outside world, she was a tough woman, but she loved us fiercely and she was the only soft spot in our world. She always took our side against our father; she cared and quietly nurtured us, wanting more for us than what my father did. It was because of her I had such a strong bond with Luca.

I picked up my coffee cup and drained it. "How does she propose I settle down? I'm at one of the casinos, the vineyard, or meetings all the time. My schedule is crazy. It's not as if I have time or desire to date. I have no interest in a relationship. I'm happy as I am."

"She is not. Her greatest dream is both of us settled, a couple of great-grandbabies on her knees, and then *she* will be happy. She was pretty damn adamant."

I clasped his shoulder, giving it a shake. "Tell her you talked to me and I am going to try to make her dream come true. That should ease her mind. I'll make a point of going out a couple times and being photographed. You can show them to her. That should appease her."

"The only thing that is going to appease her is a ring and some babies, brother."

"You work on the babies. I have no interest in that. Or a wife. Nonna is going to have to give up on that dream."

He lifted his eyebrows. "You know she won't. And you are her favorite, so she's not going to let this go. If I fail in my mission, she'll make it hers."

I groaned. "Maybe I should send her on a trip for a while. Home to see her sister for a few months. Get her thinking about something else."

He shook his head. "Not going to work."

"Fine. I'll speak to her myself."

"That's another thing. She says she is lonely in that big house of yours and you're never there."

"I've been busy with Aldo away and the new build. Plus overseeing the casinos."

"She would tell you to reprioritize and hire more people. She wants company—aka great-grandbabies."

A smile pulled on my lips. "So she wants me to marry someone and knock her up so she has company? I could just hire another companion for her, although I've lost count of the number I've gone through."

"We tried that. She scares them all away."

I laughed. She did. Gemma Volare suffered no fools. If she liked you, you were accepted. If not...

"She stays busy with the vineyard and overseeing the house and grounds. She bustles around there like she is fifty, not seventy-six."

"You are still her favorite, Roman. Nothing makes her happier than spending time with you."

His statement was true. I was Nonna's favorite, yet it caused no bitterness between us. She loved us fiercely, but Nonna and I had a bond that was strong and unbreakable. She lived with me for that reason. I would never allow her to be on her own. She'd looked after us as children, and it was my job to do so as she aged.

"I'll talk to her. I'll go see her tomorrow."

I hadn't been home in a week, except to see her quickly. I had been living in the suite beside my office because my hours were so erratic. I'd been on the floor more than usual and busy with the plans for the new casino in Ottawa and some other projects. I would have to do better for Nonna.

And I would.

But the wife and kid thing… That wasn't going to happen. It wasn't in the cards for me. Now, I would just have to figure out how to convince her of that.

I was back at the casino early—before five the next morning. I went through numbers, checked reports, and once satisfied, decided to head to the house and see Nonna. I felt badly that I had been neglecting her, but with my right hand, Aldo, away on his honeymoon, problems with the build in Ottawa, and the general craziness of running the businesses, I had been too busy. Much to Carlo's chagrin, I had him stay at the casino and I drove myself. My personal car was bulletproof, and I wanted to be alone. Due to the roadwork, I ended up driving past the small diner again. Without thinking, I pulled over and parked, heading inside. It was busier, the breakfast crowd getting their morning nourishment and coffee. I sat down at one of the few tables, waiting.

Effie walked out of the kitchen, carrying a tray. She served the customers, refilled their coffees, then turned to me, her smile fading a little when she saw who it was.

"Oh. You."

I smiled at her. "Me. Not happy to see me?"

"Not really."

"Shame. You look very pretty today."

She snorted. "Yeah. Right. Now why are you back again?"

"I enjoyed my bagel."

"I see. You know, there are lots of bagel places. I can recommend one a little more upscale for you."

I shook my head. "No. Your coffee is excellent. So was the bagel. I would like a dozen to go."

"Whole wheat?"

I smirked and shook my head. "Cinnamon raisin."

"Anything else?

"Do I get another cookie?"

"Those are for lunch orders only."

"Every lunch gets a cookie?"

"Yes."

I stroked my chin. "Interesting gimmick. Did your sister contact you?"

She frowned and huffed. "I really don't see what business that is of yours."

I regarded her steadily, and she began to fidget, breaking her silence. "Yes, okay, she did."

"Tell me you said no."

She sat down, leaning close. I found her eyes as mesmerizing as the day before, the color indescribable. Blue. Violet. Amethyst. It changed with how the light caught her irises. "She told me she was in trouble and needed money. I offered her what I had in my account, and she said it wasn't enough."

"Still generous of you. You are aware you wouldn't get it back, correct?"

"Yes. She wasn't very happy. Then she informed me it was all my fault, which is her usual go-to when she is upset. She left, and I haven't heard from her since."

The last word I had from my men was that Marianne was in her apartment and had been there since last night. No doubt she was concocting a scheme to run. I had half a mind to let her go. The money meant nothing—it was the principle. And although I didn't like her, hurting women was a no-go for me. I planned on putting the fear of God into her and making her work off her debt, but in the end, that would probably be too much trouble. I would figure something out.

I stood. "Good. Best you don't."

She stood as well, barely coming to my chest. I felt like a giant beside her.

"Do you know what sort of trouble she's in?" she asked.

I nodded.

She leaned closer, and I caught her scent. Sweet and floral. It was as delicate as she appeared to be, and for some reason, it made my cock twitch.

"Are *you* the reason she's in trouble?"

"*Marianne* is the reason she is in trouble. Nothing else."

She pursed her lips, making me want to kiss them. I blinked at the thought. This woman was not my type at all.

"My bagels. And a coffee."

She turned and walked away, and I admired her round ass. Her yoga pants showed it off to perfection, and I wondered how it would feel cupped in my hands as she rode me.

I shook my head as my cock got right on board with the idea, my pants getting tighter by the second.

A moment later, she came from the kitchen, a bag in one hand, a coffee in the other. I approached the counter, smiling as I stuffed another fifty in the tip jar. Then I did something I hadn't planned. I reached into my breast pocket and pulled out a simple white card with my name engraved on it. I wrote my cell number on the back and pressed the corner, then slid it into the pocket on her T-shirt. "If anything happens, or you need something, that is my private cell. Call me."

"Why would I—"

I cut her off. "Anything. Call me."

And I left.

I opened the windows, resting my arm on the door as I drove down the familiar back roads. It still amazed me that sandwiched between Toronto and Niagara Falls were many large, rolling estates. The soil and climate here made excellent wine, produced amazing crops, and made you think you were in the middle of a vast countryside, not a few miles off one of the busiest highways in the country. I slowed as I came to the gates, admiring the stonework that ran the perimeter of the grounds. To the average eye, my estate looked much the same as many. To someone really looking, they would see the differences. The higher stones, erected in such a way they were insurmountable. The gates that were shut. The active guards who were visible. We hosted no wine tastings or large groups. Picnics were not allowed. You needed an invitation to come on to my grounds.

And I rarely extended one.

The gates rolled open smoothly. Henry smiled down at me. "Good morning, sir."

"All well?"

"Quiet as usual. Your nonna was out here yesterday, deciding on new flowers for the garden."

"Please tell me she was driven down."

His lips quirked. "She drove herself in the golf cart. Brought us lunch and told us all what we needed to be doing."

"Of course she did."

He shrugged. "Well worth pulling some weeds for one of her killer paninis."

I chuckled. "She is a tyrant."

He stood straight. "Wouldn't have it any other way."

I nodded and drove up the long, winding driveway, looking at the vineyard, spotting the workers who were busy. I pulled up to the house, sitting for a moment to look at it. The expansive courtyard with the fountain bubbling was surrounded by flowers. The house was shaped like a big U. The center contained the spacious kitchen, dining room, and living area. To the right were my nonna's rooms, a couple of guest rooms, a gym, and a spare office.

The left was my wing. A huge primary bedroom, en suite, my office, and three other bedrooms. The back of the house boasted a large pool, sitting areas, and a grilling kitchen. All were surrounded by trees and flowers. There were more vineyards toward the back of the property, as well as our wine-making rooms and storage.

I had bought three estates and turned them into one, guaranteeing my privacy. I loved wine and though the art of making it was still much of a mystery to me, I hired the best and I was slowly learning. I found it fascinating. We had won some awards for our vintages, and we were gradually building a good reputation. I stepped out of the car and headed to the house, finding Nonna at the back under a shaded spot, a pot of coffee on the table and a plate of flaky croissants beside it.

I bent and kissed her cheeks, greeting her with affection. There were few I showed any to, but she was the top one.

"Nonna. You are looking well."

I sat down, putting the paper bag on the table.

"What is that?"

"Bagels. The kind I know you like. I had one yesterday, and it was delicious. I brought you some for your breakfasts."

She nodded. "Thank you, *piccolino*."

I laughed. "I am not a little boy anymore, Nonna."

"You will always be to me." She poured me a coffee, pushing the cup my way. "Nice you recalled I am still alive and here."

I shook my head. "Nonna, I saw you three days ago. I'm a busy man."

"Three days," she sniffed. "You live here, yet you are never in your bed. For days, you are gone. I should go into a home. At least others are there to talk to."

I leaned back, sipping my coffee. "You would hate it. You have plenty of people here to talk to. I know you've been at the gates, ordering the gardeners around, and no doubt in the vineyards telling everyone how to do their jobs." I sniffed the air. "The kitchen too. I smell the sauce."

She waved her hand. "I have to stay busy to avoid the loneliness."

"Do you want to go to Italy? See Zia Mary?"

"No."

"I'll hire you a companion."

"No!"

I leaned forward. "Nonna. I am trying to run a business. Many of them. It is crazy right now. But I'll be around more. I promise. I will come home three nights a week. We will have dinner."

"Four."

"Three, and I'll find a companion for you. Someone to play cards with and gossip."

"I do not gossip. Nor do I require a stranger as a companion. I prefer family." She met my eyes. "My own family."

I sighed and took her hand. It felt paper-thin, the spider web of veins underneath it almost purple in color. The skin was becoming translucent, looking fragile. But her grip was strong and sure. "Nonna, I am not getting married or settling down soon. Luca is married now. So is Aldo. They will have little ones soon. I am sure they will be happy to have you bounce them on your knee."

"I want *your* children on my knee, Roman. I want to know you are settled and happy. I cannot leave this earth and join my Roberto until I know that."

I shook my head. "If my being single keeps you here, I'm selfish enough to become a monk, Nonna."

That made her laugh. She cupped my face. "You deserve to be happy. Settled with a wife. Fill this house, these grounds, with your bambini. Live, Roman. You are not living. You are existing."

I had no idea how to respond to her. My phone rang in my pocket, and I ignored it. It went silent and rang again. Then again.

Nonna dropped her hands.

"Take the call. It must be important."

I stood, answering. "What, Franco? This better be important."

"Boss, that woman is on the phone for you. She says if she doesn't talk to you, you'll kill her and it'll be on my head. She's called five times."

I didn't have to ask who. No doubt, Marianne was calling to beg. Nonna picked up the bag and carried it into the kitchen.

"Patch her through." I waited until I heard the line click. "Ms. Warner."

"Finally," she snapped. "I'll have your money—all of it—tonight by nine. I'll bring it to your office."

I was surprised at her words, and I wondered who she had hoodwinked this time.

"Your sister came through?" I questioned.

"In a manner of speaking. She gave me an idea."

I furrowed my brow. "I will text you a number. You call it when you're at the casino. Someone will come out and get the money. You wait while we count it."

"I'm not going to stiff you. I have a plane to catch. I'm leaving this country. I got a chance at a new start."

I pitied the man she'd talked into helping her. His life was about to become a nightmare.

"You have until nine. Be grateful I'm being lenient."

I hung up.

At nine fifteen, Franco came into my office. "Counted, boss. It's all there. I put it in the vault in your office downstairs. I cleared her marker."

"Not counterfeit?" I asked.

"No."

"Was anyone with her?"

"Some goon. I didn't recognize him."

"Did we get the exchange on surveillance?"

He looked at me like I was crazy. "Of course."

"Get it for me."

I sat at my desk, waiting for the feed. I watched it closely. Marianne got out of a nondescript car, waiting beside it. A man came from the passenger side, holding an overnight bag. I zoomed in, studying his face. I didn't recognize him at all. His expression was dour, he was dressed in black, and he didn't look any happier about being with Marianne than she was with him. He hardly looked like a new lover, but maybe he had simply sent her protection. I zoomed out and watched the rest of the exchange.

Franco came on to the screen, and he took the bag and Marianne's arm. She appeared to argue with him, but her escort said something and she walked with Franco, who handed the bag to another one of my staff. Ten minutes later, he answered his phone and said something to Marianne. She tossed her hair and threw her hands up in the air, talking and gesturing. I doubted anything she had to say was complimentary. She looked at the camera and flipped the bird with both hands, then marched to the car and got in, slamming the door. They drove off.

I sat back, rubbing my chin. Something felt off. Where did she get the money? Who bankrolled her?

Then I shook my head. It didn't matter. She'd paid her debt, she'd been banned from my casinos, and I'd had my security head send her photo and information to other owners I knew. She was going to have to find a new way to feed her addiction.

I reached into my pocket, my fingers encountering the small, plastic-wrapped item. I pulled out the cookie, looking at it. Before I'd left, I helped Nonna wrap her bagels. She liked them cut in half and would freeze them so she could toast them whenever she wanted to.

She loved the dense bread for breakfast. We finished, and she reached into the bag, holding up the cookie.

"What is this?" She frowned. "It seems strange to put a cookie in a bag of bagels."

I took the cookie from her hand. "Must have been a mistake."

I distracted her and slipped the cookie into my pocket. I was certain a pretty violet-eyed woman had purposely put it in there.

And the thought of her doing so brought a smile to my mouth that didn't belong there.

I returned to my desk, clicking on a program, and checked the location of the tracker I had in the card I gave Effie Warner. It blinked, slow and steady, at the location where her diner and home was located. She was there. Safe.

Then suddenly, it stopped. Vanished. I refreshed the program and got nothing. I picked up the phone. "Bring me that bag. Now."

Franco arrived a few moments later, handing me the bag. I snatched it from his hands, opening the zipper. I grabbed a stack of the cash, pulling a hundred from it. I held it under the light, examining it. There was nothing. I breathed out a sigh of relief, then tried another. My heart dropped when I saw it. The tiny mark in the bottom right corner. I looked at another. Pulled stacks from the bag, checking them. Most of them were marked. It was a mark I recognized. Loathed beyond anything else.

"Get my car. Now!" I roared.

Moments later, we were driving toward the Bagels and Bites shop. It was dark, but I headed up the stairs I had noticed the other day at the side of the building. The door at the top was ajar, and I pushed it open, stepping inside, my worries confirmed. The place was a mess, indicating a struggle had happened.

And Effie was gone.

Marianne had taken my angry words to heart.

"You have confused me with the Santinis. Go peddle your offer to them."

She had done exactly that. How she found them, I had no idea, but she had.

Once they finished with Effie, she wouldn't be recognizable. Her life was over.

And it was my fault.

Marianne might have pulled the trigger, but I'd put the gun in her hands.

And I couldn't take it back.

CHAPTER 4
EFFIE

I shut the door of the diner and locked it, a sigh of relief escaping my lips. For a moment, I rested my head on the cold steel frame, then straightened and turned to look at the small space. I was tired today. I felt…off, I supposed was the best word. Tense. I had felt that way since yesterday.

Since the moment I'd walked out of the kitchen and met the gaze of the stranger.

My first thought was two-fold. He was incredibly handsome. Tall. His hair was a chestnut brown, the ends tipped in gold as if he spent time in the sun. His skin had the same golden hue, kissed by the outdoors. His shoulders were broad, tapering to a lean waist, and he looked fit. His eyes were green. Dark. Intense. The second thought was that he was also frightening. When he spoke my name, it sent a shiver down my spine. Well-dressed and looking out of place in my little shop, he had an air of authority about him. He exuded power. A hint of malevolence.

You didn't cross this man.

And while he never smiled, and there appeared to be no change in his rigid demeanor, I was sure he had teased me. But his gaze remained intense, and his lips never curved into a smile. Not even a small one. Oddly enough, I wanted to see him smile.

Instinctively, I wanted him out of my shop. Away from me. Why he was there, I had no idea, but I wanted him gone. When he asked about Marianne, my suspicions were confirmed. What he wanted or needed, I wasn't interested in.

His warning caught me off guard. He spoke as if I should listen to him. Obey him. That pissed me off.

I had heard his order. Simple. Straightforward businessman. Bagel and coffee. Nothing rich, sweet, or fatty. Just to be a pain, I dropped in one of our cookies. Normally, they only were given out with lunch orders. Soups, sandwiches, that sort of thing. But because I felt he wouldn't want it, I put it in the bag. I didn't expect him to eat it, but rather be annoyed by it. I had a feeling he didn't like "extras."

Marianne did come by after I closed the diner. As usual, she breezed in, launching into her latest diatribe. It was always about Marianne. Her troubles. Her life. She was always the victim, and whatever was occurring, it was never her fault. She never bothered to ask about anyone else. Especially me. I was used to it.

"I need money."

"Again?"

She frowned. "I haven't asked for a while."

"You didn't pay me back the five thousand you needed last time. Or the loan before that."

She crossed her arms. "Look. I'm in serious trouble. I-I crossed the wrong people this time. They're threatening to hurt me. You have to help me." She paused. "Please."

I was surprised at her tone. She never said please. I studied her. Under her makeup, she looked ashen. She seemed genuinely upset.

I sighed. "I have five thousand you can have."

She shook her head. "I need seventy."

I felt my eyes widen. "Seventy grand? I don't have that sort of money."

"You must. You invested a bunch of money from Mom."

"Into this place. I bought this building."

She shook her head. "Stop holding out on me."

"I can't help you."

She got mad. "So now I have to suffer. This is all your fault!"

I rolled my eyes. "My fault? You're the one who owes someone seventy thousand dollars. Marianne, what have you done?"

"Give me the five. I'll take it and hit the casino."

"No. That's what got you into trouble in the first place, isn't it?" I knew she liked to gamble, but I had no idea it was to this excess.

She grabbed her purse. "I should have known coming to you was useless. I thought you'd help me. You're my sister, for God's sake." She paused dramatically. "Mom would be so disappointed."

I shook my head. "She would be glad one of us has a level head."

She dropped her act and glared. "Fine. You leave me no choice. You brought this on yourself."

And she rushed out of my apartment.

As usual, a run-in with her left me tired. I heated up some soup left over from the day and sat on my sofa.

Marianne and I were only half sisters. Same father, different mothers. Her mom died when she was seven, and her father married my mom. I came along about a year later. It was always a competition with her. She had to be more loved. The center of attention. Our father doted on her, but it wasn't enough. She had to be number one with my mom as well. There was always drama. Odd illnesses, problems with bullies at school, anything to get the notice she craved. It irked her that Mom treated us equally. Our lives were different growing up. Marianne was always the star, and I was the shadow in most cases. Unlucky, my dad had muttered once since I was prone to accidents— even as a baby.

When our dad died, Marianne acted out, which kept Mom's attention on her. I was sad about our dad dying, but I kept it to myself, trying to be a help to Mom. Marianne demanded constant reinforcement that Mom loved her. As I grew older, I wondered if, at times, it drained my mother. I knew it certainly drained me, and Marianne's demands for affection from me weren't frequent. Usually only when she wanted something. It took me a while to figure out that pattern and to learn to say no.

When Mom passed four years ago, Marianne went off the rails. She acted as if the inheritance we received made her a millionaire and was unending. I bought this building and opened my diner. The rest I invested for my future. She blew it all on trips, shady deals, and, lately, a gambling addiction I suspected had grown larger than I knew, if today's visit had been any indication. I knew if I cashed in my investment, I would never see a penny of it back, and for the first time, I refused her.

Then this morning, the mystery man had shown up again. Once again, his presence overtook the space he was in. He was dressed more casually today, his shirt sleeves rolled up, no suit jacket on, but still he was overwhelming without even trying.

He almost teased me about the cookie, but I wasn't sure he knew how to tease. It was more a question. Why I added a fresh-made cookie to his bag of bagels, I had no idea. For all I knew, he was taking them home to feed his children. Although the thought of him being a father seemed ludicrous. He was cold and removed. Emotionless, almost. I highly doubted he was a doting father or husband. He questioned me about Marianne again, and when I asked him if he was the reason she was in trouble, he summed it up perfectly.

"*Marianne is the reason she is in trouble,*" he stated firmly.

Then he did the oddest thing. He tucked a business card into my pocket and told me to call him if I needed him. For anything.

I couldn't imagine ever calling him. I rather hoped he wouldn't come to the diner again. He made me edgy and tense. Yet when he left, I felt melancholy instead of relieved. It was very strange.

Still, for some reason after I showered, I slipped his card into the pocket of the loose shirt I changed into. I read his full name. Roman Costas. I had called him Mr. Roman, and he hadn't corrected me. He probably couldn't be bothered.

I ate my soup and rinsed the bowl and spoon, sitting on the sofa, making a list of things I needed to do. I heard footsteps on the stairs outside, and I sighed. I was sure I knew who they belonged to, and I braced myself for another argument with Marianne. Except the sound of heavier footsteps followed the lighter treads, and I frowned. Maybe it wasn't her.

Except, it was her knock. Always impatient. Three sharp raps that sounded suspiciously like "let me in." I always knew it was her.

Yet I was cautious before I opened the door. I looked through the peephole, confirming it was Marianne. I didn't see anyone else. She looked angry.

"I'm not in the mood for an argument, Marianne."

"I'm not here for one. I'm leaving town, and I wanted to say goodbye."

I frowned, still hesitating. "Are you alone?"

"Yes," she snapped. "Just open the damn door."

Every instinct in me screamed not to believe her. "I heard two sets of steps," I replied.

"My ride followed me partway. Making sure I didn't trip. You can wait in the car," she said to someone over her shoulder.

There were retreating steps, and I sighed in relief. I had been reading too much into this.

I opened the door, and she stepped in. But as I turned to follow her, pushing the door shut behind me, something stopped it. I spun around, but before I could do anything, a large man pushed his way inside. I stumbled back with a gasp, staring at Marianne.

"What's going on?"

"You should have said yes." Her eyes narrowed. "At least you'll be useful to me. Finally."

The man advanced, and fear shot through me as I saw the rope in his hands. I turned and ran, crying out as he grabbed my braid, jerking me back. I fought against him, clawing at whatever flesh I could find. He howled as my nails found purchase on his face, and he dropped me. I raced to the other side of the sofa, staring at him. Marianne leaned against the wall, looking bored.

"You're only making it worse," she said.

He lunged and I dodged, desperate to put space between us. I needed to get to my cell phone on the small dining table. He crashed into the side table, knocking over the reading lamp and sending it and my pile of books to the floor. I grabbed my phone, pushing buttons, hoping to hit emergency. He yanked it from my hands, grabbing my wrists and pulling me, my cell phone falling to the sofa. I crashed into him, lifting my knee to get his balls, but he moved too fast, spinning me. My leg knocked the other table, sending my knickknacks and purse to the floor. I fought, my terror building. I caught his face with my elbow. His groin with my foot. I struck out everywhere I could, knowing if he got me out of the apartment, I would never see it again. My life would be over.

"Stop this, Marianne!" I pleaded.

She rolled her eyes. "You had your chance."

The man yanked my hands, tying them up behind me. I lifted my head, butting his face, and he grunted, letting me go. That was all I needed. I rushed for the door, thinking I would make it, except Marianne stuck out her foot, and I fell, hitting my head, my face taking the brunt of the fall.

The last thing I heard was her laughter.

I woke up to the dark. I blinked, wincing, the pain in my head and my face a throbbing beat. I tried to move, but it made me nauseous. Closing my eyes, I took in some deep breaths, confused.

Where was I? What had happened?

My eyes flew open as my last memory hit me. Marianne. A strange man. Rope. Falling.

Other images hit me. A second man. Marianne tossing my apartment, screaming she needed five minutes. The sounds of drawers opening, items being thrown around. Glass breaking.

"Where is it?" she shrieked.

"No more time. We have to go," one of the men replied.

I felt pain as she kicked me, her high heels pointed and dangerous as more agony radiated through my body. I was lifted like a sack and tossed into a trunk, drifting in and out.

Then I woke up here.

Slowly, inch by inch, I checked my body. I could feel my legs and arms, although they were heavy. I opened my eyes again, carefully lifting my head. The rope was gone from my hands, but one leg was chained to the floor, the heavy links rattling as I moved. It took everything in me to get into a sitting position. I let my head hang to my chest, breathing in the dank smell. The floor beneath me was damp and cold. I felt the walls behind me—they were cement as well. I was in a basement or underground somewhere. Chained up. As my eyes adjusted, I saw a small window set up high, but it was boarded over outside. I could make out the faintest glimmer of light, so I knew it was now daytime. What day or the exact time, I had no idea.

My breathing became erratic, and I forced myself to calm down. I had to figure a way out of here. Out of this.

Except I wasn't sure exactly what *this* was.

Only that it was bad.

I swallowed, my throat dry and painful. I felt along my head and face, wincing as my fingers brushed my skin. I tasted the coppery tang of blood in my mouth.

Tears formed in my eyes, and I let them fall.

What did these men want? I lived a simple life. Kidnapping me did them no good. All they would get was a few grand and a mortgaged diner. I had nothing of great value. My investments were small.

Surely Marianne didn't think holding me here would make me give those to her?

A shiver ran down my spine. Maybe in her mind, she thought I would.

Maybe she was desperate enough to try.

A door opened, and heavy footsteps pounded my way. I pushed myself back against the wall, bracing myself.

A light came on, and I shielded my eyes.

"Well, look who's awake."

I didn't answer.

"Cat got your tongue, baby?" a voice sneered.

I swallowed. There were two of them.

"Where-where is Marianne?" I forced the words from my dry throat.

They laughed. "Long gone."

"What do you want?"

"Money. Lots of money."

"I don't have lots of money."

"The men your sister sold you to do. They're paying us lots to keep you here."

The words crashed over me. I looked up, the two men standing a few feet away. One carried a gun. They both wore dirty hoodies and looked as if they needed a shower. One had claw marks on his face, and he glared at me with hatred.

"W-what?"

"You've been sold, baby. Your life as you know it is over." The one with the claw marks laughed, the sound making me shudder. "And I highly doubt you're going to enjoy it."

Sold.

Marianne sold me? As if I were a piece of furniture?

"No, please. Let me go."

They laughed. "Sorry, we get a big payday once we turn you over."

"No, you're making a mistake."

The one I'd clawed advanced, grabbing my shirt and hauling me to my feet. He was close enough I could smell his putrid breath and unwashed body. I tried not to gag, turning my face. He grinned, pushing closer. "The only mistake is that I don't get to have a go at you," he sneered. "But I can check out the merchandise," he added as he grabbed my breasts, squeezing them hard. I gasped at the pain as he increased his hold. "Get used to it," he advised. "I have a feeling pain is going to be in your future." He groped me again, and I sobbed. I managed to push him away, and he slapped me. I dropped to the floor, rolling into a ball as he kicked me.

Then he hauled me to my feet again, and something fell to the ground between us. He frowned. "What you got here?" He picked up the card that had come from my pocket, holding it up and squinting to read it. To my shock, he stepped back, handing it to the other man.

"What the fuck?" he said, then grabbed my face. I braced myself for more pain, but I saw the fear in his eyes.

"Why do you have a card from Roman Costas in your pocket? Whose number is on the back?"

The words were out before I could think. I grasped the only lifeline I had.

"That's his number."

"Why would you have his number?"

I lifted my chin. "Because he's my fiancé."

The man gaped and stood back. "Liar."

"Call the number and tell him you have me. See what happens." I bluffed.

They looked at each other and hurried away. They snapped the light off, leaving me in the darkness again. I crumpled to the floor.

I prayed with everything in me that my gamble was going to work. I'd seen the terror in his eyes when he read Roman's name. That terror was all I had.

ROMAN

I returned to the casino, furious. Livid. I headed straight to the computer room, opening the door so hard it slammed against the wall. My head guy looked up, lifting his eyebrows.

"Careful, Roman. Expensive equipment in here. Maybe have your tantrum somewhere else."

I ignored his words. Gordon was one of the few employees not scared of me. He knew how valuable he was to me.

"Why did the chip on one of the white cards you gave me fail?"

He sat back, regarding me. "If you recall, it's still being developed. It's not perfect. It could have been destroyed. Malfunctioned."

"It was on my screen one second, gone the next."

"Then the card was moved." He tapped on his screen, peering at it. "It shows it is active but undetectable right now. It's somewhere the system can't find it."

"Keep your eyes on it. I need to know the second it's back online. I need the location."

"Sure."

"Can you tap into traffic cams by Fireway Drive?"

He sighed, turning to another computer, typing away. "Not many around there. There is one on the corner by Third and Fireway."

"Perfect. Bring up the footage for the last two hours. Put it on the wall monitor."

He did as I asked, and we scanned the footage. It was grainy and dark, but I found what I wanted. A car pulled up outside the diner, and a man wearing dark clothes and a hoodie got out. A second car pulled up, and another man got out, dressed the same. A woman joined them, and I knew without a doubt it was Marianne Warner. I recognized the coat she wore from earlier. I checked the time stamp. They'd taken her before Marianne dropped off the cash.

"Fast-forward again until they come back."

My suspicions were confirmed when they reappeared, one of them carrying a sack over his shoulder that he put in the car trunk and sped off. Marianne got in the second car, and they pulled away, heading, I knew, toward the casino.

"Fucking bitch," I snarled. "That fucking cunt!" I slammed my hand on the desk. "Find that car, and tell me where it goes."

"I was about—"

I cut him off. "Now. I don't fucking care what you had planned. Until I tell you to stop, you're on this, you understand?"

He held up his hands. "I hear you. Relax, Roman."

I stormed from his office and headed upstairs.

Until I found either Effie or Marianne, relaxing was the last thing I could do.

CHAPTER 5
ROMAN

Midafternoon the next day, I was pacing my office. I'd been up all night. I had no idea why I was so upset. Marianne had done something horrendous, but the bottom line was, it didn't affect me. I didn't know Effie. We had no relationship.

Except, every time I shut my eyes, I saw her face. Those eyes. That sweet smile. The fact that I had inadvertently caused this chain reaction didn't sit well with me. Knowing those eyes would soon be pits of despair and that mouth would never smile again bothered me on a level I didn't understand.

The car Marianne was riding in showed her getting off at the bus station. I had no doubt she was headed to Toronto. Gordon dug around and found a plane ticket. She had departed late last night for Costa Rica. I couldn't find her there, but I had him tag her passport. If she came back to Canada, she would pay for her crime.

The car that contained Effie had disappeared quickly, and Gordon couldn't find it. The license plates of both cars were unreadable. No doubt purposely dirtied up or damaged so they couldn't be read.

The chip on the card I'd slid into Effie's pocket remained dark.

I had no doubt this was the Santini brothers. The one choice I had was to contact them. Offer to buy her back if I could get them to admit they had her.

I dragged a hand through my hair in frustration.

A knock at my door made me look up from my desk. "In."

The door opened, and Aldo walked in, tanned and relaxed-looking, his large frame filling the doorway. "What are you doing here?" I asked, surprised. "You're not due back for days." I hugged him. We had grown up together, and he was my closest ally and my right hand. I trusted him as much as I trusted Luca.

"I was getting restless. Vi thought we needed to come home early. From the look of you, I'd say I made the right choice. Gordon says you're furious over something, and you look as if you're about to explode."

"I fucking am."

He shook my shoulders. "Tell me."

I poured us a scotch, and he listened to what I had to say. He sat on the sofa, his large frame taking up almost half of the space. Growing up, we had always been similar in our build. But when we turned sixteen, Aldo hit a growth spurt and packed on muscle and inches. I was tall at six foot two. He hit the six-foot-five mark and outweighed me by forty pounds. He was a deadly shadow, at my side whenever I needed him.

When I finished telling him what had happened, he frowned.

"Atrocious, I agree. But when have you bothered before, Roman? We've seen and heard lots of horror stories. You walk away."

"I caused this."

"You care about this woman?"

"I care I destroyed her life for no reason other than my stupid mouth."

"You had no idea her sister was that horrendous."

"She is diabolical. Psychotic, I would say."

My intercom sounded, Gordon's voice filling the room. "The chip just came online."

"I'll be right there."

Aldo came with me, and we rushed to the computer room. "Can you get a lock on it?" I asked as I hurried in.

"I'm trying."

He tapped away, doing whatever computer geniuses did. He moved from keyboard to keyboard, mumbling to himself. "Just a little longer."

"I got the area. Not a good part of town. Way toward the west."

"Not surprising."

My phone rang. My personal cell phone. The one very few people had the number for. The caller ID said unknown number and I was going to ignore it, but knowing I had given it to Effie the day before, I glanced at Gordon. "Trace this. It could be her."

I waited until he nodded, and I answered.

"Costas."

"We have something of yours."

The voice didn't belong to one of the Santini brothers. It had no accent, and he was too young. I decided to play along.

"Something of mine?" I questioned.

"She says she's yours," he responded.

"If that something is five foot nothing with dark hair, it better be unharmed." I paused. "Or you're a dead man walking."

"How much is your fiancée worth to you?"

I blinked. *Fiancée?*

"What is your price?" I asked, realizing Effie had told them we were engaged. It was probably the one thing she had to bargain with. My name.

"The people who want her won't be happy if they don't get her."

"Not as unhappy as I will be," I ground out. Gordon indicated to keep talking. "What is your price?"

"We'd have to disappear."

He had no idea he and his accomplice would be disappearing permanently. As soon as I was close enough to put a bullet in their heads.

"We're not greedy. We just want to live comfortably. Two million." He paused. "Each."

Aldo's eyebrows shot up.

"It'll take me a little to get the cash."

"We're supposed to deliver her at six a.m. tomorrow."

"You'll only be delivering her to me. I'll have it by midnight. You can get a red-eye anywhere you want to go."

"We'll call with the meetup address."

He hung up.

I looked at Gordon. "Tell me you have that."

He nodded. "I assume whoever you're looking for is being held at 188 Warrington." He brought up an image. "The cell phone and chip both agree."

I stared at the run-down house. It was falling apart. I could see the basement windows were boarded over. The front door hung on one hinge.

"We'll be meeting sooner than that, boys." I glanced at Aldo. "You with me?"

He looked grim. "As if I'd miss this."

At nine-thirty, we drove past the house slowly, circled the block, then pulled up a few spots before the driveway where they couldn't see us. The neighborhood looked mostly deserted, but I wanted to be careful. The SUV had blacked-out windows so no one could see in, and with darkness encroaching, it was the perfect camouflage. I glanced at Aldo. "You ready?"

"Yep."

I turned on the video in the car parked two streets over. It was old and had a fake pizza delivery sign on it. "Set?"

John nodded eagerly. "I'm going to the door with the pizzas. They'll either lie and take them or say they didn't order them. I'll step back, and you'll come behind me. I'll disappear."

"Yes. Do not stick around."

A voice beside him spoke. "I'll slip into the SUV, and when you call me, I'll back it up into the driveway. You'll come out with the package, and we leave."

"Yes. Anything happens and you don't get my signal, you get the fuck out. Understand?"

"Yes."

I turned to Aldo. "Thanks for coming with me."

He nodded. "I always have your back. Even when you're starting a war."

"They won't know. The witnesses will be dead."

"Let's hope they're the only ones who know."

He was right, but I had to do this. I had no choice.

The old car pulled up into the driveway, and John got out, carrying two pizza boxes. "Let's go."

We followed closely, hiding to the side. John rang the bell, and a voice inside yelled out, "Who is it?"

"Pizza delivery," he sang out cheerfully.

There was a brief conversation inside. "We didn't order pizza."

"What? Is this 188 Warrington?"

"Yes. We didn't order it."

"Dammit, that's the second one this week. Look, do you want it? I have to throw it away, so if you want it, it's yours."

"What do you mean?"

"If someone's ordered and not given the right address, we have to chuck the pizza."

"Leave it on the step."

"Sure. No problem." He waited.

"What now?" the voice yelled.

"Don't I get a tip? You're getting free pizza. All I'm gonna get is a cuff upside the head for no delivery and then have to go back out to the right address. Bastards."

Even though this was a serious situation, I bit my lip at his whine. He was doing a convincing job.

"Fine." The door opened a crack, and a bill was shoved out.

"Thanks!" John jogged past me, grinning, a ten held in his hand. He hopped into the car and pulled out of the driveway. I snuck up the steps, waiting, Aldo right behind me.

A moment later, the door opened again, and a pair of hands appeared to grab the pizza. I pressed my gun into the head bent over the boxes. "Slowly now," I advised. "Unless you want your brain matter all over the front steps."

He cursed, backing in. I followed, my gun still against his head. Aldo trailed me, his gun pointing at the other man in the room. I pushed at the one I had. "Stand. Slowly, with your hands where I can see them."

He did so, backing away. The two men were shocked. Both were ruffians, dirty and unkempt. One had claw marks on his face and a bruise on his cheek. "What do you want?"

"Nice try, boys. Where is she?"

They were silent. I cocked my gun. "I'll ask again. Nicely. Next time, you'll be eating my bullet. Where is my fiancée?"

Their eyes widened when I confirmed I was who they thought I was. The one with the clawed face pointed to the left, and I glanced at Aldo. "Watch them."

I found the door, locating the light switch, and went down the stairs cautiously. The basement was damp and cold. Musty. Dirty from years of neglect.

It took me a moment to locate her. She was in a corner, a small bundle of misery on the floor. Chained there, like an animal. I knelt beside her, rolling her over, narrowing my eyes at the sight of her injuries. Her face was bruised and torn. Her neck showed signs of fingerprint-shaped bruises developing on it. Her lip was cut. She was ice-cold and unconscious, but she was breathing. I pulled off my coat, wrapping her in it. I left her for a moment, rushing up the stairs.

"Whoever has the fucking key, give it to me before I count to five." I held out my hand. It took to three for the key to be dropped into my palm. I shot the asshole in the knee for taking so long and, ignoring his scream, raced back downstairs, unlocking the chain and gathering Effie into my arms. She roused a little, gasping and moaning. "Stay still," I murmured. "You're safe now."

Upstairs, the men watched me as I set her on the sofa. It was disgusting but at least warmer than the fucking basement floor.

"Two million each and this is how you treat her?" I asked, my voice quiet and deadly calm.

"She fought us," the one with the claw marks said. "She fell. It was her fault."

I crouched in front of him. "She do that to your face?" I asked.

"Yes."

"Fought like a little tiger, did she?" I said, lowering my voice, sounding as if I were sharing a secret. "The little ones, they always fight, am I right?"

A sick grin split his face. "Yeah. They do. I like it."

My bullet froze his face with that grin on it. A perfect hole in the center of his head that gave me a great deal of satisfaction.

I stood, eyeing the one who'd given me the key.

He was holding his knee, openly weeping like a little girl. "I didn't know, man. That she was yours. I wouldn't have touched her."

"Is that a fact?" I asked.

"Look, just give me a hundred grand so I can hide somewhere. It was all his idea, you know. The two mil, and even this job. Not me."

I rubbed my chin as if contemplating his words. He seemed to think he actually had a chance.

"One hundred," I mused. "I'll make it two for a little information."

He nodded eagerly.

"Was it the Santini brothers?"

"Yes. They bought her from her sister. They said she was a virgin and not to touch her. I guess they lied."

I stepped closer. "You know something I discovered today about the Santini boys?"

He waited, not speaking.

"They hire the dumbest fucks I've ever met." I shot his other knee, and his mouth opened, a soundless scream frozen on his face as I bent closer. "And that two hundred grand? I lied too."

He was dead before he hit the floor.

Aldo spoke. "Finished having fun now, Roman? We need to get out of here."

I turned to lift Effie into my arms, startled to see her eyes open, the blue-violet color dull and vacant. She looked at me and the two men bleeding on the floor. A small whimper escaped her mouth.

I scooped her up, holding her tight. "Close your eyes, Little Tiger. You've seen enough for now."

Her body slumped in my embrace.

"What are we doing with them?" Aldo asked.

"Leave them to rot. It'll send a message."

And I headed to the SUV.

CHAPTER 6
ROMAN

I n the vehicle, Aldo glanced at me. "She needs medical attention."

"I already have Sims on standby. Head to the General," I instructed.

Dr. Sims met us at the entrance, and I carried Effie to a private room. She had been in and out of consciousness the whole trip, at times staring up at me, her hand fisting my shirt. Even when she would pass out again, her hand stayed clutched to me. I held her close, not understanding the intense sensations raging within me. Anger, worry, fear, and desperation swirled inside me. Anger, I was used to. Worry over Nonna, I felt often. The rest, never. And all at once? Certainly not.

It was hard to release her from my arms. Dr. Sims shook his head as he looked at her. "I'll take care of her."

"She hit her head."

"I'll get a CT as well as seeing what other injuries she has."

"Gently," I ordered.

He lifted his eyebrows. "Of course."

He said something to the nurse, who left the room, then returned, handing me a pile of material.

"What is this?" I asked.

"You might want to change before going to the waiting room," he said mildly. "And clean up."

I looked down with a grimace. I was covered in blood and dirt. In the corner of the room, I watched as he began to check out Effie. I shucked off the shirt and pants I was wearing, pulling the scrubs over my head. I washed my hands and arms, then bundled the soiled clothes into a bag the nurse also had given me.

"Wait outside," Dr. Sims instructed, inserting an IV and starting fluids.

Aldo grabbed my arm, dragging me from the room.

The small waiting area was empty, and I paced, edgy and angry. When the room became too small, I paced in the hallway.

Aldo watched me silently. I heard a noise, and I turned to head back to the room. Aldo stopped me. "Let him do his job." He pulled me back into the waiting room. "I think we're done here," he announced.

I waved my hand. "Yes. Go home to Vi."

He stood, stopping my pacing. "No. *We're* finished here. You've accomplished what you set out to do, Roman. Be done with it. She is free. Let the doctor examine her, and we'll make sure she has the best care. Leave it now."

"No."

"I'll post a guard. You said you did this because you felt guilty. You've made amends. You rescued her."

"Leave it."

"Why? What hold does she have on you?"

"Nothing," I snapped.

"Feels like something. You're not acting like the Roman I know."

"You're seeing things that aren't there."

"Better to leave her now than later when she starts asking questions."

He was right, but I wasn't leaving this hospital.

"I'll take it from here. Make sure she's okay. We'll pay her off, and you can stop this. I'll go tell the doc to keep me in the loop." He began to move away.

"I will drop you where you stand," I hissed, my gun drawn without thinking.

Aldo stared at me. I lowered my weapon.

"I-I apologize," I said formally, shocked at my behavior. "I have no idea what came over me."

He crossed his arms. "I have no idea," he mimicked, shaking his head. "Good God, Roman. Listen to yourself. Look at you—pulling a gun on me for suggesting you leave the hospital."

I met his gaze. It was confused, curious, but not judgmental. "I can't leave her, Aldo. I can't explain it, but I still owe her. She needs my protection."

His eyes widened. "Well, good thing you're not catching feelings. God knows how erratic you'd be." He lifted his eyebrows in jest, trying to defuse the tension between us.

I dropped my head, laughing. I shoved my gun behind my back and stuck out my hand. "My apologies, my friend. It was a moment of madness. It's passed."

"Passed," he snorted. "Right. Apology accepted, though." He shook my hand. "I have a feeling the next while is going to prove to be interesting." Then he grinned. "Leave you alone for a while, and this is what happens. Vi is gonna piss herself laughing."

I ignored him.

Dr. Sims came out, and I strode toward him. He held up his hand. "She is all right. She has a concussion, is bruised and frightened, but nothing permanent other than the mental trauma. She can go home as long as she has someone to look after her."

I nodded. "She does. She'll be with me."

Behind me, Aldo started humming. I glanced over my shoulder, glaring. He was being annoying tonight. He stopped, but he kept smiling. Bastard.

"You can see her. She can leave once the IV is done. Make sure she eats and has fluids. If she gets a headache or anything looks off, call me, and we'll get her back in."

I nodded and headed for the room. Effie was in bed, the blankets drawn up around her. Her eyes were closed, her bruises ink stains on her pale skin, and she looked tiny. Alone. It did something to my chest to see her that way, and the odd sensation made me angry.

I walked to the bed, her eyes flying open at the sound of my heavy steps.

"Hi," she whispered.

"Hello."

"The doctor said I can go home." Her voice was rough and painful-sounding.

I barked a laugh. "The doctor said you could be discharged. There is a difference," I said, my voice brusquer than I meant it to be.

"Um, I have nowhere else to go."

"Unless you want to end up back in the same situation I pulled you from, you will not be going home."

Her already-pale face turned ashen, and I cursed myself for being short with her.

"You're going somewhere safe to recover."

"My diner. My employees," she protested.

"I will arrange it all."

"But—"

I leaned close. "Do not argue with me, Effie. I will arrange it. That is what a fiancé does, is it not?"

"I'm sorry. I panicked."

I sighed. Why was I being so curt with her? This was my fault, not hers. Calling me her fiancé had only helped me find her faster. I tempered my voice.

"We'll talk about it later. Rest."

"Where am I going to go?"

"Where you'll be safe."

"Which is where?"

"Where I am."

Aldo kept humming some familiar tune, but I couldn't place it. It was pissing me off to no end, though. When the doctor told me Effie could leave, I picked her up off the bed, wrapped in the blanket and hospital gown, and carried her out to the car. She was sedated and exhausted enough not to protest or try to get away. Instead, she rested her head on my shoulder, once again finding purchase with her fist clutched to the scrubs I wore.

I sat in the car, holding her, feeling oddly relieved at her closeness. I wasn't much for touching people, but with her, it felt right.

"Do you want a room for her?" Aldo asked.

"No."

"Where—"

I shot him a glare, and he shut up, although he started humming again.

At the hotel, Aldo followed us upstairs, and we headed to my private office and suite. I carried Effie to my bed, laying her down carefully. I noticed her grimace of pain at times, and I didn't want to cause her any undue discomfort.

I pulled the scratchy hospital blanket off her, frowning when I saw the mottled bruises on her upper thighs. Without thinking, I pushed up the hospital gown, my anger growing again at the sight of more bruising on her hip.

She made a distressed sound, and I looked up, meeting her gaze. Clouded in pain, her eyes were a gray-violet, and she looked terrified.

"I'm not going to hurt you," I assured her, using the quietest voice I could. "I'm just looking. How did these bruises get here?"

"First Marianne, then one of them—the men," she whispered. "I fought them in the basement, and one got mad and he kicked me."

I shut my eyes, trying to calm my rage. I should have shot them both a few times and let them suffer instead of ending their lives so quickly. And Marianne no longer fell into the "do not touch" category. If I ever found her, she would suffer.

The feel of Effie's hand on mine made my eyes fly open, and she shook her head. "You stopped them. Thank you."

She shouldn't be thanking me. It was because of me this happened. Once she found out, she wouldn't be so sweet.

I pulled down the gown and reached for the blanket, but she stopped me. "No. I'm dirty and—"

"It doesn't matter."

"Yes. Please. I'll shower."

I barked a laugh. "You can barely stand, Little Tiger."

"Please."

Once again, I lifted her, carrying her into the en suite. I set her on the bench in the large shower, turning on the water. I aimed the spray at her once it was warm and set the soap and shampoo beside her. "Do not try to stand. Get clean, and I will get you something to wear."

Aldo was waiting for me in my office. "You can go."

"And what is going to happen when I do?"

"I'll get her settled, then check in downstairs. I have to keep waking her every two hours, so I won't be sleeping much tonight anyway."

"Playing nursemaid now too."

"Paying my debt."

He looked as if he was going to say something but refrained. That was a good choice since my temper was barely under control.

"I'll check in downstairs and tell them to call with any issues. Try to get some rest, Roman."

He left, and I picked up the phone, barking some orders into it, then went back and checked on her. She was out of the shower, wrapped in one of the massive towels, standing in front of the vanity, staring at her reflection. There were marks on her shoulders and arms, no doubt from being manhandled. Her hair was a long streak of black down her back, and I saw the tremors that ran through her body.

"The bruises will fade," I assured her.

She nodded, not speaking. I set a T-shirt and boxers on the vanity beside her, along with a toothbrush. "I'll get you new clothes tomorrow."

I paused when she didn't move. "Do you need help?"

"I don't know," she whispered, the sound barely audible.

I drew in a bracing breath, picking up the boxers and standing behind her. "Lift your leg."

It was a slow, painful process for both of us. By the time I dropped the shirt over her head and pulled the towel away, she was shaking and tears leaked from her eyes. I held her chin in my hand and brushed her teeth. She continued to cry silently, the sight of it fanning my fury.

"Stop," I hissed, then shook my head, realizing I had said that out loud and now she thought I was angry at her. So then I did become angry at her.

I threw the toothbrush into the sink and bent, lifting her, the sound of her exhaled pain once again hitting me. I carried her to the bed, sliding her under the blankets but leaving her sitting upright. "Are you hungry?"

"N-no," she stammered out.

"You should eat. I got you some soup. You will eat it."

I headed to my office, the tray already waiting for me. I returned to my room and slid the tray over her lap. I lifted the lid, the savory aroma of creamy chicken soup wafting up. I handed her the spoon, waiting.

She tried. Goddammit all to hell, she tried. She clutched the spoon, dipping it into the soup, but her hand trembled so hard she couldn't lift it. She tried again, taking only a small amount on the spoon, barely enough to taste, but I could see even that wasn't going to happen. "Stop," I said again.

She looked at me, the fear, pain, and exhaustion so blatant, I swore I felt them. I took the spoon from her hand, dipped it into the soup and lifted it to her lips. "Eat."

She let me feed her the mouthful. "Good girl," I murmured. "You need this, Effie. Your body needs this."

I got about half the bowl into her before she laid her head back, shaking it when I tried to feed her more. She hadn't spoken a word, but her tears had stopped, which was a good thing. I couldn't handle them. I had never seen my nonna cry—not once—and I wasn't used to that emotion. I had experienced it on occasion with women I dated—usually when I was breaking up with them—and their waterworks didn't bother me as a rule, but Effie's tears did.

I was starving, so I finished off the soup, ate the sandwich, and drank the milk. That made me grimace. I disliked milk.

Effie sipped the ginger ale I offered to her, and I slipped two pills into her mouth. "To help your pain," I said to her silent question.

I carried the tray back to my office and returned. "You are safe. Nothing will harm you, and no one is going to get close to you again. Sleep, and we'll talk in the morning."

I reached for the light, and she whimpered in distress. I went to the opposite corner and snapped on a light, then turned off the one beside her. "All right?"

She shut her eyes. "I-I can't… There are no words…" She trailed off.

For some reason, I ran my hand over her head, touching the long, dark tresses on the pillow. She sighed, turning her head into my caress.

"I know," I replied.

I did a quick check of the casino. Spoke with my managers. All assured me things were fine, the night was busy, but everything was under control. They also told me Aldo had been around, checking on everything. My right hand had been annoying but, as usual, highly efficient.

Effie was on her side, curled into a ball, almost defensively. But she appeared to be asleep, so I grabbed fresh clothes and took a shower. I came back into the room, finding her in the throes of a nightmare. I stood beside the bed, trying to help her. I had no experience offering comfort, but I vaguely recalled my mother's soothing touch as a child, and I carefully touched her shoulder and ran my fingers through her hair. It was like silk to touch but knotted. It needed a brush, but she'd been too exhausted for me to suggest that. I would bring up someone from the salon in the morning to help her.

When she quieted, I looked around, unsure. I had to wake her every few hours, and I had planned on sleeping on the sofa in my office. It wouldn't be the first time I'd crashed there. But it felt too far away in case she had another nightmare. Instead, I pulled a chair away from the window, bringing it close to the bed. I sat down and lifted my legs to the bed, then I set my alarm to wake me to check on her. I would be close if she needed me.

I'd intended to close my eyes, but I couldn't take my gaze off her. Small and delicate-looking in the large bed, she was bruised, scared, and an unwelcome distraction. Yet, despite the bruises, the fear, and the fact that she was nothing like the women I usually preferred, there was something about her I found intriguing. Captivating. I felt a draw to her I couldn't deny.

And one I had to forget. Nothing could come of this. She was, without a doubt, a relationship girl, and I didn't do relationships. I did brief stints. Sex. A few dates, maybe a weekend away. A pretty piece of jewelry I let them pick out at the shop downstairs and a goodbye. No one lasted. I was never interested enough, and I was always honest from the start. I felt nothing for them but the lust of the moment. It always passed.

And this draw would as well.

Of that, I was certain.

CHAPTER 7
EFFIE

I woke, my eyelids flying open. I'd had the most terrible nightmare. I pressed a hand on my heart to calm the racing, only to realize, as I took in the dim room, it hadn't been a nightmare. This wasn't my room or my bed.

And I hadn't dreamed the man currently asleep in the chair by the foot of the bed. It had been his voice waking me, lifting my head for sips of water, asking me my name and his.

Roman Costas.

I took a moment to study him in the muted light. Asleep, the stern countenance was softened. His full lips were parted, his breathing deep and even. His dark chestnut hair spilled over his forehead, and scruff dusted his chin. He looked younger. Not so dangerous.

He was in a simple T-shirt and sweats, and I blushed thinking of how he'd dressed me the night before.

I had no idea what to make of him. One moment, he was kind; the next, he seemed angry. He refused to let me leave yet let me know he was as unhappy about it as I was.

Still, he touched me with nothing but gentleness. His voice all night was low and concerned. I swore I felt his hand running over my head, and I heard him hushing me, telling me everything was all right. It comforted me greatly.

I must have imagined that.

I needed to get up, and I gingerly lifted the blankets, pushing myself into a sitting position, a low groan escaping my mouth. Roman's eyes flew open, and he shot from the chair as if the room was on fire.

"What is it? What's wrong?"

"I have to get up."

"What do you need? I'll get it."

I huffed a breath. "I have to pee."

"Oh." He straightened. "Right. Of course." He ran a hand through his hair. "Do you need help?"

"No. I'll do it."

It took me a moment, but I swung my legs out of bed, holding in my hiss of pain. It felt as if I had been hit by a Mack truck. I pushed off the mattress, the room around me spinning. Before I could take a step, Roman had me in his arms.

"You can try again later, Little Tiger. Enough."

He carried me into the bathroom, setting me on my feet. "Okay now?" he asked.

"Yes." There was no way I was peeing with him in the room. I needed to maintain a little pride.

"Call me when you're done."

I planned on walking back to bed myself. But I stayed quiet, relieved my bladder, and carefully stood, waiting until the dizziness had passed before shuffling to the vanity to wash my hands. I glanced in the mirror, my face as frightening as I thought it had looked last night. The bruises were vivid and dark. My lip was split. I saw marks on my neck, and when I looked down, my stomach and legs showed trauma as well. My head ached, the constant pounding a dull roar in my ears. I gripped the edge of the sink and took in some deep breaths. I moved to the door, opening it quietly. Roman wasn't in the room, but I heard his voice, so I knew he was close. It took all my energy and effort to walk toward the bed. My legs ached and I felt exhausted. I was almost there when he stepped back into the room.

"So stubborn," he muttered, winding his arm around my waist and helping me the last few feet. I leaned into him, relying on his strength, but I was grateful to feel the plush mattress under me. He pressed two more pills into my mouth and let me sip the cold water until the glass was empty. It felt good on my throat. "Back to sleep," he ordered. "I'll get you some breakfast when you wake up."

I was too tired to argue, so I shut my eyes. I heard his sigh, and I felt his eyes on me.

"What am I going to do with you, Little Tiger?" he mumbled.

Keep me, were the words that drifted through my head as I succumbed to the exhaustion. Where they came from, I didn't know. And it didn't matter. That wasn't what I really wanted.

Was it?

The next time I opened my eyes, Roman was gone. In his place was a woman roughly my age. She was tall and slender, her dark hair short. She was curled into the chair Roman had slept in, and she was reading. On a table beside her was a steaming cup of coffee. I wondered if the aroma of it had woken me up.

I gingerly sat up, and she snapped her Kindle shut. "Hello," she greeted me. "I'm Vi. Violet if you prefer, but I prefer Vi. And you're Effie. The breathing miracle."

I blinked. "The breathing miracle?"

She laughed, waving her hand. "Private joke between Aldo and me."

"Aldo?"

"My husband. He was the other guy last night with a gun. The big one."

"Oh."

"You probably have to pee, don't you? Roman said last time you woke up, it was five. That was six hours ago."

"Oh. Ah, yes."

She approached the bed, flinging back the blankets and extending her hands. "Come on, then. Can't have you leaving a wet spot in Roman's bed." She started to laugh. "At least not yet."

I was confused but took her proffered grip and got out of bed, barely holding in my grimace.

"Wow, you are tiny," Vi said. "You have a lot of power for someone so compact. I always wanted to be short. But Aldo loves that I'm so tall. He says it makes us perfect for each other." She helped me stay steady on the way to the bathroom. "I think what makes us perfect is his massive dick and my willing snatch, but there you go." Once again, she laughed gaily. Then she glanced at me. "You want a shower while you're up and fresh clothes? Roman had me get you some. They might be a little big. He said small, but I didn't expect *small*, you know?"

"I'm five one," I protested.

She chuckled. "I'm five ten." She extended her leg. "Over six feet with my heels. And I love my heels."

"Oh." I frowned. I rarely wore heels. They made my legs ache. "Yes, I would like another shower," I said. "I still feel dirty."

Instantly, she was sympathetic and bustled around. "You get in the shower. I brought conditioner because Roman was worried about knots in your hair. Believe me, I howled every time I thought about him saying knots. *Roman*. Worried about knots." She snickered.

I was even more confused, but I let her set the shampoo and conditioner on the bench, a fresh towel on the vanity and a hairbrush. I wondered how hard she would laugh if I told her Roman had brushed my teeth for me last night, but I decided to keep that to myself.

"I'll get you some breakfast. I'm under strict instructions to make sure you eat."

Then she was gone.

I sat under the spray, enjoying the heat. I used the expensive shampoo and conditioner, recognizing the name. It was one I could never afford.

I wrapped myself in the towel and began the process of detangling my hair. The conditioner had helped, but I was tired when I was done. I opened the door, and Vi sprang from the chair. "Feel better?"

"Yes."

She walked beside me and indicated the clothes on the bed. "You change, and then we can eat."

The loose pants and shirt were soft and in a pale blue. There were socks for my feet, which I wanted to put on, but the pain when I bent over was too much. I walked to the door, leading down a short hall and into what I assumed was Roman's office. Vi sat on the sofa, her legs tucked under her. She indicated I should join her, and I sat down. She handed me a plate. "Eat that."

"That" was a plate of fluffy scrambled eggs with toast. There was cheese on top of the eggs and a plate of bacon on the table. Vi was tucking into a large omelet, humming in satisfaction.

"Coffee?" I asked hopefully.

"Oh, sure." She poured me a cup and added the cream and sugar I requested. She sat back, eating, not talking.

"Where is Roman?" I dared ask. "I want to thank him before I leave."

She almost choked. "Honey, you ain't going anywhere. I'm sitting with you until Roman the Warrior returns." She shook her head, taking a sip of coffee. "I value my life, thank you very much, and I'd appreciate it if you didn't make it difficult to keep it."

"I'm sorry?" I asked.

"Don't try to leave. If I have to call him and say I lost you…" She grimaced. "I'm not sure even Aldo could keep him from going berserk."

I decided this woman was crazy. "Will he be back soon?"

"I suppose. He said he was making sure some bakery ran smoothly for a while. Putting men on it to watch it."

I blinked. "You mean my diner?"

"Ah," she said around a mouthful. "That explains it. I wondered why he cared about a bakery."

"Who is he?" I blurted.

She grinned, not missing a beat. "If I were a betting woman, I'd say your future."

Then she went back to eating her omelet, leaving me more perplexed than ever.

We finished breakfast. I ate as much as I could. My throat was sore and my appetite off, but I did my best. Vi didn't look happy, then shrugged and made a call. Not long after, someone came and cleared the dishes and handed her a tall to-go cup. She thrust it at me.

"What is that?"

"A smoothie. That'll make up for what you didn't eat, and I won't have to lie to Roman."

"Have you known him long?"

She lifted one shoulder. "Not a long time. I was hired as a waitress in the casino restaurant. Roman wasn't part of the interview process, but I did meet him on my first day. He and Aldo meet every new employee. I would see Aldo on occasion and I heard about him from other employees, though I didn't really know him. But we were attracted to each other, and eventually, we gave in. We had an affair, but I expected nothing from it. Then one day, a customer hassled me really hard, and Aldo stepped in. Threw him out. The asshole didn't like that very much, and he came back another time and attacked me."

"How awful."

She nodded, but she had a smile on her face. "Aldo stopped him. He carried me inside and took care of me. He started checking on me, walking me to my car, dropping by the restaurant to make sure I was okay. We grew closer, and I realized I'd fallen. So had he. The rest, as they say, is history. We got married really fast. In fact, we just got back from our honeymoon."

I had a feeling I was hearing a very toned-down version of their story, but I didn't pry. I licked my lips, leaning forward. "Is he dangerous? Like Roman?"

She was quiet. "Aldo is lethal. They both are. To other people. To the people they love, they are the best. I realized Aldo was only dangerous to me because of the fact that he held my heart in his hands. But I learned very quickly those hands were perfect for such a delicate job. My heart has never been safer." She smiled softly. "We got married last month. Roman sent us to Fiji for our honeymoon. We came back the day you were kidnapped."

"I'm sorry, I—"

She waved her hand. "I love Aldo, but I also know him. He was done with the beach and the drinks and lazing around. It was time to come home, and when I suggested it, he couldn't pack his bag fast enough. He'll take me away again soon. I think I would rather have lots of short trips with a happy husband than long ones where all he wants to do is pick a fight or shoot someone to relieve his tension." She winked. "A girl can only do so much with her magical holes, you know."

I blushed and she laughed. "Oh, I like you. I'm glad the Warrior has crumbled. This is gonna be fun."

I had no idea what she meant, and I was too tired to figure it out. I drank some more smoothie, humming at the flavor. Mango, pineapple, and strawberry. It was a rich, tasty treat. I set down the container and yawned.

"You need to go back to bed."

"No, I'm fine. I really need to make some calls."

"Once Roman is here."

"Which will be?"

She shrugged. "When he arrives."

And that was all she said.

I woke slowly, voices drifting in and out. I only caught the occasional sentence or word.

"Perfectly good bed."

"I told you to look after her."

"Pretzel."

"…how you talk to my wife."

"Stop it, boys."

"You gonna keep her, Roman?"

I recognized Vi's voice. Roman's as well. He had a commanding tenor to his speech, but right now, I would add pissed off to the tone. The other voice, I was unsure of, except I thought it belonged to Aldo.

I opened my eyes, startled to see Roman crouched in front of me. His head was turned, and he was speaking to Vi and Aldo. I recognized him from last night. Roman's voice was quiet but firm.

"She needs to rest and recover. I am not moving her."

"I need to go home."

Roman's head snapped around, and he met my eyes. For a moment, I saw his emotions clearly shine in his eyes. Then, as if a veil descended, he distanced himself.

"You'll go home when I say so." He stood. "And you should be in bed. Twisted around like a snack to go isn't doing your injuries any good."

"I bet he wants to eat her like a snack," Vi murmured.

Roman glared, Vi laughed, and Aldo turned his head, trying not to join her. Roman glanced my way, and I had to hide my amusement. He almost looked embarrassed.

"Sometimes the snack-sized pretzels are the best," Vi continued.

"Stop it," Roman said, dropping his voice. I knew it was meant to sound scary, but it only made me want to laugh too. Vi was ridiculous, and he was taking her far too seriously.

I stood, planning on gliding past them all and heading to the room down the hall. Except I moved too fast, and the room spun. I gasped, reaching out to grab something to steady myself and found Roman's arm already going around me. He lifted me up, practically growling in anger. "She. Needs. To. Lie. Down."

He stomped down the hall, ignoring Vi's giggles. Aldo began humming something familiar, and Vi's chuckles turned into laughter.

"Let yourselves out," Roman snapped over his shoulder.

I sighed, letting my head rest on his shoulder. I wondered why I felt so safe in his arms. *Lethal*, Vi had admitted.

Unless he cared.

But I doubted that was the case.

Right?

I wasn't sure how to ask him.

CHAPTER 8
EFFIE

I woke up again, and it was early evening. I wondered if I had slept as much the entire past year as I had the last couple of days. I got up, pleased when my body didn't scream as loudly in protest at being moved. After using the bathroom, I shuffled down the hall and into Roman's office. He wasn't there, but I heard his voice in the hall talking to someone. I looked around the large space. His desk was dark wood, heavy and solid. The shelves that lined one wall matched. The sofa and chairs in the corner were covered in a deep russet leather. His chair and the ones in front of his desk were black. A small table had chairs tucked under it, and I assumed he used that if he was eating a meal in here. I approached his desk. Piles of paperwork, a thermos of coffee, and a glass of amber liquid sat on top of the dark wood. On top of the paperwork were a pair of tortoiseshell frames. But what caught my attention was the wall of windows behind his desk. I walked over, staring at the Falls. They were, as usual, majestic. Riveting. The colors changing every second. Blues, greens, grays, whites. Swirling and rushing, the power of them enormous. Even growing up here, I never tired of them. I loved them in all seasons. Fall was my favorite with the colors of the trees against the backdrop of the rocks and water. Winter was incredible with the ice and mist that hung in the air. I tended to avoid them during the height of tourist season, but up here, that didn't matter. You couldn't hear the voices, the cars, or the constant click of cameras. All you saw was the beauty.

I leaned my head against the cool glass, mesmerized.

I startled at the sound of Roman's voice behind me. "Spectacular, isn't it?"

I nodded without turning around. "It is. I never tire of it."

"Did you grow up here?"

"Yes."

"Once again, you are not where I left you. This seems to be a habit of yours."

I met his gaze in the reflection. He was perched on the edge of his desk, the glass I had seen now in his hand. I turned and met his eyes. He had a slight smirk on his face.

"I woke up and came to see if I could go home yet."

Instantly, his face changed. His expression became dark. "That isn't happening for a long time, Effie. Get used to the idea, and stop asking me."

"Why?"

He tossed back the alcohol in his glass and slammed it on the top of the desk. "Because of your goddamn sister."

"Did you"—I swallowed—"did you have a relationship with her? Is that why you're so mad?"

He scrubbed his face. "Absolutely not."

"Oh."

"Why would you think that?"

I shrugged. "She's so pretty and—"

He interrupted me. "Pretty is not the word I would use to describe your sister. Hard. Cold. She didn't appeal to me at all. In fact, I imagine having sex with her is akin to throwing a hot dog down a hallway. Useless."

I felt my eyes widen. "Wow."

He shrugged. "Just being honest. You want pretty, Effie? Go look in the mirror and see past the bruises. You are incredibly lovely."

I blinked, unsure how to respond. I swallowed, my throat dry. "So how did you get, ah, involved?"

"*I was not involved,*" he stressed. "She gambled in my casino and lost a huge amount of money. Somehow slipped away from the manager without paying her debt. We found her, and I gave her a chance to pay it or suffer the consequences. She chose to go to the most despicable men out there and trade you for the money she owed."

"So what those men said was true—she sold me."

"Yes."

I felt my knees start to tremble. "And they were going to…?" I trailed off.

He met my eyes. "Sell you off to the highest bidder as a sex slave, no doubt."

My legs buckled, but Roman was right there, catching me. He sat me in his chair, holding my face. "Deep breaths, Effie. Take some deep breaths."

I realized the noise I heard was me. I clutched at his wrists. "But—but, how—you?" I stuttered out.

"I figured it out. The money she paid me back with was marked. She had mentioned going to you for the money. I found you."

"Where—where is she?"

"I don't know. But I will find her."

"What will you do to her?"

He shook his head, refusing to answer. I gripped his wrists tighter, everything he said overwhelming and scary.

"You have to stay here for now, Effie. There is no choice. I can't let you go. The men I stole you from might come looking."

A long shiver went through me. A hysterical laugh burst from my lips. "So the man who rescued me from my kidnappers is my new kidnapper?"

"For now."

"Why?" I asked quietly, tamping down my panic.

He regarded me in silence. "I don't know," he admitted.

I stared down at the food on my plate, my appetite nonexistent.

"Eat," Roman said, his tone brooking no argument.

After my question, he had moved away, informing me dinner was coming. I sat on the sofa as he worked at his desk for a while, my mind racing. I always knew Marianne was selfish and cold. I knew she didn't care much for me. But for her to do *that*. To be willing to sell me just to pay a debt, I realized she must hate me. I couldn't get the thought out of my head. My whole life, I had tried to get her to love me. I adored her when I was little, and although she barely tolerated me, I always hoped that would change as we grew up and became adults.

Apparently not.

I picked up my fork, slicing off a bite of chicken. It was tender and, I was certain, delicious, but it tasted like ash in my mouth.

"Would you prefer soup?" he questioned. "Is your throat still too sore?"

"No, this is fine."

He made a noise of distaste. "Yes. So fine, you've eaten three bites. Your body needs the nourishment to heal. There must be something you'd like."

"No, I'll eat this."

He sat back, picking up his wine, swirling it in the glass as he studied me. I felt his stare everywhere.

"My diner?" I asked, trying to distract my thoughts.

"I went there this morning. Spoke with Margi. I explained you'd been in a car accident. She assured me that she and Anne could keep the place running. I offered one of my chefs, but she said she could handle it. She did say there was payroll and supplies to be ordered." He took a sip of wine. "I told her to give it all to me and I would make sure it was looked after." He indicated a bag by his desk. "It is all in there. You can look at it tomorrow. I did leave two men to watch over and help out. Just in case."

I wasn't sure how to respond. "Thank you."

He eyed me pointedly, then shifted his chair and sat closer. He pulled my plate over and cut a small piece of chicken, added some of the creamy potatoes to the fork and pressed it to my lips. "Open."

I was so shocked by his actions, I did as he directed, chewing slowly. He readied another fork.

"Why bagels?" he asked.

"My mom's favorite food. She made them all the time and taught me. They became one of mine too. I wanted something different for my diner, and I liked the idea of using bagels."

I let him feed me another mouthful, and I chewed and swallowed.

"Bagels and breakfast go hand in hand. I decided the gimmick would be bagels for everything. No toast or muffins. Bagels with breakfast, bagel sandwiches. We make five kinds daily. All from scratch. Two kinds of soup. And breakfast. We open at six and close at three."

"Long days," he observed.

"Yes. But it has grown and caught on. I employ six people, and I am proud of that."

"And the cookies?"

He fed me another bite, and I shrugged as I chewed. "Another fun thing. My mom made sugar cookies all the time. It gives me a creative outlet. I make them in huge batches on the days the diner is closed. You get a cookie with every lunch order."

He set down the utensils, and I was surprised to see I had eaten a lot of the food on my plate. At least enough to satisfy him.

He didn't move his chair but continued to ask me questions about the diner. I told him how I had invested the money my mom left me. I bought the building in the neighborhood I grew up in and started the business, watching it grow.

"How old are you?" he asked.

"Twenty-seven. How old are you?" I responded.

"Thirty-six."

I looked around the sumptuous office. "I think you might be doing better than I am in the business department."

He threw back his head and laughed. The sound was loud and rich, and it made me smile with him.

"Family business, Little Tiger. It helps when you're rich to start with. I inherited a fortune, and I kept it growing."

"Was your family, um…" I wasn't sure how to finish my question. "Mafia?" I had heard rumors.

"An arm of it. A syndicate." He took a sip. "Still are, but things are different now."

I wanted to ask how, but I couldn't get the words past my mouth.

"Will you kill me?"

He shook his head. "No. I will protect you. I never hurt women or children." He frowned as he studied the contents of his glass. "Unlike your fucking sister, I do have some morals."

My smile fell at the mention of my sister.

"What?"

I shook my head.

"Tell me," he demanded.

"After Marianne tripped me—"

He cut me off. "She tripped you?"

I nodded. "I was trying to get to the door. I thought if I could at least scream, maybe someone would hear me. But she stuck out her foot, and I fell instead."

He shut his eyes, a string of curse words, some in English, some in what I assumed was Italian, escaping his mouth. His hand curled into a fist on the table, and it took a moment before he gathered himself.

"What happened after she tripped you?"

"I was lying on the floor, and she was tossing my apartment. I wasn't sure why until you said inheritance. Mom left me a necklace that was my grandmother's. Marianne wanted it. She always wanted it, and she hated the fact that Mom gave it to me."

"But you're your mother's biological daughter. It makes sense."

I shrugged. "Marianne's wants rarely made sense. Mom gave Marianne her wedding rings, which were worth more, but she wanted both."

"Always selfish, I see," he said dryly.

I lifted one shoulder in agreement. "She must have been looking for it. I guess she thought I'd be dead soon enough, she might as well have it."

My voice caught on the last part, and I had to swallow.

"Where did you keep it?"

"In a box I had taped to the back of a drawer. I was always worried she'd try to take it, so I never wore it. I wonder if she kept it or sold it."

Suddenly, I was overwhelmed again. The memories of those moments and the hours that followed hit me hard. I could feel my emotions threatening to swamp me. Knowing my sister had been at the center of all of this was too much to handle. I stood so fast, my chair toppled, and the room spun. Roman was on his feet instantly, but I held up my hands. "No, please. Don't." I swallowed the thickness in my throat, desperate and frantic. "Excuse me."

I gripped the table until the dizziness passed. I turned and stumbled from the room, needing to be alone.

Roman didn't follow.

ROMAN

I let her go, the strange feeling of helplessness hitting my chest. I had seen the sudden realization in her eyes. The pain of her sister's actions hitting her. Understanding had dawned—hurt and betrayal had set in. I watched it all happen in the kaleidoscope colors of her eyes.

I walked to the window, the lights on the Falls changing and reflecting on the waters. Much the way Effie's eyes changed and swirled in the lights.

I listened, not hearing anything. I wondered if she was crying. Or if she had simply collapsed on the floor, too exhausted to give in to the emotions tearing through her.

I wondered why I cared so much.

I picked up the glass on my desk and poured in some scotch. Nothing had prepared me for the events of the past few days. I had no clue how to go forward.

What to do with Effie.

Except, until the danger had passed, I had to keep her safe. That much, I knew. It was my responsibility to do so since it was my anger that had put the idea in Marianne's head.

The thought that one day Effie would know that made me take a deep swallow of my scotch. She would be so horrified, she would walk away. She'd been betrayed by her sister and, in a way, me as well.

The idea of that made my chest ache in a particularly painful way.

I rubbed at it, wondering if the wine sauce on the chicken was giving me heartburn. That made more sense than Effie's rejection. Because that was exactly what she would do.

Reject me.

I checked on her an hour later, concerned when I didn't find her in the bed or the chair. The bathroom door was shut and the light off, and I listened before turning the handle. Effie was on the floor, curled into a ball, a towel piled up on the floor with her. I crouched down, shaking my head. She'd come in here and sobbed into a towel until she fell asleep from exhaustion.

Alone.

I knew with a certainty that she'd been alone for a long time.

Carefully, I gathered her into my arms and carried her to my bed. With the brighter light, I could see how hard she'd cried. There was still wetness under her eyes, the traces of the salty tears on her cheeks. Her nose was red, and her lip had bled some, no doubt from biting it while crying. She was so pale that the bruises were vivid on her skin.

My constantly simmering anger roared to life, and I wished her sister were in front of me. My no-hurting-women policy was canceled when it came to Marianne. If I ever found her, my punishment for this heinous crime would not be fast or pleasant. And I would enjoy every moment of it.

I pulled the blanket over Effie and stood back.

I felt weary—something that was rare for me. I only required a few hours sleep. I was up late with the casino and usually awake and at the gym before dawn. But at the moment, I felt as if I could sleep for days. No doubt the night spent in the chair had something to do with it.

I showered and changed, then returned to my desk. I finished the paperwork, approved payroll, then scanned the items Margi had given me. Effie was organized and efficient with her bookkeeping. She ran a tight ship, with no huge expenditures and careful budgeting. She had a modest monthly profit, and she paid her employees a living wage. Living upstairs, she kept her expenses low, and she practiced the same budgeting for her personal life. I was impressed by everything I looked at. The difference between the two sisters was night and day in their ways of living, attitudes, and values.

I heard a noise, and I hurried down the hall. Effie was whimpering in her sleep, and I hushed her, running my fingers through her hair. It was silky and full. Every time I stopped, she began to frown, making little noises in her throat. Reaching a decision, I rounded the bed and carefully lay beside her. I rolled onto my side, touching her hair again, and she relaxed. I shut my eyes, enjoying the quiet of the room. Her soft breathing. The scent of her hair was light and floral.

I breathed it in, planning on staying for a short while then going back to my desk.

At least, that was the plan.

CHAPTER 9
ROMAN

I woke up, something tickling my nose. I fisted the thick material in my hand, slowly realizing what I was holding was not material, but hair.

Someone—a woman—was in bed with me, and I was holding her hair. She was lying across my chest, snuggled tightly against me. And she smelled really good. I opened my eyes, confirming I was in my private suite.

I searched my memory. I never slept with a woman. If we made it to a bed, once sex was done, I was gone. There were rarely repeats, and I never brought them here. Ever. And I never snuggled.

I blinked away my confusion when the woman cuddled into me made a little noise. I recognized that noise.

Effie.

I was in bed with Effie. I had come to comfort her and lie down to make sure she fell asleep again, only to fall asleep myself. How we had gotten into this position, I had no idea. But now, I was awake, and so was my cock. He had no objection to Effie being so close. In fact, he wanted her closer.

And naked.

I lifted my free arm, shocked at the time. It was past seven. I had come in here at midnight.

I had slept for seven hours. That never happened.

I lifted my head, wondering how to extract myself before Effie woke up and discovered we'd slept together and my morning wood was hoping to make her acquaintance. Intimately. I decided I would carefully slide out from under her and leave.

Except as I lifted my head, she did too. Her eyes were sleepy, still too drowsy to be scared or filled with memories. They were a lovely violet-blue in the morning light, and for a moment, I lost myself in her soft gaze.

Then I cleared my throat. "Morning."

She blinked. "Morning?"

"I came to check on you. I guess I fell asleep."

"How did I get here? With you?"

"Well, you cried yourself to sleep on the floor, and I couldn't leave you there. I brought you to bed. How you ended up on my chest, I have no idea. Gravity, I suppose." I managed to slide out from under her, feeling a strange loss when we were no longer touching. I dragged the pillow with me, hiding my erection. "Nothing happened."

She was calm. "I had a nightmare. I remember that."

"Yes. Hardly surprising."

She sat up. "Thank you."

I really wished she'd stop saying that. She had nothing to thank me for. If it weren't for me, she wouldn't be in this situation.

"Whatever. It means nothing," I snapped. "I have to get ready for work. Excuse me." I spun and walked to the bathroom. I locked the door behind me and headed to the shower. I needed relief and some space.

Maybe then I'd forget how good it felt to wake up next to that tiny woman. How right she felt snuggled into my side.

It wasn't happening again.

But as I scrubbed my face, all I smelled was her on my skin.

And it was her name I groaned into my arm as I came under the hot spray.

And that pissed me off.

Royally.

EFFIE

I had never known anyone like Roman Costas. Then again, my world was small, so perhaps lots of wealthy people were the same as him.

But to me, he was an enigma.

Severe and scary, yet at times, when he let his guard down, I saw a different side to him. Something almost gentle.

Waking up this morning, wrapped in his embrace, was a surprise. How it felt was even more so. The sensation of being safe, protected, and…as odd as it sounded…*home*.

The look that passed between us when I woke had been nothing less than intimate and intense, all at the same time. He looked at me with a fierce tenderness and almost wonder. Then the shutters came down, and he rolled from the bed, dismissive and angry.

He stormed into the bathroom, and I heard the shower come on. Unsure what to do, I got up and pulled on the robe I had found and padded into his office to give him privacy to dress, although the closet was certainly large enough for him to do so if he chose.

I sat on the sofa, waiting patiently. I heard him moving around and some cursing, then he appeared in the doorway, half dressed, his hair chaotic. "What the hell are you doing?" he snapped.

"Giving you privacy."

That seemed to surprise him. He grunted and disappeared again. When he walked back into the office, he was Mr. Costas. Perfect suit, hair in place, scowl firmly set.

"I'll order breakfast. Give you some privacy as well," he said, sounding dismissive. "I have meetings all day. Vi will come and visit you."

"She doesn't have to babysit me. No one does. If your driver could just—"

He lifted his head, glaring. "You aren't going anywhere."

"You expect me to sit in this room day after day? Without even a book or a TV? Let me go home."

"You. Are. Not. Safe," he ground out.

"When will I be?"

"When I decide." Then he paused. "You still need to recover."

"May I at least call Margi and check in with her?" I swallowed, hating that I had to ask permission. "I won't say anything. I'll stick to your story I was in an accident."

He regarded me for a moment, then nodded. "Yes. You may." He held up his finger. "I'll trust you once. Betray me, and you'll be sorry."

I had no plans on finding out what that entailed. "Thank you." I looked around the room. "Is there something I can do?"

"Like what?" He frowned.

"Some bookkeeping, organize a supply cupboard, or inventory? Anything to keep my mind occupied."

He stared, perplexed. "I'll see what I can find."

"Okay."

I headed to the bedroom. "Um, have a good day."

He didn't reply.

When I got out of the shower, I didn't want to redress in the outfit Vi had brought me, but I was wondering how to ask for something else to wear. I was already indebted to Roman, and I hated adding to that debt, but I couldn't wear the same clothes all the time. I peered in his closet, seeing a pile of gray T-shirts on the shelf. I took one, noticing the casino logo embroidered on the front over the pocket. Small, classy. Not like a touristy shirt. Deciding to risk his outrage, I pulled it over my head and tied a knot in the side. My leggings were still fine for today, but at least I felt better in a clean shirt.

I headed back to the office, surprised to find Roman still there. He glanced up, freezing when he saw me, his green eyes locked on the shirt.

"Um, I'll pay you back. I don't have another clean one."

"It's fine. I'll get Vi to get you a few more things."

"I have clothes at home—"

He cut me off with a shake of his head. Then he indicated the table. "Breakfast."

I sat down, pouring a cup of coffee. He sat beside me, lifting the lid on his plate and cutting into a large omelet. My plate contained pancakes and scrambled eggs.

He pointed to the meal. "I thought your throat might still be sore."

"That was very thoughtful."

He didn't reply.

He finished his breakfast before pouring himself a cup of coffee. I laid down my utensils.

"Is that all?" he asked.

"I ate most of it."

He lifted his eyebrows in disbelief but didn't argue. He finished his coffee and stood. "Vi will be here soon. You can make your call. Your books are on my desk. I expect you to show respect and not snoop."

"I have no desire to see what you have in your drawers," I responded.

I swore his lips quirked at my unplanned quip.

"The elevator works, but my men are posted at the bottom."

I rubbed my head, already feeling the headache. "I said I wouldn't try."

He ignored me. "If you need something, press zero-one-one on the phone. That will reach my private staff. They will get you anything you want. If you are feeling unwell, my cell phone number is on the desk." He waved his hand. "Or if you get nervous or anything."

"All right."

He paused, looking at me. His tone was steely. "One move, Effie. Don't disappoint me."

This time, I dared. "What will you do?"

"You don't want to know."

I felt a shiver run through me.

His gaze fell to something behind me, and he leaned over, picking up the socks from the corner of the sofa. I had never put them on yesterday. He held them up in question.

"It hurts too much to bend and get them on my feet," I admitted.

Before I could blink, he kneeled in front of me and lifted a foot to his knee. He pulled on the soft socks and briskly rubbed my foot. He did the same with the other one, and I sighed at the warmth. For a moment, he held my feet in his large hands, staring down at them. When he lifted his gaze, our eyes locked. That same fierce tenderness raged in his stare. I felt the hitch in my breathing. The intensity of his grip on my feet. The change in the air around us. Then with a low curse, he stood and walked out of the room, shutting the door behind him loudly.

I sat, shaking.

And this time, it had nothing to do with being cold.

ROMAN

We sat in yet another office I had. It was a space I shared with Aldo, where we did a lot of decision-making. Plans of the casino hung on the walls, graphics and other items scattered around. It was secure and functional, our desks facing each other. We called it our war room. The windows looked out to the casino floor below. It was a great place to survey the empire I had built. People looking up only saw glass. I saw them.

"What crawled up your ass this morning?" Aldo asked. "Bad night?"

I felt like laughing. I'd had the best sleep I could remember. My mind was clear, my body refreshed, and it pissed me off because of the reason.

Effie.

I hadn't slept beside a woman in years. I was never comfortable with someone in my bed, yet last night, not only had I slept beside her, apparently I had hauled her up on my chest and held her all night.

"No," I said shortly. "I'm fine."

"As a newly married man, I now have a new appreciation for the words 'I'm fine.' They mean anything but."

"I said I'm fine."

"Okay, then. Whatever you say." He picked up a stack of papers. "We need to go through these renovations you want done to the restaurant."

"It's looking tired. I want it spruced up."

He glanced at the file. "A two-million-dollar paint job? Seems a bit excessive."

I had to smirk. "That's an entire overhaul. Walls, floors, ceiling, windows, seating. I liked their concepts. They want to make the view and the food the focal points, not the drapes and carpet. It's clean and simple, yet classy and understated."

"I agree. We'll lose business while it's closed."

"It'll be a month. I'm paying extra for round-the-clock crews. And the kitchen will still be open. We'll serve in the overflow area. Smaller, but make it so hard to get into, everyone will want it for a month. Meaghan is planning a whole new menu."

"You've been busy while I was gone."

I lifted a shoulder. A sound came from my computer, and I glanced at the screen. Effie was at my desk, going through her paperwork. Her hair fell around her face, a curtain of ebony. She pushed her hair back and leaned on her elbow, cupping her chin. I studied her face. Even bruised, she was lovely.

"Roman?"

"Sorry, I was thinking about something else."

"You want to reno the spa too?"

I shook my head to get my mind back on track. "No reno unless needed. I want to improve it. My secret shopper said the Conroy is more luxurious. The masseuse there is supposed to be incredible."

"He is, according to our sources. But he is a package deal. His wife is their aesthetician. And from what I was able to find out, they have it good there."

"I can make it better," I said confidently. "We have an incredible area, the view can't be beat, and I can offer more money and give them some say in how the spa is run. I want this to be the best."

"I'll arrange a meeting."

His phone rang, and he stood to answer it. I glanced back at the screen, seeing Effie was on the phone. I hit speaker, wanting to know what she was saying.

"Thanks, Margi. No, I'm recovering." She listened for a moment. "Um, it's complicated. Mr. Costas is being very kind and helpful." Another pause. "No, I'm fine. Really. I'm being well looked after. I can't recall the last time I slept this much." She nodded absently. "Yes, I was very lucky he was there when I was hit by the car." She shut her eyes. "Yep, such a huge coincidence he'd been at the diner and recognized me."

She asked a few questions about the diner. Listened again. "Um, I'm not sure. Maybe next week? If you need anything…" She trailed off and looked around. "Well, you have Roman's number. My cell phone is in my apartment." She pressed her lips together, and I was surprised to see the tears in her eyes. "I have access to my email, so you can send anything that needs my attention. Okay, I have to go, Margi. Thank you for stepping up. I'll make sure you're rewarded."

She hung up and buried her face into her hands. For a moment, her shoulders shook, and then she stopped, wiped her eyes, and straightened her posture. I wasn't sure what was making her cry, but I didn't like it. And I hated the fact that I didn't like it.

A knock sounded, and I heard Vi's voice sing out a greeting. Effie smiled at her, and I muted the speakers.

A throat clearing brought me out of my musings.

"Watching your girl?"

"She isn't my girl."

"Your prisoner, then?"

I hated that descriptor even more.

"Your wife just arrived."

"I know. She was in the kitchen getting Effie a smoothie. She gets the chef to add protein powder since Effie's appetite isn't great."

I rubbed my eyes. "I know. I had to hand-feed her last night to get food into her."

There was silence, and I looked up. Aldo was staring at me. "You *hand-fed* her."

"She wasn't eating."

"I often don't eat, and you don't feed me."

"You don't look like Effie," I replied.

"And how exactly does she look?"

"Like she needs to be looked after."

He stared again. I met his gaze. "I have to make sure she is okay before I let her go."

"Which will be when?"

I reached for a file. "When I decide the time is right. Now, are we working or gossiping?"

He chuckled. "I'd say we're falling, but I don't want to get slugged."

"Fuck off."

"Okay, boss. Now, what is next on the list?"

A couple of days later, we were back in the same office, planning. Effie was still upstairs in my suite, and Vi was coming to see her again. Effie had been sleeping a lot, and I made sure she ate, ensuring the kitchen sent up a couple of the protein drinks to her during the day along with her meals. She checked with her staff a few times, but they were handling the place well in her absence. Effie told me she liked to read, and I bought her a Kindle and a subscription to an all-you-could-read service she liked. It kept her happy and quiet, and I often glanced at the computer when I was out of my office to see her asleep over the device. I liked watching her sleep for some reason. Her peaceful naps seemed to help calm me. I knew she was looking forward to seeing Vi today, though. Last night she'd been restless, asking about going home again.

She hadn't liked my response.

Aldo's phone rang, and he stood, strolling to the other side of the office. He leaned against the wall, a tender smile on his face. "Hey, baby. How's your day going? Having fun?"

Covertly, I watched him. His indulgent tone, the smile, the softness of his actions with Vi were something I was still getting used to. He had totally changed since he'd met Vi, his protective nature coming out full force. The emotions he had always kept under wraps were evident in every aspect of their relationship. Nonna adored Vi and was thrilled Aldo had found someone. He had been around so long, he was another one of her boys.

He listened for a moment, his gaze skittering to me, then back to the carpet he suddenly found interesting. "I don't think that's gonna fly, baby."

I could hear Vi's voice, the tone pleading. He glanced my way again.

"Are you really gonna make me ask him?"

"Ask me what?" I demanded.

He pulled the phone away from his ear. "Effie needs some things. Clothes and girl stuff."

"Tell Vi to order whatever she wants."

"Vi wants to take her shopping."

I shook my head. "No."

Vi began to yell, and Aldo put her on speaker. "You can't keep her in this room, Roman! And women like to look at things and try them on! Not order all of it online and get shit off Amazon. The outlet mall has lots of great places. We'll take a couple of men."

"No. She is not leaving this building," I snapped.

"You stubborn bastard," she snarled. "All right, then. I'll take her downstairs to the hotel boutique and the spa. We won't leave the building."

"You still get two men."

Vi huffed out a long, annoyed sigh. "Fine." Then her voice changed. "Aldo, I'm going to spend some cash."

"Go for it, baby."

"Love your face."

He glanced my way, grinning sheepishly. "Love yours more."

He hung up.

I signed a few pages and glanced at the computer. Effie and Vi were walking out of the suite, two of my men following closely. I nodded, pleased. They were following instructions. Not leaving the building. They were protected and—

I turned to Aldo. "*Holy fuck*. Your wife just played me."

Aldo didn't look up. "Wondered when you would catch on."

"She had no plans on going to the outlet mall."

"Probably not."

"I said Effie couldn't leave the suite. She conned me into doing exactly that."

Aldo grinned. "Why do you think she wins our arguments every time?"

"Fucking con woman."

"*My* fucking con woman. And watch your tone when you call my wife names."

I had to laugh. "My apologies, my friend. I meant no disrespect."

His lips twitched. "Of course not."

"She is your ideal partner."

The twitch became a full-out smile.

"That she is. All one hundred percent of her evil, conning ways."

We both laughed.

That she was. Perfect for him on every level.

I ignored the whisper in my head that maybe it would be nice to find that sort of match.

Or the other one that laughed and said I already had.

I couldn't concentrate. Knowing Effie wasn't across the room or a few feet away down the hall seemed to have short-circuited my thinking. Even though she was in my building, with my men and Vi, I was still worried. I wasn't beside her.

Aldo was on the phone, talking to the masseuse I wanted to steal, setting up a meeting. I was sure once he saw what I was offering here, he and his wife would jump ship. A private suite, incredible salary, and trips to other hotels I owned, they would have a good life. I wanted this hotel and casino to be the very best. I hired the elite and demanded loyalty. I protected them and made sure they were happy. It was a two-way street.

I clicked on my computer, bringing up the security feed. Nothing new, but this time, I focused on the lobby. It was busy, people coming and going. The space was perfect, the flowers fresh, the iced fruit water sparkling in the massive crystal urn. The coffee station close to it was immaculate. Our guests could help themselves around the clock. There was a selection of pastries, fresh all day and night, to snack on.

Without thinking, I clicked on the expansive boutique down the hall. It was run by a gay couple I'd hired away from a designer clothing store. Their taste and elegance were incredible, and the boutique carried high-end clothing and accessories. The mail-order portion alone brought in a huge chunk of change. They ran the store with the same grace and panache they exuded as people, and I treated them well.

I scanned the store, finding Effie and Vi. My men were at the back, not bothering anyone but tracking all the customers, their eyes fixed on the two women. I frowned as I watched Effie. Vi held up clothing, each piece lovely and suitable, but Effie shook her head, clearly saying no.

I picked up the phone, punching in the direct extension. Gerry answered. "Silken Lace, how may I help you?"

"It's Roman."

"Hey, boss man. What can I do for you?"

"The lady with Vi."

"Oh, the Snow White beauty with the eyes?"

"Yes, that one."

"She yours?"

I didn't want to explain, so I took the easy road. "Yes. Why isn't she picking anything?"

His voice dropped. "I think she is too overwhelmed."

"Overwhelmed? Women love to shop."

"She glanced at one price tag and froze."

"Fuck," I swore. "I should have told Vi to tell her there was a discount."

"She tried. I heard Snowy say it was still out of her reach."

"She's seen things she likes?"

"Without a doubt. Those eyes of hers give her away. My God, if I were straight, I'd be all over that." He paused. "No disrespect, boss."

"None taken."

"Once the injuries from her car accident heal, she'll be stunning. I called Claire in the spa. She has healing oils that will help with the bruising. They're headed there next."

"Good. Anything she looks at and likes, send up to my suite. On my account."

"Got it."

I hung up, watching the screen again. I zoomed in as close as I could, focusing on Effie. Gerry was right. Her eyes gave her away. Even on camera, I could see when she liked something, no matter whether she was shaking her head no.

A throat clearing made me glance up. Aldo was watching me with a grin.

"Done your stalking?"

"I'm not stalking."

"You've been staring at her for five minutes straight."

I was about to protest when Effie's headshaking caught my eye again. I stood, buttoning my jacket.

Aldo didn't say anything but stood with me. We headed to the elevator and got in. He began to hum, and I glared at him. "What is that tune?"

He shrugged, his eyes dancing. "Just something in my head."

"It's annoying."

He kept doing it.

We got out in the lobby, heading to the boutique. Gerry and Curt saw me, both men smiling. Vi noticed me. Effie was carefully looking at the marked-down rack at the back, still nothing in her hands. I resisted rolling my eyes. I saw the pile at the counter, and I knew Vi had no issue buying all those clothes, knowing I would pick up the tab to say thank you for being with Effie.

Effie held up a purple shirt, and I stood behind her. "Pretty," I observed. "Matches your eyes."

She jumped, turning my way. I leaned close. "You need clothes, Little Tiger. I own this place. Everything you're touching, I pay for, so pick anything you want. The price is for customers, not you."

She frowned, starting to open her mouth. I did the strangest thing. I leaned forward and pressed my lips to hers to silence her. "Pick anything you want. No arguing."

She looked as shocked as I was. I never kissed a woman, aside from my nonna's cheek. It was too personal. Too intimate. But it felt natural to kiss Effie. Her lips were warm and soft under mine. Sweet—like her. I did it again as if to check and affirm the feeling I got when we kissed.

It felt the same.

"Please," I said against her mouth. "Pick something."

She blinked. "Okay."

Then she looked around. "What are you doing here?"

"Oh. I'm on the way out. I wanted to make sure you're okay. I'll be back later."

"I'm fine. Vi has stuff planned."

"I bet she does." I studied Effie. She looked a little pale. "Don't overdo it." I glanced at Vi, who was watching me with an indulgent smile and a gleam in her eyes. "She is still recovering. I don't want her tired."

"We'll be done shortly. She can nap after lunch."

I focused on Effie again. "Take it easy." My eyes dropped to her mouth, and I bent, kissing her for a third time. "I'll see you later, Little Tiger."

She nodded.

I stopped at the register. "Anything she likes," I stated again. "Got it?"

Gerry nodded, his eyes dancing. "Got it."

In the private elevator, Aldo grinned, not saying a word as we headed to the garage. The door opened and we stepped out. "Where are we headed?"

"To the diner and to see Nonna. She called earlier and said she was lonely. I wanted to go see her and thought she'd enjoy seeing you too."

"And the diner because?"

"She loved the bagels and wants some different types to try as well. And I want to look for something for Effie."

"Your 'little tiger'?"

"Fuck off," I ordered, not understanding why his words made me smile.

We checked on the diner, and I was pleased to see everything was in order. I was surprised how many people came up to me asking about Effie. She was obviously well-liked by staff and customers alike. The fact that they even approached me was a bit disconcerting, but perhaps they had no clue who I was. Normally, people avoided me like the plague.

We got Nonna some bagels and headed upstairs to the apartment.

"We breaking in?" Aldo asked.

"I took a key when I left."

"Of course you did."

Inside, he looked around. "Wow. Someone destroyed the place."

"Marianne. She was looking for something, but Effie wasn't sure if she found it. I thought I would look for her."

He blinked. "Okay. Where?"

"Taped to the back of a drawer. You look in here and the kitchen. I'll look in her room."

I pulled out the drawers in her dresser, then the bedside table. I went into the bathroom and tried the two drawers in the tiny vanity. I found it on the bottom drawer, taped well with duct tape. I carefully peeled it off and opened the lid. A necklace was nestled on the faded velvet. Nothing vastly extravagant and probably not worth a huge amount, but I knew the emotional attachment to the piece was deep. The long gold chain held a pendant containing a blue sapphire surrounded by filigree and set with pearls. It was pretty and delicate.

Aldo came in.

"Found it?"

"Yeah." I showed it to him.

"Pretty."

"Sentimental." I slipped the small box into my pocket.

"Sometimes sentiment is more valuable than money. Vi loves my mother's ring more than the big diamond

I gave her. I thought she'd want that, but she prefers the little pearl ring. She says it means more."

"She wears the big diamond."

"Of course she does. I gave it to her. But check out her hands when we're at home. The pearl ring is on her finger all the time. The diamond is in the safe."

As we were walking past the bedroom, Aldo stopped. "Should you take Effie some of her own clothes while we're here? She might feel more comfortable."

That was a good idea, and I was pissed I hadn't thought of it.

In her room, I found a small bag and stuffed some things from her dresser into it. I opened her closet, adding some shirts and a couple of dresses. I hesitated, then opened the top drawer, staring down at the lacy items it contained. It appeared Effie had a thing for pretty lingerie.

I fingered the silky material of one of the camisoles, then with a low curse, shoved the entire contents into another bag I found. As I was closing the zipper, I saw the frame on her nightstand, and I picked it up. It held two photographs, one of her as a baby with a woman I assumed was her mother, and another taken a few years ago. She resembled her mother, her eyes similar but the color more vivid. She had the same dark hair and smile.

Aldo came up behind me, and I showed it to him. "I wondered if she might like to have that with her."

He nodded. "I think she would."

I added it to the bag.

Nonna was thrilled to see us. She hugged Aldo as hard as she hugged me, cupping his face and nodding in satisfaction. "You look happy."

He grinned. "I am, Nonna V."

"Good." She side-eyed me. "Maybe you can talk some sense into this one."

He laughed. "He has never listened to me before."

She rolled her eyes. "Stubborn. Just like his mother."

I ignored them, walking ahead. I sat down at the table, waiting for them to join me. Nonna went to the kitchen to ask for refreshments, and I glared at Aldo.

"Thanks for having my back."

"I do. But I agree with Nonna V. You need someone."

"For fuck's sake. Not you too. Nonna, you, Luca. Love and babies. Blah, blah, blah. None of that is for me.

Aside from my family, I have no feelings except for hate."

"Uh-huh."

"It's true. I have no interest in it either."

"Uh-huh."

I shot him a look as Nonna sat down. She opened her hand. "Another little cookie in the bag."

I leaned forward and took it, sliding it into my pocket.

Aldo began to grin. I didn't like the look of it and decided we were going to make this a short visit. Very short. But before I could open my mouth, he leaned close to Nonna, his eyes dancing with mischief and spoke.

"Nonna V, did Roman tell you he is seeing someone?"

Nonna's head snapped in my direction, her green eyes narrowed. "No, he did not. Roman?"

I wanted to pull out my gun and shoot him. Not dead, but in the knee or somewhere equally painful. But we were never armed around Nonna. A glare was all I could do. My denial died at the look of utter delight on her face. I huffed a long breath.

"It's still new, Nonna."

"He is crazy about her," Aldo insisted. "Taking care of her."

Her gaze never left my face. "Roman? The other day you said… Why have I not met her?"

Aldo sat back with a wide grin.

Internally, I groaned. Both of his knees were in jeopardy now.

"She, ah, was in a car accident, Nonna," I said, continuing the lie. "Her face is badly bruised, so she is shy about meeting you until that clears up."

"What is her name?" she demanded.

"Effie," Aldo replied for me. "She's a pretty little thing. Vi adores her."

"Vi has met her and not me?" Her voice indicated her dismay.

"She has been helping me care for her. Effie is a private person, and I didn't want to embarrass her."

Nonna nodded. "Good boy. Now you bring her Sunday for lunch."

I opened my mouth to say no, but she shook her head. "I do not care about bruises or prettiness. The heart matters."

"She's got a huge heart. Everyone loves her," Aldo insisted. "She makes Roman act human."

She nodded firmly. "Sunday." She glanced at Aldo. "You too."

"I wouldn't miss it for the world."

I was going to kill him—and he knew it. Nonna stood to go get something in the kitchen.

"You are going to pay for that stunt."

"Really?" he said, not at all worried.

"Your kneecaps are in danger of meeting my bullets."

He picked up another pastry from the plate, humming. "Your nonna and her pastries. Those are dangerous. You, not so much."

"How do you figure that? My gun is far more painful than a few pounds."

He grinned. "You shoot me in the knees, you'll be dealing with my wife. A very angry, very frustrated wife. She likes it when I go down on my knees for her. You shoot me, I won't be able to. Then she is gunning for you. Probably your balls. My knees will recover. You can't sew balls back on, so I suggest you keep your gun safely where it is."

I cursed, taking a pastry. He was right. Vi was scary when she was pissed. And I liked my balls right where they were.

"Watch it," I growled.

He laughed.

The bastard *laughed*.

"Oh, I am. And it is so fucking amusing to watch."

I ignored his remark.

We were silent on the car ride back to the hotel. Part of me was fuming. Another part annoyed. And strangely, a small part didn't mind the thought of taking Effie to meet Nonna. Maybe if she thought I was doing what she wanted and seeing someone seriously, she would leave me alone.

"I was wondering something," Aldo mused.

"No doubt you're going to share," I muttered.

"Just thinking, Effie is feeling better? The danger of a concussion has passed?"

"Yes."

"Why haven't you moved her into Nonna V's room? Or another suite?"

I had asked myself that a hundred times. The past few mornings, I had woken up draped in Effie, with a raging hard-on I had to take care of myself. Those moments were torture, yet I had slept perfectly content with her wrapped around me. The thought of her sleeping next door or, God forbid, on another floor, made me anxious.

"I'm being cautious."

"Cautious. Right," he drawled.

"Shut it, Aldo."

He glanced out the window, humming again. It pissed me off, but I stayed silent.

We arrived at the hotel, and I glanced at my phone. "I need to check in with Alfred. He has a question."

"You want me to handle it?" Aldo asked, his eyes still far too amused.

"No."

He followed me through the busy floor, the machines and tables already full. Piped music filled the background as we left the louder part of the casino for the more private blackjack rooms.

I stopped, the tune once again familiar. It was the same one Aldo kept humming. The one annoying me to no end.

Except now, hearing it, I recognized it. "Feelings" by Morris Albert. A sentimental, sappy love song from the seventies.

"Good thing you're not catching feelings," Aldo had quipped.

The bastard had been making fun of me all this time.

I spun on my heel, glaring at him. He instantly knew why.

"If it looks like a duck and quacks like a duck…"

It wasn't taking out his knees, but it felt good to punch him in the face. My fist wasn't thrilled with it, but I would live with the pain.

"You talk to Alfred," I snapped and walked away.

"So worth it," he called with a laugh.

I shook my hand in the elevator.

Then for some reason, I began to laugh.

CHAPTER 10
ROMAN

I opened the suite door, pleased to see the cases I had sent upstairs by my desk, waiting. I picked them up and headed to the bedroom. It was empty, but I knew Effie was there. A small bag was on the bed, and the shoes Vi had brought her were neatly by the door. Effie was very tidy with everything she did. I had noticed that.

The bathroom door was shut and I waited, but she didn't come out. I listened at the door, hearing some odd sounds and became concerned. Was she ill? Crying? Without hesitation, I flung open the door and stepped in, freezing.

Effie was climbing out of the tub. The air was heavy with steam swirling around us. She stopped her movements, shocked into immobilization. I stared, transfixed. She was exquisitely formed. Her legs were shapely, her ankles and feet small. Wider hips set off the sweet curve of her waist. Her breasts were surprisingly large for someone so petite. Her nipples were rosy, a dark pink color, and the narrow thatch of curls between her legs matched the deep raven color of her hair, which was piled on the top of her head. Her mouth formed a shocked O. My cock hardened instantly, and in the flash of a moment, I decided the type I had sought my entire life was incorrect. Effie was my perfect type. She became irresistible as she blushed, the color suffusing her body, turning her skin pink and her nipples a darker hue. I was mesmerized.

Neither of us moved. Our gazes were locked, mine intense and hungry, hers wide with shock and uncertainty. My heartbeat picked up, my body tightening. Her chest heaved, her breath escaping in short, sharp rasps. Injured or not, I wanted her. Reluctant or not, I wanted her. I stepped closer, grabbing the towel off the vanity and pausing.

I looked one more time at her sensual beauty. The beauty she kept hidden under loose clothing. I wanted to take a picture of her, yet the thought of anyone seeing her this way, anyone but me, was abhorrent. I burned her image into my mind. It was one I knew I would revisit often.

I handed her the towel, then I turned and walked out before I gave in to my desires.

A long time later, Effie walked into my office, looking decidedly nervous. I was working on a stack of paperwork, trying to find a solution to an ongoing problem. I needed to occupy my mind and hands and stop myself from returning to Effie and throwing her on the bed and tasting her pretty pink skin— everywhere.

I glanced up, trying not to laugh. The shirt she wore was old and shapeless. The leggings covered her right down to her feet, and she wore socks. The shirt was buttoned up to her neck. As if by covering herself it would erase the memory of my eyes on her. Her gaze drifted to the table, and I smirked. She was braving the lion in his den because she smelled the pasta. The aroma of garlic and basil had been tickling my nose since it arrived a short while ago, and I had wondered if she would join me or hide all night.

"Hungry, Little Tiger?"

She nodded and I stood. She scurried to the table, sitting down so quickly she almost missed the chair. She grimaced, and I shook my head, sitting across from her.

"Don't hurt yourself. I won't touch you."

My nonna had drummed it into our heads from young boys that women were to be respected. Admired. Treated with the utmost care. My father's teachings had been drastically different, but even he held to the one simple truth. No means no. I never had, nor would I ever, force a woman.

Especially the tiny one sitting across from me.

I poured some wine and lifted the lids. "I thought pasta would suit," I explained. "Soft on your throat but filling."

She looked at her plate, a delicate alfredo on one side, a Bolognese on the other, both with fresh pasta.

She glanced up. "They are my favorite."

"Then eat. You need the strength." I winked at her. "And my chef is directly from Italy. It is amazing."

She chewed and swallowed, tasting each one. I liked watching her eat. She enjoyed her food, and I was pleased to see that. Eating was one of the joys in life.

"So delicious," she murmured. "Perfect sauce and pasta."

"I want that plate clean."

She ate slowly, savoring the meal. She sipped a little wine but drank more water than the red liquid.

"You don't like wine?"

"I rarely drink."

"I can order you something else."

"No, thank you." Then she laid down her utensils. "And thank you for my clothes. And the picture. That was very thoughtful of you. Or should I thank Vi?"

"No, I didn't ask Vi. I went to check on your diner and thought some of your own clothes would be more comfortable for you than the ones I sent upstairs."

"I saw the garment bags. You can send them back."

"No." I drew in a deep breath, wondering when I had become nervous about telling someone, especially a diminutive woman, what I expected them to do. "You will need them."

"For?"

"You will be coming to my nonna's for lunch on Sunday. Well, my place, but Nonna lives there and basically runs it." I paused. "She wants to meet you."

"Why?"

I took a sip of wine, bracing myself. "Nonna has been worried about me. She thinks I need to settle down. Aldo got smart this afternoon and told her I was seeing someone."

"Who?"

"You."

She blinked. "Was he drunk?"

I threw back my head in laughter. "No, Little Tiger. I can't explain his reasoning, but she now thinks we are dating. And since I know she will like you and you are here, you are now going to come to lunch and let her think we are, in fact, together."

"And how exactly will that work?"

I shrugged. "We will hold hands, smile at each other, throw out a few stories about our relationship, and make her happy."

Effie stared at me. "She'll never believe that."

"She will if we play our parts."

"And if I say no?"

I didn't want to force her. I didn't want to use her misguided gratitude, but I did.

"You owe me, Little Tiger. I'm collecting. Your life and freedom for a few hours spent with an old lady who wants me to be happy. It will only be on a couple of occasions. Not much to ask, really."

She blanched, and I knew I had won.

"When you put it like that, how can I refuse?" she murmured.

"You can't. Pick one of the dresses and wear it. I would especially like to see you in the one with the blue flowers. It will bring out your eyes."

"My eyes?"

"They, like the rest of you, are beautiful."

She almost snorted. "Fine." She went to stand, a grimace crossing her face.

I stood. "Did the massage not help today?"

"I didn't like it. I asked them to stop."

Something inside me flexed. A burn began in my gut. "Why? Was someone inappropriate with you? Give me their name. *Now.*"

She frowned. "I was in pain, Roman. I couldn't get comfortable on the table, and when they tried, it hurt too much. I asked them to stop the massage, and they got some special ointment and used it instead. Then they told me to have a warm bath, which would help it. I was just getting out when you, ah, burst in."

"I heard a noise. I was afraid you were ill."

She met my eyes. "You didn't leave when you saw I was fine."

"Forgive me."

"Are you truly sorry, or is that lip service?"

Her snappy comeback made me smile. It showed, under the pain and fear, she had a backbone. I had seen it when I went to the diner the first day, and I was worried it had been lost.

"I am sorry if I embarrassed you, but if you are asking me if I am sorry I saw you naked, the answer is no. You are exquisite, Effie."

She scoffed. Actually scoffed at me. "Exquisite. *Oh yes*. Wide hips, boobs out of proportion with my frame, short arms and legs. Such a stunner."

I stepped closer, so close I could feel her breath on my skin. Feel the heat of her body so near to mine. I tilted up her chin. "I have never once in my life called a woman exquisite before. You are. Your hair and skin are beautiful. Your face is lovely, your smile sweet. Your eyes are indescribable. And your naked form is far too beautiful to be covered in these oversized rags. I have seen what they hide, and I will never forget it. Wear the clothes I got you. Enjoy them. Consider them a gift for having to pretend to like me." I paused, staring into her mesmerizing eyes. I pressed the box I had found earlier into her hand. "And wear this."

She looked down, gasping.

"But how…?"

"Marianne didn't find it. I did. It's safe with you, just as you are with me."

"Thank you," she whispered, then rolled up onto her toes to press a kiss to my cheek. But I turned my head and captured her mouth. She stiffened, then melted against me, fisting my shirt in her hand. I slanted my head over hers, deepening the kiss, dipping my tongue in and tasting her. She whimpered low in her throat, and I caught her against me, holding her tight. I explored her, groaning. I slid my hand under the too-big shirt, spreading my fingers against the skin of her back. It was warm and soft. I dipped under the waistband of her pants, running my hand side to side, wanting what was under the material. She shivered, and I gathered her closer. She moaned, but this time, the sound was painful. Distressed. I released her, stepping back. "Forgive me, I forgot about your injuries."

She touched her lip, not saying a word. Then she backed up. "I-I'm sorry."

"It's fine. I was out of line. Sit and finish your dinner."

I took my plate and went to my desk, hoping she would eat if I left her alone. I entered more data, still angry that I couldn't solve this puzzle. I studied the screen, almost growling in frustration. I was missing something.

"You wear glasses."

"Yes," I responded shortly. "For reading," I added.

She hummed. "I see."

I hit the keys with a little more force than needed, my frustration getting the better of me.

"What are you working on that is making you so irritated?"

I glanced up. "A puzzle."

"What kind of puzzle?"

I saw no reason not to tell her. "We have three bars here. All well monitored. But suddenly, one has dropped in sales. Nothing drastic, but steadily. I can't figure this out, neither can Aldo," I mused. "How the numbers have changed. Everything was fine until a couple of months ago. No new staff, no missing liquor, and although the crowds have stayed the same, liquor sales have dropped. Then they rebounded. I want to know why so I can stop it happening again."

She was quiet for a moment, then approached the desk. "Do you monitor the staff?"

"Yes. I see them start their shift, end it. We can't watch every move all night, but their manager gives them their tips when they check out."

She frowned. "I had a small drop in sales. I thought nothing of it until I noticed it remained consistent."

I nodded for her to go on.

"I installed a camera and caught nothing. Then one day, I accidentally set the recording to start early and caught an employee bringing in their own store-bought bagels and selling them in the shop. He would stock the shelves, slotting them in. Then he pocketed the sales. He did it so well, it took me a while to figure it out. I didn't miss it when it was five, but the twenty dollars a day caught my eye, and I certainly noticed the eighty dollars, then the hundred as he started doing it every day and adding in more bagels. In a month, he was pocketing over four hundred bucks." A small smile twitched on her lips. "Less the cost of the cheaper bagels, of course."

I stared at her. I picked up the phone. "Get me the feed from Breakers the past month two hours before they open. Line it up. I'll be there soon." Then I texted Aldo.

I stood and rounded the desk. She didn't expect it when I cupped her face, and I kissed her again. Deep, long, passionate. "You are fucking brilliant, Effie. Exquisitely beautiful outside, smart and capable in that brain of yours." I kissed her again. "Brilliant."

She clutched my wrists. "You're not going to kill someone are you?"

"I will teach them a lesson."

"Roman, there could be a reason—"

I cut her off. "Do not tell me how to run my business, Effie. You steal, you pay the price."

"Maybe the person doing this had no choice."

"There is always a choice."

She lifted an eyebrow, and I knew what she was thinking. I hadn't given her a choice. I hated that she was in my head. That she made me question my ways. I tugged my shirt sleeves down, ending the conversation. I stepped back. "Don't wait up."

In the elevator, I rolled my neck, anger coursing through me. Stealing from me was an unforgivable offense in my world. The person doing this needed to be taught a hard lesson.

And my lessons were rarely forgotten.

CHAPTER 11
ROMAN

Aldo and I watched the video feeds, finding exactly what I anticipated seeing after Effie told me her story. I was surprised to see the culprit was Connor, one of our younger staff. He'd been with us for over two years and had always been steady and reliable. The one time he'd ever not shown up had been when his parents died in a car accident, leaving him and a younger sibling with only each other. He'd only missed a week of work and was very private about his grief and life. We'd sent flowers, and Aldo and I had gone to the memorial out of respect.

It didn't take long to find his methods. He came in early before his shift on a Friday and Saturday, carrying his backpack as usual, but instead of stowing it away and returning to the bar, he slid a bottle of Crown Royal and Absolut Vodka onto the shelf. Just one bottle of each on his side of the bar. Not enough to get noticed. Inventory would have been done earlier in the day, so no one would be the wiser. Then he would put his backpack on his shoulder and leave, reappearing closer to his shift, waving at his manager and coworkers. Every shift, he'd pour drinks from those bottles, disposing of them quickly by hiding the empty bottles in his backpack. He only did it on weekends, when it was crazy busy, and he covered his tracks by ringing in one drink instead of two, pocketing his money quickly and evenly. A ten or twenty slipped into his pocket regularly. Each bottle gave him a tidy net profit.

And dipped into mine.

"Get him," I commanded Aldo after checking that he was in the bar. "Bring him downstairs."

Aldo nodded and left, and I paced, fuming. I treated my employees well. Paid them above a living wage. Provided benefits. Bonuses. And this was how he repaid me? Stealing?

I tucked my gun into my waistband and checked that I had a knife in my ankle holster. I hadn't decided what to do with him, which shocked me. The last person who'd attempted to steal from me had lost all the fingers on their right hand and the ability to walk for months. The one person who succeeded didn't get to spend a penny before my gun wiped the satisfied smirk off their face.

Why I couldn't decide what to do with Connor was no doubt simply the how. It had nothing to do with the woman upstairs.

Yet somehow during the elevator ride down to the basement, I kept seeing Effie. Thinking of what she said. How she would react. She had fired the boy stealing from her, she'd told me. Made him help in a soup kitchen to work off the debt. She tracked him until he had "paid her back" in volunteer hours. He had apologized and told her he learned his lesson. He left town after that, and she hoped he'd change his life for the better. I thought her incredibly naïve and far too kind.

I was waiting when Aldo stepped into the room with Connor. How he got him there, I had no idea, but Connor suspected nothing until he saw me and viewed the enclosed room. He paled and stopped walking.

"You've been busy," I stated, crossing my arms.

Connor tried to bluff, then became belligerent and, finally, teary and pleading. I let him dig his own grave, not speaking, listening, watching. Silence always unnerved the guilty. It worked with him, and he admitted to stealing money. He even told me how he did it.

Aldo totaled up the sum of what we estimated he had stolen and presented it to him. Connor swallowed, straightening his shoulders. "I can't pay you back. I don't have it."

"Where is it?" I asked, my voice cold. Unfeeling.

His bravado disappeared. "I used it to pay my sister's tuition and living expenses. She's going to be a doctor. When my parents died last year, they had no insurance. It took everything they left to bury them and pay off their debts. It's my responsibility to help her. I was desperate—she'd worked so hard to get into medical school. I only did it until I had the money. Check the past couple of weeks. I haven't taken a dime!"

Internally, I cursed at his words. His excuse and his request. He hadn't brought a bottle into the bar the past while. But that didn't justify his theft.

"So, your excuse is it was a limited time? What about when she needs it next year? The year after?" Aldo snapped.

Connor shook his head. "I got another job—days. I'm saving all that money for her." He turned to me, pleading. "I didn't want to, Mr. Costas. I didn't think you'd miss it." His eyes were terrified. He swallowed. "Please make it fast. Make it look like an accident so my sister gets my insurance." He hung his head.

"You should have come to me. Asked me," I snapped.

"I didn't think you would care."

"So instead, you stole?"

He nodded, not meeting my gaze.

I met Aldo's eyes. He nodded at the tablet he was holding. He'd asked for all the information on Connor's sister's education and the supposed debt, verifying it. I had no idea about either issue, but then again, I never got involved in my employees' personal lives. Aldo lifted a shoulder in deference. He knew the decision on punishment was mine.

I wavered again. My pause surprised both of us. I couldn't let this go—we all knew it. Connor had stolen from me. He needed to pay for what he had done. It was simple in my world. You did the crime, you paid the consequences.

But he was a kid. Desperate to help his sister. That did count for something. Because it was *family*.

That was the word that won out.

"I'm not going to kill you," I informed him. "I don't murder people for being stupid."

"What do you do, then?" he asked.

"You will pay your debt plus interest. You'll no longer keep your tips. You will be monitored closely. You quit your other job, and you'll work here exclusively— under watch. If I think, even suspect, you are skimming, stealing, taking advantage, there will be no other chances. You will forfeit something you cannot get back."

Connor's eyes widened.

"My life?" he asked.

"Don't find out."

"I won't." He paused. "So, that's it?" he asked, relief making him stupid. "The rumors of the scary Roman Costas were just that? Rumors?" He blew out a breath. "Kinda funny—"

He never finished his sentence. He screamed as his arm snapped, and I pushed him into the wall, holding him by the throat.

"Don't push it, boy," I hissed. "I'm holding back by a thread. Say one more word, and you will not walk out of here. You hear me?"

He nodded, unable to speak with my hand wrapped around his throat. I tightened my grip, my anger getting the better of me. I smashed my fist into the wall by his head, and I held his eyes. "One more squeeze and you're done. Do we have an understanding?"

He blinked, unable to move or speak. I let him go, and he crumpled to the floor, gasping for air and crying. He wet himself, the scent of the urine hitting me.

I shook my head. "Get your arm fixed. Be grateful it was your left one so you can still work. Be doubly grateful it wasn't your neck."

I headed for the door. "Tony will take you to the doctor. Don't make me regret this."

I walked past Tony in the hall. His bruising was still evident from the beating he'd taken from me, but he was walking. "Take care of it."

Aldo's phone rang as we stepped into the elevator. I was angry. Pissed with myself. Furious for the reason. Goddamn Effie had gotten into my head. It had to stop.

"What?" I snapped as he held the phone from his ear.

"Ben Maverick is here. He wants more credit."

"Too fucking bad. If he can't pay tonight, beat the shit out of him and toss him over the Falls."

Aldo's eyebrows lifted. "I'll call you back," he said into the phone.

He hung up. "May I remind you how much he spends here? How much money you make off him? The yacht you got when he couldn't pay one time?"

"I don't give a fuck."

He shook his head. "Maybe you should come to the casino with me. Find someone to spend some time with."

I knew what he was saying. Find someone to fuck my frustration out of me.

"Not interested."

"You want me to call Larry? Have him spar with you?"

"No."

"You wanna spar with me? We can go a few rounds."

"I'm going to my suite."

"In the mood you're in—"

I cut him off as the door opened. "Fuck off, Aldo. Do your job. Stop playing mother. I don't fucking need one."

He didn't back down. "Maybe Effie should stay in Nonna V's room."

"She's not fucking going anywhere."

"Is she safe?" he asked quietly.

I dropped my head. "Yes." I strode out of the elevator.

"I'll take care of it, boss," he said dryly. "I'll check in later. Everything better be okay. I'd hate to take you on for doing something you'd never forgive yourself for."

I was still glaring as the doors shut.

I headed past my suite and went to Nonna's. They were connected by a door Effie hadn't seen or noticed yet. Nonna rarely came to the casino, but when she did, she had her own room, decorated by her. It was feminine and looked nothing like a hotel suite. I used the shower in her en suite and washed off the altercation with Connor. I let the hot water pour over my shoulders, sluicing down my back and loosening the tight muscles, but I was still tense. I dried my hair with a towel and wrapped another one around my waist. I took my clothes and walked through the large closet and into my own, dumping them in the hamper. I pulled on some sweats and a T-shirt and headed into the bedroom, surprised not to find Effie in bed. I went to the office and found her asleep on the sofa. I sat on the coffee table, studying her face. The creams from Vi and the spa were helping the bruising on her face. The blue-black was fading, a tinge of green and yellow showing through. I reached out to tuck a stray lock of hair behind her ear, grimacing at the bruising on my own skin. I had torn the skin on my knuckles when I'd smashed my fist into the cement wall beside Connor's head a short while ago. I had been tempted to hit his head, but instead, injured myself. That didn't improve my mood much.

A voice brought me from my musings.

"Are you all right?"

I looked down at Effie. She looked sleepy and soft. She gazed at me, concerned. Worried. For some reason, that angered me more. I wanted her to stop looking at me like I was a good guy. I was anything but.

"I'm fine." I indicated the sofa. "You prefer this to the comfortable bed in the other room? This is my office. It's for business, not naps," I said, sounding exasperated.

She frowned. "I was waiting for you. I didn't mean to fall asleep."

"You should be in bed resting. If you'd listened to what the doctor said, you'd know that."

She crossed her arms. "I was a little out of it when he was speaking."

"Hence the rest."

She tilted her head. "Did you kill someone?"

"Don't ask me questions like that," I snapped and stood. I paced the room, anxious energy and anger coursing through me. I had too much adrenaline roaring through my body.

"I have to know."

"Why?" I shouted. "Why is it so fucking important to you?"

"Because if you did, it's my fault. I told you what to look for."

Her words stopped me. I huffed an exasperated breath and shook my head. "Stop taking the blame for the decisions of others. You are not responsible for his actions, any more than you were responsible for Marianne's. And to answer your question, no, I did not kill him. In fact, you are what held me back. I showed leniency. Gave him a chance to make restitution."

"Why?" she asked.

I smacked my hand on the top of my desk. "I don't fucking know," I roared. "I should have killed him. Or cut off his fingers to teach him never to steal from me again. But all I could hear was your voice telling me how you handled the same situation. I could see how fucking desperate the kid was."

"And that made you angry?" she asked, rising from the sofa and walking toward me.

"Yes."

"Why?"

"He stole from me. He deserved to be punished."

"Did you? Punish him?"

"Yes."

"And then?"

"I gave him a chance at restitution."

"Did he take it?"

I nodded.

"And you think that makes you weak?"

I blinked at her question.

She kept talking. "I think it makes you compassionate."

"Stop making me out to be a good man, Effie. I am anything but that."

"You can be powerful, scary, and intimidating and still be compassionate, Roman. It doesn't make you less."

"It does in my world."

"Then you need to change your world."

I stared at her. The light behind her highlighted her curves through the thin material of her shirt. She wasn't wearing a bra, and I could see her nipples under the fabric. Her hair was loose and hung down her back in waves of ebony. Her eyes were staring at me. Through me. The idea she saw me, the part of me that I kept hidden from the world, hit me, and I grasped the back of my chair, forcing myself to stay where I was. Not to cross the space between us and feel her against me. Take my anger out on her. Aldo was right. I wouldn't forgive myself for that.

"Go to bed, Effie."

She shook her head. "No, I want to keep talking to you."

"I don't want to talk to you. Get out of my sight."

"Why?"

"I am barely holding on. Get out of my sight before I do something we both regret."

She lifted her chin. "You don't scare me."

I pushed off the chair. Walked toward her. She never wavered. She met my gaze, steady and sure. "You're mad at yourself, not me," she said.

"Pretty sure it's you irritating me."

"What have I done that is so irritating?"

I leaned close, laying it on the line. "I can't get your voice out of my head, Effie. I can't stay away from you. You are all I think about. Worry over. Your opinion matters to me. I don't usually give a fuck what anyone thinks, but your thoughts somehow have become a priority. You have gotten under my skin, and I'll be damned if I know how to get you out."

"And you hate that?"

"Yes."

She drew in a deep breath. "You hate me?"

I let my shoulders drop. "No."

"I don't hate you either."

I had her in my arms before I could think. As soon as she was close, the anger, the anxiety I was feeling drained away. I felt calmer. Focused.

"Fuck, Effie, what are you doing to me?"

"I don't know."

"Me either. A month ago, I would have shot that boy without a thought."

"Why does what I think make a difference?"

I tilted my head and studied her. I cupped her face, stroking the skin gently. "I don't know. Perhaps to win your favor. Make you see me as something other than someone to fear."

"I don't fear you."

Our eyes locked and held.

"Maybe you should. You did when you met me."

"No. I see more to you now."

"What do you see?" I asked, trying to tamp down the new energy humming through my body. It replaced the anger, ramping up the desire I was feeling having her so close.

"I see Roman, the man."

I pulled her closer. "Do you like what you see, Little Tiger?"

She wrapped her hand around my wrist, gripping me hard. Her voice was barely a whisper. "Yes."

I covered her mouth with mine, kissing her. She snuck her hand around my neck, sliding into my hair, twisting the strands. I shivered at her touch, tugging her to me and deepening the kiss. She tasted of sweetness, sugar, cinnamon, and something unique. Something special. Effie.

She was hesitant at first, but I coaxed her tongue with mine, groaning as she learned to kiss me back. Everything in my life ceased to exist but this moment. Nothing mattered but her. Me. The two of us.

I dragged my mouth down her neck, kissing the tender flesh. "Am I your first kiss?" I asked, the caveman in me rejoicing when she nodded.

"Like that, yes." She paused. "My first everything."

"Effie," I murmured, her words affecting me somehow. "Don't tell me that."

"Why?" she asked. "You should know that I have no experience."

That statement only made me want her more.

"I want you," I rasped. "Don't tempt me."

"Why?" she repeated.

"I don't know. I shouldn't, but I do." I pulled back, meeting her wide gaze. "I want you more than I have ever wanted another woman."

"I-I want you too."

I towered over her. "I feel like a live wire," I said quietly, truthfully. "I don't know if I can be gentle with you." I met her gaze. "I don't know if I *can* be gentle."

"You won't hurt me."

"Fuck," I cursed. "I need you, Effie. When I'm with you, I'm calmer. I need that right now."

"I don't understand."

"Neither do I. You unlock something inside me. I can't stop thinking about you. Thinking about being with you."

"I-I think about you too," she confessed. "When you kissed me earlier, I liked it."

I gazed down at her. "If this happens between us, it will change everything."

"It doesn't have to."

I laughed. "Yes, Effie, it does." I already knew it would. It already had. I couldn't explain it; I didn't want to think about it, but I knew it was the truth.

She gazed up at me, her wondrous eyes bright in the dim light. Wide with desire. Nervous, yet she met my gaze with determination.

"Do you feel it?" I asked. "This connection between us?"

"Yes. With every breath in my body."

Those words sealed her fate.

CHAPTER 12
ROMAN

I lifted Effie, taking her with me and covering her mouth with mine. I carried her down the hall, laying her on my bed, my body following hers to the plush mattress. I was careful to stay away from her injured side as I kissed her, our tongues tangling together, her taste filling all my senses.

I pulled away, looking down at her, my breathing fast. "I should send you to another room. Away from me."

"Will that stop this?" she asked, reaching her hand up to cup my cheek.

"No." I shook my head. "You shouldn't do this, Effie. You shouldn't give yourself to me. There is no future here. I have nothing to offer you."

She didn't withdraw her touch. "It is my choice, Roman."

"Why? Because you think I saved you? I'm not a hero."

"No, you're a man." She smiled, her fingers tracing small circles on my skin. "A complicated one. But you make me feel something I have never felt until now. I want you. I want you to be my first."

"I'll be your only," were the words that blasted through my head. I stared down at her, wondering if she had any idea of the power she held over me. Of the emotions she stirred within me. From the moment I saw her, it started. And I couldn't control it. I didn't want to control it.

Aldo was right. Somehow, somewhere, I had "caught feelings." How far, how deep, I didn't know, but they were there. And they were changing me.

And I didn't want to fight them or her.

EFFIE

Roman loomed over me, his expression once again fierce yet tender. I saw the war going on behind his eyes, felt his tension and need. But the fury, the anger from before, was gone. I had seen it dissipate the closer I went to him. The longer I spoke. It ebbed away, leaving room for another emotion. Desire.

His eyes were dark, the pupils eclipsing the green. His muscles bunched under his sun-kissed skin.

"Are you sure?" he asked.

I met his gaze. If anyone had told me that in the short time span since he'd walked into the diner for the first time all that would transpire, and that I would be under him in his bed, I would have thought they were on drugs.

But here I was.

"Yes."

He lowered his chest to mine, the hard planes of his torso pressing into my softness. His mouth covered mine, kissing me. When he had asked me earlier if I had been kissed before, I had been truthful. Other men had kissed me, but not the way Roman did. His mouth was demanding and possessive yet tender and giving, all at the same time. He took control, sweeping in his tongue and exploring me. Making me whimper as I slid my hands into his thick hair, pulling him closer. Being kissed by Roman, I decided, was highly addictive.

He took great care not to press on my injuries, holding his full weight off me. But I wanted to feel him. I wanted him pushing me down into the mattress. I tugged on him, and instead of coming closer, he lifted away.

"I don't want to hurt you."

"I want to feel you."

He grinned, the action changing his countenance. With his hair messy from my fingers, his lips wet, and a wide smile tugging on his lips, he was sexier than ever.

"Oh, you're going to feel me, Little Tiger. Every damn inch of me."

He grasped the bottom of my T-shirt and tore it in half. One wrench of his hands and the material tore up the middle. I gasped as he stared at my breasts, slowly tracing his fingers over my tightened nipples.

"Fucking exquisite," he muttered. He yanked his shirt over his head, tossing it somewhere behind him.

Then he slid his arms under me and sat up, enfolding me in his embrace. His mouth descended once more.

And I was lost to him. To this moment.

It didn't matter how I got there. Who did what and what had happened to bring me to this moment. I was in his arms. He wanted me. I wanted him. That was all that mattered.

His chest rubbed on mine, my nipples sensitive and aching for something. He pulled me up, closing his lips around me and sucking. Licking, gently biting. The sensations were incredible, and the ache shot into my center, making me whimper for him. He kissed his way back up my neck, covering my mouth again. He held me close with one arm, the other hand roving over my back, cupping my ass and sliding between my legs.

He dragged his lips to my ear. "Are you wet for me, Effie?"

"Yes," I managed to say.

"You want me?"

"Yes, Roman. Please. So much."

He smiled against my lobe. "I'm going to get you wetter. Then I'm going to make you come. Twice. Then I'm taking you. Once I do, there is no going back. You understand me, Little Tiger?" He stroked the spot between my legs that was aching for him, pressing into the material.

"Yes," I repeated, knowing I would probably agree to anything he wanted if he would put out the fire.

"Has anyone made you come before?"

"No."

"Have you made yourself come?"

"Not very well," I groaned. I tried, but it always left me unsatisfied.

He chuckled, making me realize I had spoken out loud. "Trust me, Effie. You'll be fully satisfied tonight." He bit on the juncture of my neck. "Several times."

ROMAN

Her breathless voice. That fucking sweet, breathless voice. Her little sounds of pleasure. I had never wanted or needed to hear sounds like that until this moment. Until her.

I wanted to hear her cry out my name. I wanted to feel her wrapped around me. To bury myself inside her and know the warmth and feel of her body holding me so intimately. I was desperate for it. For all of it. Her sounds, her body, her release.

I laid her back on the bed and stared down at her. She was a vision. Her hair was spread across the pillows, spilled ink on white paper. Her cheeks were flushed, her wet lips swollen from mine. Her chest moved rapidly, her skin a delicate pink everywhere, the color soft against the deeper rose of her taut nipples. She had five freckles, five perfect spots of coffee-colored flesh beside her belly button. I bent and kissed them, tracing the shape with my tongue. She shivered, and I smiled against her skin.

"Shivering is good," I murmured.

I glanced up, meeting her eyes. They were wide with curiosity, nervousness, and desire. They fluttered shut as I tugged on her pants, pulling the soft fabric down her legs, taking her lacy underwear along with them. I was transfixed as I took her in. Curves where there should be, a small patch of dark curls I wanted to touch, and lots of creamy, pink skin that beckoned to my mouth. Effie's body trembled, and I looked up, shaking my head. "Don't, Little Tiger. Don't be afraid of me now. Afraid of what is happening. I'll make it good."

"What if I can't do the same?" she whispered. "I have no experience."

I braced my arms on either side of her head, bending low to kiss her. I had never liked kissing much before. It was intimate and too much. But kissing Effie was different. It felt right. Our lips molded together felt as if they should always be that way.

"You'll be perfect."

I kissed her deeply. I kissed her until I felt her relax, sinking into the plush mattress, her body softening in relief. She sighed as I caressed and licked my way down her body, learning everything about her. How she tasted everywhere. Reacted to my mouth on her breasts, gasping in delight at the nips from my teeth, the swipes of my tongue. She whimpered as I sucked on her nipples, traced my fingers along her abdomen and trailed them down her pretty legs. I lifted one foot, then the other, kissing her ankles and calves, slowly opening her wide so I could see all of her. I felt the heat of her blush under my fingers as I gazed in rapture. Pink, glistening, and mine. All of her was mine. And I planned on claiming every last inch. I lowered my head, wrapping my hands around her thighs and pulling them farther apart. I lapped at her, hearing her fast inhale of air. I groaned at the taste of her. It was rainwater, quenching my thirst, yet leaving me wanting, needing more. She was sweet and musky, perfect on my tongue. I teased her clit, listening to her reactions. As I sucked the nub, she cried out, grabbing my hair then dropping her hand.

I looked up, shaking my head. "No, baby. Hold me. Show me what you want. Pull on my hair. Scream my name. Let me hear you." I grabbed her hands, sinking her fingers into my hair, and went back to her pretty little pussy. For a moment, she did nothing, then she began to move, flexing her hips, moaning quietly. She moved her fingers restlessly, murmuring my name as she lost herself. Twisting the strands of my hair as she grew more comfortable. Pressing on my head when I found a spot she liked. Groaning as I slid in one finger, then two, pumping slowly as she crested, her back arching with her release. She cried out my name, and

I rode it out, lapping gently, slowly pushing my fingers into her until she began to tighten around me again. I went faster, pushing harder, sucking deeper, licking and nipping at her pussy, thrusting quicker, pushing her over the edge again. She was beautiful in her release, and before she had time to process anything, I stood, dropping my sweats. Her eyes grew rounder as she took me in. I wrapped a hand around my aching cock, stroking it, and climbed back on the mattress. I grabbed a condom from my bedside table, stopping when Effie told me she was on birth control. The thought of taking her bare was too much to resist. I ran my cock through her wetness, groaning at the sensation. She was going to be spectacular. I grasped her thighs, pulling her up my legs, positioning myself.

"Last chance. I can stop right now."

"No," she whispered. "I want you."

"Once I start, there is no going back," I warned, my desire and need beginning to overtake me, but knowing I would stop if she asked.

"Please," she asked.

I slid into her, pushing past the tight barrier. Her head fell back, eyes wide in panic, her neck stretched, her back arching. She grabbed my forearms, her nails sinking into my skin. I didn't move, using every muscle in my body to stay locked down. She let out a shuddering sigh, flexing slightly. A small hiss left her mouth, and a tear rolled down her cheek, disappearing into her hair. I bent and gathered her into my arms, lifting her onto my thighs. The angle took me deeper, and I groaned at the sensation. Tight, hot, pulsing around me, she was perfect, exactly how I knew she would be. I held her close, stroking my hand through her hair, whispering words of praise. Sweet words of affection I had no idea I could say fell from my lips. I kissed her crown, her forehead, her nose, and mouth. She wrapped her arms around my neck, leaning her head on my shoulder. "Please," she said again.

I began to move. Gentle strokes, then faster. Harder. She wrapped herself around me, feeling the rhythm, moving with me. The heat built between us. I grabbed her face, kissing her, keeping her close with my other arm. Guttural sounds filled the air as I fucked her. Deep growls, passionate groans mixed with her sighs and whimpers. Her pleas, my demands.

"More, Roman."

"Move, Effie. Like that. Hold me inside you. *Fuck*. Yes. Like that. Squeeze my cock. *Jesus, yes*." I kissed her wildly. "You are fucking perfect, strangling my cock. So fucking good."

Her head fell back and she cried out, her body going taut. I grasped her hips, holding her tight as my orgasm hit me. It was a tidal wave, sucking me under and leaving me floundering, not knowing which way the sky was. I was tossed and spun, my breathing erratic, my limbs not my own. I buried my face into her neck, inhaling the sweetness that was her.

Effie.

My Effie.

I held her close. Felt the tremor that went through her. Knew before I saw her face that she was crying. I rocked her, pressing kisses everywhere I could reach.

I framed her face with my hands, making her meet my eyes. Her eyes swam with tears, the color so blue and beautiful. I kissed her trembling lips.

"Thank you," I murmured. "For your gift."

She covered my wrists with her fingers, the pale skin delicate and soft against mine.

"That was…" She shook her head. "I have no words. I didn't expect…" Again, she trailed off.

I kept her against me as I lay down, holding her. I didn't recognize this man or his actions.

But then again, this man had never bedded Effie or been given such a priceless gift. The last time I'd been with a virgin, I had been one also. We'd both been bad at it.

I pulled a blanket over us, not wanting her cold.

I knew I should talk to her. Make sure she was okay. That I hadn't hurt her.

That she wanted to do that again.

Several times.

Or perhaps, for always.

I blinked at those thoughts.

Then Effie let out a little snore. I glanced down, unable not to smile. Her long lashes rested on her cheeks. She was nestled on my chest as if that was where she belonged. Her hand rested over my heart. And she was smiling.

I shut my eyes.

I was pretty certain I was doing the same thing.

CHAPTER 13
ROMAN

I felt the bed shift, and I tightened my grip on Effie.

"Where are you going?" I asked, my voice rough with sleep. I had never known slumber as deep and peaceful as when I slept beside this woman.

"I have to pee," she muttered, pushing on my arm.

I pressed a kiss between her shoulder blades. "Hurry back."

I watched her fumble around, finding her robe. "No need for clothes," I said with a chuckle. "I like you naked."

Her little huff of annoyance made me smile, and I shut my eyes, inhaling the scent of her on the linen my head rested on. She was everywhere in the bed, on me, my skin, my mouth. I liked it—more than I should.

I opened my eyes, shocked to discover I had dozed, and Effie hadn't come back to bed. I sat up but found the bathroom door open. I heard noises and frowned. She had to be in the office.

But why?

My first instinct was mistrust, and I wondered what she was looking for. Then I reminded myself it was Effie, and she had access to the office all day if she wanted. Besides, she wouldn't find anything. I was far too smart to keep evidence of any kind where someone could find it. Still, I was annoyed she was in there and not in bed. I grabbed my sweats and strode into the office, stopping when I saw where she was and what she was doing. Sitting cross-legged on the floor by the small fridge under my bar, she was snacking on a cheese stick. An apple was clutched in her other hand, a few bites gone. I leaned on the doorframe, observing her. A bite of apple, a nibble of cheese. She chewed slowly as though enjoying the food, her eyes shut.

"Hungry, Little Tiger?" I asked, now amused.

Her eyes flew open, the blue bright in the light coming in from the large window behind my desk.

I strolled forward, sitting in front of her. "Are you in need of sustenance?" I asked with a smile.

"I'm hungry, yes," she replied, taking another bite of apple.

Grinning, I took the fruit from her hand, taking a large bite and chewing. She looked displeased that I had taken her snack, and I leaned forward, pressing a kiss to her mouth. "Tell me what you want to eat. I can get you anything."

"Anything?"

"Anything," I assured her. The kitchen was open twenty-four seven. Any time the guests were hungry, they were served. The buffet in the casino never closed. It shocked me how much food people consumed between midnight and morning.

She bit her lip, hesitating. "Tell me," I demanded.

"I want a chicken sandwich with tomatoes and bacon. On sourdough bread with mayo and salt and pepper. And crispy French fries." She paused. "With a cola."

"Anything else?" I asked, my amusement complete.

"Would the chicken be real or packaged?"

"We don't serve anything packaged here."

"Oh," she breathed out. "May I have pickles too?"

I stood, taking her with me. "It'll be here soon." After sitting her on the sofa, I went to my desk and picked up the phone. If the chef was shocked at my ordering food at two a.m., he hid it well. I repeated Effie's order, adding a sandwich for myself and a thermos of coffee. I hung up and studied her across the room. She was looking anywhere but at me, gnawing on the apple, the cheese now gone.

I opened my arms. "Come here, Little Tiger."

She crossed the room, and I pulled her to my lap, wrapping my arms around her. She sighed, resting her head on my shoulder. I relaxed with her so close and took the apple from her, finishing it in three large bites.

"Always tell me what you want," I said in a low voice. "Everywhere. When you're hungry. When you need something. What you like in bed. What you want me to do to you."

I felt the heat of her blush on my skin.

"Does that embarrass you, Effie? Thinking about being in bed with me? Telling me what you like?"

"No." Her eyes remained downcast, and she traced a design on my chest with her finger. "I, ah, liked everything you did earlier."

I chuckled. "Are you sore?"

She paused. "No."

I tilted up her chin. "You are a terrible liar. Your tells are so obvious, it's like a blinking road sign. Don't lie to me. If you're shy, tell me, and I'll explain something.

If you want something and don't know how to ask, show me." I grinned widely. "Like when you pulled my hair and pushed my face into your sweet—"

She covered my mouth. "Okay, I got it."

I laughed, kissing her palm, then pulled her hand away. "We'll eat, and you can have a bath if you want."

"It's the middle of the night."

"People have baths in the middle of the night too. It'll help you feel better in the morning. You can sleep in too."

"What about you?"

I leaned my forehead to hers, confessing. "I rarely sleep well, Effie. But beside you, a few hours rejuvenates me. I sleep better than I can recall doing for years."

"Why?" she asked, sliding her hand to my neck, stroking the skin.

"I have no idea. The same way you calm me when you're close. It's just you."

A knock startled us. We'd been so deep in conversation, so attuned to the other person, neither of us heard the elevator. I stood, putting her on her feet. "Go to the bedroom. I'll bring in the food."

She didn't argue.

We sat cross-legged on the bed, the tray between us. Effie was voracious. She attacked her sandwich as if she'd never seen food before. The mayo and tomato juice hit her chin, and she wiped it away with a carefree smile, continuing to eat.

I bit into my sandwich, enjoying the fresh ingredients and taste. I chewed slowly, simply enjoying watching her eat. She sipped her cola, wrinkling her nose at the bubbles. The French fries were liberally salted and dragged through the ketchup she'd squirted on the plate.

"If I had known that you eat this way after sex, I would have fucked you sooner," I said dryly. "I've been struggling to get a few mouthfuls into you every day."

She paused, some of the light fading from her eyes. "Is that what we did? Is that all it was?"

I slid my fingers under her chin, shaking my head. "No."

The light returned. "I am hungry," she mused. "Usually, I would just have some crackers and go back to bed."

"You can have anything you want, any time you want." I bit and chewed, swallowing. "Do you often get up in the night?"

She furrowed her brow. "If I was worried about something, I would. When my mom was sick, I stayed up with her in the night. She said the dark was the hardest to handle. So I would sit with her. We'd talk or listen to music. Sometimes I would read to her."

I finished my sandwich. "And where was your sister while this was happening?"

"Off being Marianne. She would drop in, pull some crying stunt, or tell Mom and me all her problems, then leave. She'd tell people how she'd been nursing Mom, which was a joke. But I let her do whatever she wanted as long as she stayed away. Somehow even though it was Mom dying, Marianne made it all about herself. It was exhausting."

"Selfish narcissists do that. They excel at it."

"She wasn't always bad. I remember growing up, she was actually nice. A good big sister. I was somewhat prone to accidents, and she saved me more than once. I fell in the pool, and she rescued me. She pushed me out of the way once when a limb broke off a tree." She looked sad as she spoke. "Sometimes it felt like something was out to get me, but it seemed to stop as I got older. My dad called me unlucky, but I think I grew out of it."

"Or you became more adept at avoiding whatever was causing it," I replied, suspicious.

She nodded and finished her sandwich.

"You miss your mother."

"Very much."

"I think you'll like my nonna," I offered.

"Will she like me?"

"Definitely."

"Why?"

I smiled at her. "Because I do."

"Really?" she whispered.

I stroked her face. "Really." I stood. "Bath time, then bed."

"I don't need a—"

I cut her off. "I'm not asking."

She piled the plates onto the tray, carefully adding the napkins and her empty glass. I tried not to smile at her actions, but she was so endearing. Nonna was going to love her, which, in some ways, would be great. In others, not so much. I had a feeling she'd be planning a wedding that was never going to happen. Once I made sure Effie was safe, she would return to her life, and I would go back to mine.

It was inevitable. I wasn't the marrying kind, and she wasn't the on-and-off affair kind of girl. I found her enchanting and enticing now, but I was certain that would fade. She would find me tedious and unable to make a commitment to her. My attention would wither, and she would cease to care. That was guaranteed.

Yet, the thought alone made my chest burn.

I might have turned the taps on too hard in the bathroom, the water splashing on my chest, dripping down onto my sweats.

I ignored it and the fact that a voice was whispering something I didn't want to hear.

That maybe, just maybe, I could be wrong.

CHAPTER 14
EFFIE

I woke up, the sound of the bedroom door clicking shut waking me. I sat up, looking around confused for a moment. Roman was gone, his side of the bed still slightly warm from where he slept. I knew I had been nestled close to him in the night after our impromptu picnic and bath. We had soaked in the warm water, the heat relaxing my sore muscles. Roman had been gentle as he dried me off, and in bed, he had kissed me, then we made love again. This time, it was slow, soft, incredibly intimate in the dark, with only his voice and touch to ground me. I had never experienced the sensations he caused within me. The pleasure his hands and mouth gave me. And when he was inside me, my body couldn't get enough. I hadn't slept with anyone prior to Roman simply because no one captivated me. I hadn't planned on being a virgin at my age, but I'd never met anyone I felt desire for.

The desire I felt for Roman was overwhelming. He wasn't the sort of man I would ever have thought I would be interested in, but there was no denying the attraction. He was intense, serious, focused, and driven. Dangerous. I had recognized that the moment I met him. But he was also incredibly gentle, thoughtful, and kind—at least to me. Vi thought the world of him. I knew Aldo was loyal, and Vi insisted they were great friends. But she was honest and admitted they were both dangerous men.

Still, that didn't stop the feelings that were developing within me.

I scrambled from the bed and rushed into the office, dragging the blanket around me. Roman was just about to walk out the door when he heard me and stopped. He turned, looking bemused as he saw me. He stepped back in, observing me. "Effie?" he asked with a smile. "What is it?"

I had no idea what to say. Why I had rushed out here. Except I hadn't wanted him to leave without seeing him again. Convincing myself that last night had happened. I gathered the blanket closer. "Um, I just wanted to say, ah, good morning. And have a good day."

For a moment, he said nothing, simply staring as he ran a finger over his bottom lip, that odd expression of fierce tenderness on his face. Then he strode forward, wrapping his hand around my waist and dragging me to him. He bunched the blanket up in his hand, cupping my butt, and crashed his mouth to mine, kissing me until I was dizzy. I whimpered, threading my hand through his thick hair and tugging the way I knew he liked. He groaned low in his chest as he released me, pressing his forehead to mine.

"Thank you," he murmured, dropping a kiss to my head. He released me, and I gripped the edge of the wall for support, watching as he walked to the door. He looked over his shoulder, throwing me a smile. "Have a good day, dear," he said with a smirk. "Stay out of trouble."

Then he was gone, leaving me with his scent on my skin and his taste in my mouth.

I was restless all morning. I showered and washed my hair. Stared out the window. Looked at the diner paperwork Roman had brought me. I paced the office, did rounds in the hall outside, staring at the elevator. I wandered through the suite next door he had shown me the night before after our bath. His nonna's suite was feminine and welcoming, not resembling a hotel room at all. He accessed it through a door in his closet that adjoined hers, separated by a short hallway, much the same as his suite was laid out. He said his nonna rarely came into town, but when she did, he liked for her to be comfortable and feel at home.

"And it's safe," he added, explaining that this part of the hotel was accessible only by the private elevator and completely blocked off from the rest of the hotel floor. There was even a second staircase in case of emergencies.

"Don't people notice the short hallway?" I asked.

He shook his head. "No. Mirrors make it appear longer, and no one is looking for a hidden part of the floor. We have purposely added supply closets and a staff elevator at the one end so people don't even notice. You don't miss what you don't know is there."

"Why did you keep me in your room?" I asked, curious. "I could have stayed here. Or even a different room in the hotel. You have lots," I added, trying to keep the question light.

He frowned. "I had to watch over you. You seemed less nervous when I was close. I was only thinking of your well-being." He paused, quietly adding, "And then, I couldn't." He turned and left the room, and after a few moments, I followed.

He was intensely private. I paced some more, feeling nervous. Would his nonna like me? How was he going to introduce me? Why would Aldo tell her we were dating?

Did I want to date Roman?

I wasn't sure he was the dating sort. I didn't think I was his type either, but then again, he certainly hadn't been my type.

Until now.

Simply thinking about last night made the blood rush to my face. The butterflies in my stomach turned into a swarm, and my pulse raced. I had never known passion or ecstasy like that could exist. I'd certainly never dreamed it could happen to me. Opinions of my friends varied. Some waxed on about their sex life, others seemed blasé, saying it was only a small part of their life. I'd had no idea what to expect, but nothing had prepared me for Roman Costas. He was passionate and in control. He didn't make fun of my inexperience, but rather treated it as a gift. He was in turns rough and tender. Worried for my comfort and determined to give me pleasure and find his own.

It had been incredible.

The door opened, and Roman came in, looking concerned. "Are you all right?"

I stopped mid-pace, trying to calm my racing pulse. "Yes."

He tilted his head. "You're flushed."

I held my hands to my cheeks. "I'm fine."

He came closer. "You're upset."

"No."

"You haven't sat down since I left. You're pacing in here, in the hall. You're pulling on your hair, chewing your lip."

I knew there were cameras in here, but I was surprised to know he'd been watching me. I should be upset, yet I wasn't.

"I'm just—" I huffed, unable to explain it and hoping he didn't delve into the reason for my high color. "I'm bored. I don't hurt as much as I did, my mind is on overload, and I can't go where I want."

"Which is where?" he asked, narrowing his eyes.

I took a deep breath. "To the diner."

"No."

I leaned on the desk, rubbing my eyes. "It's my business, Roman. My home."

"It's not safe."

"Margi has questions. She doesn't understand why she can't come see me. I can't explain it to her, and she is suspicious. I just want to go and make sure everything is okay. Let her and the staff see me." I paused. "I need to check inventory, see how things are. Talk to her and the other staff. Assure them I am fine."

He frowned, looking displeased.

"How would you feel if you weren't allowed to come here? To see for yourself how your business was doing?"

His frown deepened. He began to pace in front of me, thinking. Finally, he stopped, meeting my eyes. "One quick visit. You talk to Margi, do what you have to do. And I will be with you. You stick to the story. Tell them you'll be back soon. That is all."

"Okay," I agreed quickly, not wanting him to change his mind.

"We'll go at two as the diner is closing. You have an hour. And you will not leave my sight. Do you understand?"

I bobbed my head. "Yes."

"I mean it. You are in my line of vision the whole time."

I rolled my eyes. "What do you expect me to do, Roman? Sprint away and yell for the police? I am well aware they can't protect me the way you can. I know you're worried. I'm not trying to run or do anything except make sure my diner and my home are okay." I grimaced. "I don't imagine you watered my plants. They're probably dead."

He blinked, a slow smile creeping up on his face. "I don't do plants, so no, I didn't water them."

I lifted my chin. "See? My point exactly."

"All right, Little Tiger. Stop pacing and pulling on your hair. We'll go to your diner, and you can check it out yourself."

"Thank you."

He grabbed my shoulders and hauled me close, kissing me again. His mouth was addictive, and I wrapped my arms around his shoulders, kissing him back. He eased away, leaning his forehead to mine before releasing me and heading for the door. He glanced back at me, shaking his head.

"Jesus," he muttered and walked out.

All I could do was smile.

ROMAN

I let my head fall back against the wall of the elevator.

What the hell was it with that woman? I couldn't say no to her. The last thing I needed to do was take time out of my day to take her to her little diner. I had things that needed to be handled at the casino. I needed to call my brother, who had been blowing up my texts and voice mail, telling me to get in touch. I had to deal with suppliers, staff, offshore banking, and a hundred other details.

And all I wanted to do was be locked in my suite with Effie. Buried in her tight little body. Listen to her sweet voice.

And apparently give her anything she asked for.

I pushed off the wall as the doors opened, and I strode into the planning office. Aldo was busy working on something on the computer.

"Nice of you to finally show," I muttered.

"I was here until three a.m. You, apparently, were unreachable," he stated mildly, lifting a cup of coffee to his lips. "Busy with what exactly, I wonder, Roman?"

I glared at him, taking some satisfaction from the bruise on his lower cheek. He hadn't shaved, so it blended with his scruff, but I saw it. "How's your face?" I asked dryly. "You want a matched set?"

He chuckled, setting down his cup. "If you do, Vi will be in here, and I will not be able to stop her using those stilettos she loves on sensitive parts of your body. I had to stop her from coming in here this morning and stomping on your foot. Another mark on me and I cannot guarantee your safety, boss."

I didn't hide my grin. Vi would have zero issue going after me. It was one of the things I adored about her. She was fearless, and her love for Aldo made her protective—and dangerous.

"I'll hold myself back."

He grunted. "Is Effie all right?" he asked.

"She is well," I replied, picking up a file folder.

"How well?"

"She is fine. She wants to go check on her diner, and I agreed to take her at two."

"I see. With extra men, I hope?"

I looked up. "Has there been movement?"

He nodded. "Someone was at the house. No doubt the bodies have been discovered."

"Took them long enough. They are always sloppy. I hate those fuckers."

"I am aware of that."

My phone rang again, and I rolled my eyes as I picked it up. "Luca."

"What the hell am I hearing from Nonna about you bringing a woman to Sunday lunch?"

"Hello to you too, brother."

"Don't play games with me, Roman."

I sighed, deciding to keep my story the same. "I met someone. I think Nonna will like her. I'm bringing her to lunch." I paused. "Are you joining us?"

"No, dammit. We're going to see Justine's parents in Ottawa. If I'd had some notice…" he grumbled. "You didn't mention a word of this at dinner."

"It happened quickly."

"What the hell is going on?"

With a sigh, I put him on speaker and told him everything. Our lines were secure, and so was the office. When I finished, he was silent. Finally, he spoke.

"This is a dangerous game."

"It isn't a game. Her life was in jeopardy because of me. I am simply paying a debt."

Aldo snorted, and Luca spoke directly to him.

"Is that a bunch of BS, Aldo?"

"I am neutral, Luca," he said. "Roman and I rarely discuss our personal lives. The girl is lovely, though. You'd have to be dead not to notice that. Your brother seems particularly, ah…" He paused. "Protective."

"Insane, you mean. Taking her to Nonna."

"Fucking Aldo's fault. He thought he'd be funny and throw me under the bus."

"You must be going soft, Roman. He's still alive."

"His wife is scarier than he is," I stated dryly.

We all laughed, then Luca became serious. "Roman, there could be retaliation. It could put you, this woman, even Nonna in danger."

"I had no choice."

"Are you serious about this woman?"

I shut my eyes. "Because of my big mouth, her sister put her in their path. I had to save her, Luca. She was —is—an innocent pawn in this game. She didn't deserve what would have happened to her."

"Why didn't you send her away—someplace safe?"

"She was hurt. Needed care."

"And now?"

"Now, thanks to Aldo, she is meeting Nonna. Who thinks we are dating."

He hummed. "The Roman I know would have denied it and sent the girl away. Unless she is more than an obligation." His statement was more like a question.

"I will keep her safe the way I feel is best."

"You can't keep her locked in the casino forever."

"No, she will go home eventually."

"They could snatch her again."

That was my greatest fear. "I will take precautions."

"You do that. And call me later. I want to talk about numbers."

"Dinner next week," I replied.

"Yes."

He hung up.

I looked at Aldo, and he shook his head. "She will live her life looking over her shoulder, always fearful, once you let her go."

I turned and looked out the window, cursing the day Marianne ever set foot in my building.

But I knew he was right.

On the drive over, Effie was quiet. When we pulled up to the diner, she straightened her shoulders and let me take her hand as she got out of the car. Surreptitiously, I glanced around, my men on high alert as instructed. I escorted Effie into Bagels and Bites quickly, not wanting her outside. I felt anxious even with my men around us. It was odd. I never worried about myself, but I felt the pull of fear for Effie.

Effie was greeted enthusiastically. Margi and Anne fussed over her, as did the few customers and other staff who were there. I sat at a table, letting her speak with her staff, keeping an eye on everything. I saw nothing untoward, no one out of place, and from what I heard of the conversation, no strange happenings at the diner. I disliked it when Effie went into the kitchen, and I got up and followed her. She was checking supplies, talking to Margi, every bit in control. The back door was shut and the only other person in the kitchen was busy making dough, so I left her to do what she needed to do. I sat down, and a minute later, a cup of coffee and a toasted bagel appeared in front of me. I glanced up. Anne smiled at me. "Effie said you would like that. Oh, and this." She placed a wrapped cookie next to the toasted bagel and walked away.

I slipped the cookie into my pocket, then ate the bagel and drank the coffee as I waited for Effie. She appeared a short while later, coming over to where I sat. She looked a little pale, and I stood.

"Are you all right?"

"Yes. A little tired."

"I told you that you need to rest."

She nodded, looking distracted.

"You ready to go upstairs and check your plants?"

I noticed that she gripped the back of the chair, her fingers pressing into the vinyl so tightly they were white.

"Effie?" I prompted, concerned.

"Yes. I'm done here. I need to order a few things, but I can do that later."

I followed her upstairs. My men had already swept the place, so I knew it was safe. Reaching around Effie, I used the key they'd returned to me and unlocked the door. She hesitated, then stepped inside. I followed closely. She stopped in the small living area, looking around, frowning.

"I had it cleaned up," I said.

"Thank you," she responded faintly, not moving.

"Your plants?" I asked.

She nodded, walking toward the window. The little pots were wilted, and she touched the leaves on one, stroking the green. "They need water," she murmured.

Something was wrong. Her voice was off, and she was stiff. Tense.

She turned, looking around the room, her gaze lingering by the sofa. Her breathing picked up, and her face turned ashen. I hurried toward her. "Effie. What is it? Tell me," I demanded.

She didn't speak. I wasn't sure she could. She was almost panting in distress, and suddenly, it hit me. She was having a panic attack. This was the first time she'd been here since she was ambushed and taken. She was reliving it. No doubt every single moment of what occurred that night was replaying in her head. I pulled her into my arms, holding her shaking body close.

"It's all right, Effie," I soothed. "Nothing can hurt you here. I'm with you. You're safe."

"She tripped me," she whispered, her voice cracking. "She tripped me so I couldn't get away."

I tightened my hold. "I know, baby."

"She was willing for me to be sold to God knows who." Effie swallowed repeatedly. "She didn't care what they did to me."

"She's a selfish bitch."

Her trembling increased, and her rapid breathing became labored. I lifted her into my arms, and she buried her face into my neck. The trembling had become violent, and with a low curse, I carried her down the steps and out to the car. My men sprang into action when they saw us, opening the back door and making sure I got in quickly, still holding Effie.

"Get us back to the hotel fast," I ordered.

As we pulled away, I looked over my shoulder.

Effie was never going to be able to live there again. She would never get over what happened in that room. She would never feel safe again.

I pulled out my phone and sent a text.

CHAPTER 15
EFFIE

I didn't recall much of the car ride or anything else until Roman set me on the sofa in his suite, sitting on the coffee table in front of me. He framed my face with his hands, staring at me.

"Tell me what to do."

I drew in a shuddering breath, shaking my head. "I'm okay."

"You are far from okay, Effie."

"That was embarrassing," I whispered. "For you. I'm sorry."

"What are you talking about?"

"I embarrassed you."

"You did nothing of the sort. I'm the one who owes you an apology. I should have known how you would react being back there." He stood, yanking his fingers through his hair. "Jesus. I take you back to the place you experienced a life-altering, horrific event, and you're apologizing to me?" He sat back down again, taking my hands. "It is I who should apologize to you. I should have thought that through. Refused to let you go upstairs."

"I probably wouldn't have listened." I smiled ruefully. "I am a little stubborn."

He lifted a hand, tracing my cheek. "You are," he agreed. "I like that. You talk back to me at times. Not many people do."

"Good for your ego," I quipped.

He grinned. "There she is." He leaned close, pressing his mouth to my forehead. "What can I get for you?"

"Some tea would be nice."

He nodded and went to his desk, picking up the phone. I didn't understand how he did it. In his arms, I felt safe. In his presence, I felt protected. Vi described him as lethal, and I believed her. I had seen glimpses of his anger. Felt his intense aura when he was close. Sensed the danger he carried with him.

Yet the man who made love to me last night was different. The man who held me and whispered gentle words of reassurance in my ear earlier was warm and caring. Still powerful, commanding, and intense, but softer. Kind.

I had discovered two very different sides of Roman Costas.

He returned, sitting in front of me again. "Tea and some food will be up shortly."

"Thank you." I smiled, trying for levity. "I guess my plants still didn't get any water."

"I asked Margi to go up and do it."

"Thank you. I don't think I'll be ready to go back for a few days."

He opened his mouth to say something, then shut it. "We'll cross that bridge later. I want you to eat. I can get Vi to come see you. I have work."

"I don't need a babysitter. I'll be fine. Now I know about your nonna's suite, I can watch TV. I have my Kindle. I'm good."

"Are you sure? She enjoys your company."

"I like hers too. But I'm fine. In fact, I would like to be alone, I think."

There was a discreet knock, and he opened the door, taking the tray. He slid it onto the table, indicating I should join him. He lifted the lid, looking pleased at the array of sandwiches and another one of pastries. He poured the tea into a cup, the steam drifting upward, bringing the scent of bergamot with it. He had remembered I liked Earl Grey and made sure that was what was sent up. He added some sugar to the cup and slid it in front of me.

"Drink."

ROMAN

She picked up the cup, sipping, and sighed softly. "Lovely."

I studied her face. She was still pale, and there was a slight tremor to her hand, but she was calm. She was stronger than she thought she was.

I added a sandwich and a pastry to a plate and handed it to her. She nibbled at it, eating more of the sweet than the savory, and I didn't say anything. I ate a couple of sandwiches and drank the coffee I'd had sent up.

"If I asked, would you rest?"

Her naturally smiling lips curled a little higher. "If you said please."

I slid my hand under her chin, holding it. "Please. For me."

"Then, yes."

"Good." I poured more tea into her cup, loath to leave her just yet. I was furious with myself, having not thought my actions through. Of course returning to her apartment would be traumatic for her. I should have insisted on her Zooming with her staff or only going to the diner. I should have known it was too soon for her to go back.

I doubted she would ever be comfortable there again. I knew I never would be comfortable with her being there—even if I had men stationed with her all the time. It was too isolated, too easily accessed. She had to be safer.

And no place was safer than this hotel, except for one.

My estate.

I shook my head, refusing to even think about that. I stood, holding out my hand. "I want you to lie down for a while."

She let me pull her into the bedroom, and I draped the blanket over her and ran my hand over her hair. Where all these little gestures were coming from, I had no idea, but with her, they seemed to occur naturally. I went to my desk and grabbed what I was looking for, then returned to her. I crouched beside the bed, pressing a cell phone into her hand. "If you need me, you call me, do you understand? I'm on speed dial number one. Or say my name and it will dial me."

"Yes."

"I don't care if you feel nervous or lonely or anything. You call."

"Okay."

"Vi is number two. Aldo, number three. But you call me first."

She shut her eyes, nodding, clutching the cell phone to her chest. I hated to leave her. For the first time that I could recall, I wanted to say fuck it about the hotel. Whatever family business waited for me. Any problem I had to solve, error I had to fix, or question that needed to be answered. Instead, I wanted to stay here, watch over her while she slept. Even better, crawl in beside her and hold her.

I stood, surprised at how strong those feelings were. I bent and pressed a kiss to her head. "Call me," I reminded her.

"I will," she mumbled.

I paused at the door, staring at her. I had no idea what she was doing to me.

I wasn't sure I liked it.

But I had a feeling there was nothing I could do to stop it.

I was late getting back to the suite. I rubbed my neck, tired and anxious. The casino was crazy busy with tourists, and although my managers were all experts, I always made a show of being on the floor on Saturday nights. A lot of significant people were around, and it was good to shake hands and exchange greetings. Make sure they were looked after. When they were happy and felt important, they spent more money. It was a win-win situation, although it wasn't something I enjoyed. I put on my business face and did the job. I shook hands, listened to shit I didn't care about, bought drinks, issued credit, assisted in setting up a private game, and schmoozed until I thought my face would crack. I was glad when Aldo decided my time was up and relieved me. I had seen all I needed to see and done everything I needed to do.

Effie wasn't on the sofa or in the bed. She was curled up in the chair beside the window, her Kindle in her lap, and she was asleep. It felt strange needing to see her at the end of the day. Knowing she was there, safe and waiting for me, did something to my chest. I sat on the bed, looking at her. She'd obviously had a bath, her hair still damp. I grinned when I realized she was wearing my shirt I had discarded earlier. The tray beside her had a pot of tea and an empty plate I assumed had contained toast. A small container of honey sat on the tray. She was a nibbler, and unless I was there to make her eat a meal, that was what she did. Toast. Crackers. Cheese. I saw the orders and I wished she'd eat more when I wasn't around, but I knew it was a losing battle.

I grabbed a fast shower and pulled on some sleep pants, returning to the bedroom. She slumbered away, lost to her dreams. I watched her again, fascinated. She was a mystery to me. Strong and resilient, yet incredibly fragile and vulnerable. I saw flashes of her spark, and I was confident as she moved past what happened, I would see more of it. We had been incredible together. Despite, or perhaps because of, her inexperience, being with her was incredibly erotic. Knowing she had never been touched or kissed by another man made me feel like a caveman. Possessive and carnal. Watching her learn, listening to her gasps of delight, being on the receiving end of her sexual explorations, was an aphrodisiac to me. I could barely keep my hands off her.

I crouched in front of the chair, spearing my fingers through her lovely hair. "Effie," I murmured. "Wake up, beautiful."

Her wondrous eyes blinked open, and she smiled. My breath caught at the sheer beauty of her welcoming expression.

"Hi," she whispered. "I fell asleep waiting."

I leaned forward, capturing her mouth with mine. I slid my hand around her neck, holding her face to mine and devouring her. She whimpered, letting me take control, kissing me back and wrapping her arms around my neck. I lifted her, sitting in the chair with her straddling me. I slid my hands up the backs of her thighs, slipping my fingers under the lace I discovered, ghosting them over her soft pussy. "So wet," I breathed against her lips. "So responsive."

She cried out as I stroked her clit. She rocked against my hand, and I hummed in approval. I slid a finger inside as I rotated my thumb over her clit. "That's it, baby. Ride my hand. Let me see you come."

She grasped my shoulders, undulating over me. Making those low, throaty noises that drove me wild. Her head fell back, her hair brushing my thighs. I wrapped my free hand around the thick tresses, leaning forward to suck her nipples through my shirt. "Waiting for me, wearing my shirt, Effie? Did you know how I would react, seeing you in my clothes? How hard I would get for you?" I rasped. I licked and nipped my way up her neck, covering her mouth again. She moved faster, her breathing growing choppy. I moved my hand faster, the circles becoming harder, and she started to shake. She pulled away, burying her head into my neck, crying out. I felt the sharp nip of her teeth as she fell, my name slipping like a prayer from her lips. I gentled my touch, withdrawing my hand and holding her tight. Something about this small woman made the need to have her close paramount. To show her affection and care.

She sat up, meeting my gaze, making me chuckle. I loved the innocence that still clung to her. I had a feeling she would always carry it with her. It was part of her soul.

She looked down where my erection tented my sweats. Biting her lip, she traced the bulge. "What about you?" she asked.

Before I could respond, she slid off my lap, lowering herself between my spread legs. She looked nervous as she rubbed my thighs. "I've never…"

"I know."

"I want to. Tell me how."

I almost came there. Effie between my legs, looking up at me with those beautiful eyes, pleading, trusting.

Asking me to let her suck my cock.

As if I was going to say no.

EFFIE

I was nervous in front of Roman. He stared at me with his intensity full blast. Lust, desire, and need swam in his glittering green gaze. He licked his lips, then lifted his hips. I pulled on his sweats, freeing his erection. It was thick, swollen, and as I took him in my hand, heavy and hot. One long vein ran around it, the head almost purple in color. I stroked him, running my thumb over the crown.

Roman groaned. "*Jesus*, Little Tiger."

I glanced up at him, unsure.

"Open those pretty lips and suck me in," he instructed.

I was cautious, worried about hurting him. But the hiss of pleasure he made as I did what he instructed made me braver.

"Use your tongue. Explore me. Cup my balls, play with me. Taste me," he said roughly. He placed a hand on my head, his fingers restless. "Take as much of me in as you can."

I pulled back, staring at his cock. The color. The shape. Slightly curved, the head gleaming from my mouth, a drop of liquid glistening on the tip. I licked at it, taking him back between my lips. Using my tongue, I rolled it around the shaft, alternating flat swipes with curling my tongue and teasing the head. He gripped the arm of the chair with his free hand, holding it tight.

"Fuck, what are you doing?" he groaned. "That is fucking fabulous."

I doubled my efforts. Followed his instructions and cupped his balls. Hollowed my cheeks and sucked him as deeply as I could. Listened to what made him grunt in pleasure, groan in ecstasy, and curse in abandonment. He never pushed on my head but guided me, his touch gentle and his voice gravelly. He loved it when I would curl my tongue and tease him. Suckle the crown then take him deep. His hips shifted, lifting him from the chair as he moved.

"Yes, baby. Like that. Jesus, you are good at this." Then he suddenly tugged back. "Enough."

I lifted my head, staring in surprise. "You don't like it?"

He bent, lifting me back to his lap, slouching down and using his legs to spread mine open wide.

"I fucking loved it. But I want to be inside you."

He covered my mouth as he snapped his hips, burying himself inside me. I gasped, still unused to the size and girth of him. He moved quickly, thrusting up into me hard. Gripping my hips to guide me. Kissing me so deep it stole my breath. He wrapped an arm around my waist to steady me and slid his fingers against my clit. "Come with me. I want to feel you."

It was as if he owned my body. I tightened around him, my muscles locking down.

"Yes!" he roared, thrusting harder.

I shut my eyes, a kaleidoscope of colors bursting behind my eyelids. Everything around me faded away. All I felt was him. Hard, hot, and perfect. His taste in my mouth, his hands on me. His voice in my ear as he orgasmed. The feel of him filling me. I had never experienced anything so profound. I snapped, and my body took over, spasming, gripping him. Pleasure ricocheted through me. It slithered down my spine, exploding and sending ribbons of ecstasy so great I cried out, my head falling back. Then I was in Roman's arms again, clasped tight to his chest.

Our sweat-slicked skin rubbed together. Our harsh breathing filled the air. His lips pressed on my head. His arms clutched me to him. His hands were spread wide on my back, holding me in place.

And I never wanted to leave.

CHAPTER 16
ROMAN

Sunday, Effie stepped out of the closet, sliding her hands down the skirt of the dress she wore. I paused tying my tie, looking at her. Unable to stop myself, I cupped her face and kissed her. "You are lovely."

The bruises were fading, and Vi had given her some makeup to help cover them. The ones on her arms were still darker, but her sleeves mostly hid them. The marks on her stomach and legs remained dark. My mood matched the color every time I saw them.

Her hair was down, cascading over her shoulders and tumbling down her back in a wave of ebony. The blue in the dress matched her eyes. It was pretty and feminine and suited her.

I touched her cheek. "Thank you."

She smiled, turning her face and kissing my fingers in one of her affectionate gestures. They came naturally to her, and surprisingly, they were easy for me with her. I was stunned at the intimacy of our physical relationship. How connected I felt to her. How responsive she was to me. How incredibly trusting. I enjoyed teaching her, learning what she liked. What I liked with her. It was different from any relationship I had ever been in. We were comfortable with each other, and I thought it would show to Nonna.

"She will love you," I said, addressing Effie's unspoken worries. "Vi will be there as well."

"Not your brother?"

"No, he is away this weekend, but he is coming here, so you will meet him then."

"Okay."

"I'll be right beside you."

"It feels wrong, lying to your nonna."

I studied her for a moment. "Is it a lie, Little Tiger? Are we not in some sort of relationship? I'm with you. No one else. You're in my bed. My suite. Under my protection."

She blinked. "I wasn't sure how you saw it," she admitted.

I sat on the edge of the low dresser, contemplating her words. "It's confusing," I admitted. "This is all new to me as well, Effie. I didn't expect this. Us." I shook my head. "Apparently Aldo saw something before I did, and he pushed the envelope." I took her hand. "But it's not a lie. I don't know what this is, but it is not a lie."

Our eyes met and held. "Don't ask me for a definition or a category. Can you trust me enough to do that?"

She hesitated, then nodded. "Yes."

I stood, smiling as she fiddled with my tie, straightening it and patting it into place, again her gestures endearing. "There."

"All right. Let's go."

Effie insisted on stopping to get Nonna flowers.

"She has a garden," I protested. "A huge one."

"There is nothing like receiving flowers. My mom always loved it."

"Do you?" I asked, curious.

"I've never gotten any. I imagine I would."

I followed her into the flower market. She picked various stems, putting together an impressive bouquet. I paid for it and carried it to the car, placing it in the back. My men were following at a discreet distance and would stay out front of the estate with the other guards until we departed. Effie hadn't even noticed them. Aldo and Vi would arrive in their own vehicle in case one of us was called away with an emergency at the casino. Sunday midmorning and afternoon were the quietest times of the week, so it was doubtful, but in case, we were prepared.

I liked to be prepared.

I held Effie's hand on the drive. The sun was out, the temperature just right for the day, and I had the windows down, the breeze blowing her scent into my nose.

At the gates, I chatted with the staff, who assured me everything was fine. I introduced them to Effie, using a word so they understood she was now part of my circle.

"Famiglia."

They nodded in understanding, and I drove through the gates and up the driveway. Effie stared in awe.

"Roman," she breathed out. "It is spectacular."

I helped her from the car, handing her the flowers. "Nonna is happy here."

"But it is your house?"

"Yes. I live here usually. Always in the winter and spring. The summer, I'm usually busy at the hotel and casino, but I try to be here when I can."

She stopped walking. "Am I keeping you from your nonna?"

"Lots of things are."

"I should go back to my place."

I tightened my grip on her hand. "No talk of that today. Today, we are a couple, and I need Nonna to see that. You promised me that."

She nodded, but I knew she was still hesitant.

I had to say something, even though I was uncertain of the right words. "We *are* something, Effie. What, we will figure out on our own. But today, we are Roman and Effie. Got it?"

She squared her shoulders. "Got it."

I ushered her right to the back garden, where I knew Nonna would be. She was at the table with Aldo and Vi, and I took Effie to her, bending to kiss Nonna's cheek before introducing them.

"Nonna, this is Effie."

Effie held out her hand. "I am pleased to meet you, Mrs. Volare. Thank you for having me here."

Nonna looked between us. Her gaze settled on my hand, resting on Effie's waist. A slight smile crossed her lips.

"You may call me Nonna V. Like Aldo and Vi."

"Oh, thank you," Effie murmured. "These are for you."

Nonna looked intensely pleased as she took the flowers. "So beautiful. And thoughtful."

"I know you have your own gardens. Roman told me all about them, but I thought you might enjoy some blooms you don't have already."

"Flowers are always a delight," Nonna agreed. "You picked them?"

"She dragged me around the flower market getting the perfect ones," I said with a smile.

Nonna's smile grew wider. "Come, child. You shall help me put them in water."

I began to follow, and Nonna held up her finger. "You sit. Your Effie and I can handle this."

I looked at Effie, worried, but she smiled and shook her head. "I'm fine, Roman."

I sat down, watching them disappear into the kitchen.

"God help me," I muttered.

Vi snorted. "I doubt he's gonna step in now. Nonna V is gonna grill her, and you are toast."

That was exactly what I was afraid of.

I leaned forward and poured myself a glass of wine.

I had a feeling I was going to need it.

Nonna made her risotto with garlic and shrimp for lunch. It was one of my favorites. There was also salad and a pasta. Some cold meats and breads. Antipasto. She had gone all out.

I watched Effie carefully, often leaning over to add something to her plate or whisper how well she was doing. She appeared to love the risotto, taking a second helping. She nibbled on the bread and some cheese, making me laugh and tease her about her mouse tendencies. She sipped the white wine, asking quietly if it came from my vineyard.

I relaxed back in my chair, running a finger down her cheek. "It does, Little Tiger. You like it?"

"It's delicious."

"I'll make sure to bring a couple of bottles back with us."

She turned and kissed my finger that lingered on her skin. "Thank you."

Without thinking, I brought my finger to my mouth and tapped it on my lips. I looked up and saw Nonna watching us, a delighted smile now on her face. Vi was chuckling, and Aldo dared to start humming again.

I glared and then began to laugh. This entire lunch was amusing. Effie and I were being graded, and so far, we passed.

Before lunch, I'd shown Effie the house. She marveled at the size of it, looking around in wonder at my side of the large home. "All this space for you and you stay at the hotel?"

"At the moment."

"It is so lovely, Roman."

I had to agree. It was a great house, although I rarely seemed to be there. Nonna loved it, and that was all that really mattered. We returned to the group, both of us smiling.

"How did you meet?" Nonna asked Effie.

"Um, Roman didn't tell you?"

Nonna scoffed. "He never tells me anything."

"Oh. Well, at my diner. Bagels and Bites."

"We had to take a detour one day. We were stopped by the diner, and I was hungry. I went in to get a sandwich," I interjected. "Effie came out of the kitchen and"—I spread my hands in a voilà! gesture —"the rest is history. I mean, how could I resist those eyes?"

"Ah, that is where the bagels came from," Nonna mused. "And what did you think of Roman?"

Effie swallowed the mouthful of risotto. She cleared her throat and took a sip of wine. "I thought he was arrogant and didn't belong in my diner," she stated honestly. "But he kept coming back. Kind of like a stray cat. Finally, I took pity on him."

Nonna laughed loudly, Vi and Aldo chuckled, and I grinned. I loved it when she was lippy.

"She loved me right away, Nonna. I could tell."

Nonna rolled her eyes. "Ego. Such a male thing."

Now Effie laughed. "He has a big one."

I bent close to her ear. "Are we talking about my ego now, Little Tiger?"

She blushed and pushed me away. I chuckled and picked up my wine. Nonna beamed.

After we ate, Effie and Vi went for a walk, and I helped Nonna in the kitchen getting dessert and coffees.

"She is a delight," Nonna mused.

"She makes him different," Aldo added.

I scowled at him, and Nonna smacked my arm. "He is right."

"You can go join your wife now," I instructed. "Make sure Vi isn't giving Effie instructions on how to be more like her. She is already too mouthy."

Aldo laughed, carrying the tray outside, leaving Nonna and me to wait for the coffee.

"He is right," she repeated. "You are different with her."

I shrugged, knowing she was right but not wanting to admit it.

"You care."

I nodded, refusing to discuss it.

"Is she in my suite?" Nonna asked, a twinkle in her eye.

I met her gaze. "No."

"Ah."

"She was hurt. I needed to watch over her."

"And now?" she challenged.

I sighed. "I like her with me," I admitted.

"I want to see more of her. More of you. I know you are busy, but you need to live outside work."

"I'll try, Nonna."

"You can send her to me to visit. She and Vi will keep me young."

"I will."

"She is good for you."

I sighed. "Too good for me."

"No. Just good. I like her." She smiled and slipped her hand into her pocket. She pulled out a small box and tucked it into mine. "You might need this."

I knew what it was without looking. "Nonna," I chastised.

She shook her head. "Put it away, then. But trust me, I know what I see."

And she left me.

We drove back to the hotel, the afternoon sun high. Effie was quiet but more relaxed. It had all gone well. Nonna liked her. Approved. Aldo saw Effie was fine. Vi was Vi. Amusing, disrespectful, and full of laughter. It was easy to see Aldo was crazy for her.

Effie liked Nonna. They had talked gardens and cooking. Nonna told her how much she loved the bagels I had brought her. She made Effie promise to come and teach her how to make them. She, in turn, promised to show Effie how to make the risotto.

It all went well, yet I was tense. Uneasy. It felt as if my nerves were on the outside of my body. Exposed. I didn't like it.

At the hotel, we parked and headed upstairs, Effie's expression turning sadder. In the suite, I looked at her, unsure.

"What is it?" I asked, sounding a little curt.

"How can you leave all that beauty and come here to these four walls? The sun and the breeze, the peacefulness of your estate," she wondered. "That lovely house."

I shrugged off my jacket and leaned against the desk. "I have responsibilities. The hotel. The casino."

"Don't you have people to handle all that?"

"Your point?"

"You seem to be missing out on so much life."

I rolled my eyes. "Nonna was no doubt filling your head with her words."

"She worries about you."

"I'm aware of that."

"She wants you to be happy."

I crossed my arms, studying her, suddenly annoyed.

"I am perfectly content with my life. Should I remind you today was simply an act to let Nonna think we were a couple? We're not, Effie, really. We have a relationship, but that is different. I am not looking to change my life. I am especially not looking to give up my hotels or businesses and settle down. I have zero desire for a wife or children."

I saw the look of hurt that crossed her face. But she squared her shoulders.

"What *are* we exactly, Roman?"

"I am your protector. Your lover."

"You forgot jailer."

I laughed, the sound unamused. "Your jailer is keeping you safe. You have everything you need. Everything you ask for."

"I didn't ask for this."

"Neither did I."

She swallowed. "I thought you cared. You said——"

My anger was beginning to grow. Her questions came too close to the ones I was asking myself. I pushed off the desk, cutting her off and grabbing my jacket, shrugging it on. "This *is* me caring, Effie. If I didn't, you'd be dead by now. Or wishing you were. Try to show some gratitude. I asked you to pretend to be more today. You did a good job. We both did. Let's end the acting now."

"That's all it was?"

"No," I snapped. "I like to fuck you. You amuse me. I think you're pretty. That isn't acting. But a future together isn't going to happen. It's not in the cards, so get that thought out of your head."

"I never—"

I didn't wait to hear the rest. I stormed out, unsure why I was so angry.

Why the devastated look on her face bothered me so much.

I refused to think about it.

CHAPTER 17
ROMAN

I t was dark when I returned. Effie wasn't on the sofa or in the tub or my bed. I checked in Nonna's suite and found her on the sofa there, pretending to be asleep. The rapid rise and fall of her chest told me otherwise.

But she wanted to play the injured party and sleep on the sofa? Fine by me.

I had a fast shower and slid into bed nude. I always slept nude before Effie. I had only put on sweatpants for her modesty. It felt good to have the whole bed back, and I stretched out, plumping the pillow under my head. Except the movement made the scent trapped in the fabric waft into my nose.

Effie's floral aroma hit me. I inhaled the soft fragrance, trying to ignore the way my body reacted. I rolled over, snapping off the light and willing myself to relax. Except I only grew tenser. Shutting my eyes only brought her image to the forefront.

Was she comfortable?

Had she eaten?

Did she have a blanket?

Did she miss me?

Furious, I flung back the comforter and stalked through the closet and into Nonna's suite. I went directly to the sofa, thrusting my hands under Effie and lifting her into my arms.

She pushed at me. "Let me go."

"No," I snapped. "You sleep in my bed."

"No."

I pushed my face close to hers. "Listen, little prisoner. You do what I tell you to do."

I put her on the mattress, growling in frustration when she rolled off the other side and shook her head. "I said no."

"You have no choice."

She turned and ran into the office, with me hot on her heels. She headed for the door, but she couldn't unlock it in the dark. I grabbed her around the waist, removing her from the only exit. She squirmed and called me names.

"Fuck you, Costas."

I dumped her on the desk, pushing between her legs. "*Fuck you, Costas?*" I repeated. "Men have died for saying less, Little Tiger."

"Then kill me."

"How about I fuck you instead?" I murmured, my body on fire for her.

She tossed her hair, glaring. Then suddenly, she pulled my head to hers, kissing me hard. She nipped my bottom lip, surprising me. "You want to fuck me, Costas?" she whispered. "Is that what you want? It's all I'm good for, right? A sexual relationship, but nothing else? A nice tight virgin to play with for a while?" She scored my back with her nails.

"You're not a virgin anymore," I shot back, yanking her against me, letting her feel every inch of my raging hard-on.

"Then do your worst."

I tore away the flimsy underwear she wore and ripped her shirt open at the front, the buttons scattering everywhere. I grabbed her knees, opening them wider, and snapped my hips. I was inside her, the heat and wet of her wrapped around me.

"Jesus, Effie. You want me. Even furious, you want me."

"Shut up and fuck me."

I wrapped an arm around her waist, bending slightly and bracing myself on the desk, my frustration reaching the boiling point.

She wanted to get fucked?

I was going to give her exactly what she wanted.

I drew back and sank into her, pushing her into the hard surface of the desk. I didn't hold back, thrusting into her wildly. She yanked on my hair, using curse words I had never imagined her uttering, sinking in her nails and biting at my lips and jaw. I left marks on her neck, sucking her nipples red as I rode her. Sweat poured down my back, and our hips crashed together. I was lost in a sea of sensation and emotion. Anger bled into lust. Tension into dominance. Uncertainty into the knowledge this woman was mine. I took her hard and fast. I couldn't sink inside her deep enough. I couldn't kiss her lips hard enough or delve my tongue into the honeyed recesses of her mouth far enough. Even with the curses falling from her lips, she was the sweetest thing I had ever tasted. I was more turned on than I could recall ever being, my body desperate for her.

I was disgusted with myself, and yet I couldn't stop.

But as my orgasm barreled through me, and Effie gripped me so tightly I thought my cock would break off inside her, the only thing I felt was the pleasure.

The high of the sensations. The need to keep her close.

And then we stopped.

Panting, dripping, exhausted.

I rested my head on her shoulder, my body shaking with the intensity. The ecstasy I had never experienced with anyone else was powerful. I pressed a kiss to her skin, then stilled in abject horror.

She was crying.

I had fucking hurt her, and she was crying.

"Fuck, no, Effie," I pleaded.

"Let me up."

I eased myself from her, reaching out to help her off the desk. She cringed away from my touch, and I dropped my hand. "*Effie*—"

"I'm fine. You didn't hurt me."

"But you don't want me to touch you."

"No." She skirted around me, trying to cover herself. She stopped and looked at me, her expression unreadable. "You said you liked to fuck me. I hope you enjoyed it because that was the first and last time. Ever."

She disappeared down the hall, leaving me alone. The intensity and passion of the last few moments drained away, making me feel cold and shaken. I walked to Nonna's suite and used the shower.

Effie was in bed when I went back, curled around the pillow, as close to the edge of the bed as possible. Everything about her screamed to leave her alone.

I turned and went back to the adjoining suite and stretched out on the sofa there. Effie's scent clung to the pillow from earlier, and I shut my eyes with a frustrated groan.

It was going to be a long night.

I was up and gone by five. I was in a mood all morning, walking the casino, doing an inspection with my managers. Aldo trailed behind me as I pointed out problems and items needing to be addressed.

"That is filthy. Have it cleaned. Now."

"Who allowed the table to fall into such disrepair?" I snapped, running my finger over a gouge in the wood.

"It happened last night, Mr. Costas. I have already called the repair company," one of the managers assured me. "Two tables were damaged. A patron was intoxicated and got upset when his luck turned."

"Bill whoever did it," I ordered.

"Already taken care of," Aldo said calmly. "And they have been banned for a month."

"Any uncollected debt?" I asked, turning around and glaring at the group following me.

"No."

"Good. I'd fucking fire you all if there were."

I finished, then headed to the office and went through the numbers. We were so deep in the black we'd never come out. I made some transfers to offshore accounts, worked on a few things for Luca, then saved the files.

Aldo came in, bringing coffee.

"You're in a mood," he said after a while of silence. "I thought yesterday went well."

"It did. Effie did exactly what I needed her to do. Hopefully it will get Nonna off my back for a while."

"Was that all it was, Roman? The two of you playing a part? Looked like more to me."

I opened my mouth to reply, but his phone rang and he frowned, looking at the screen.

He answered, listening and asking some questions as I looked at the feed from my suite. Effie was awake now, staring out the window of the suite. Her back was to the camera, but I could see the tense set of her shoulders.

I had no idea what to do. How to fix this. How to start the conversation.

How to apologize.

Roman Costas never apologized.

I was at a total loss.

"Roman."

I looked up at Aldo's serious expression. "What happened?"

"There's been a fire."

I stood, instantly on edge. "Where? Nonna?"

He shook his head. "Bagels and Bites. The building burned down this morning."

"Let's go."

I surveyed the damage. What was left of the building. Effie's business and home. There wasn't much. Smoke was heavy in the air. Bricks, glass, wood, and steel were bent and broken. There were smoldering embers the fire department was still pouring water on. The roof had collapsed, and everything inside destroyed.

"Did the men get in yet?"

"Yes." He paused. "At least there is that."

I nodded. Margi and Anne stood to the side, both women in tears. I approached them. "No one was inside?" I asked, knowing how devastated Effie would be if one of her staff was injured—or worse.

"No. We're closed Sundays, and I came in yesterday and worked ahead so I was later this morning." Margi shook her head. "They said it was a gas leak."

I exchanged a look with Aldo. Everything in me told me this wasn't a gas leak. This was retaliation. The Santini brothers found the bodies of their dead men and had somehow traced it back to me. Traced Effie back to me.

She was in more danger now than before.

Aldo was already walking away, his phone to his ear. He would be adding more security.

I turned back to the women. "Send me all the payroll information. All the staff will be paid for the next three months until they can find other jobs. Get me your résumés. I can find you something at the casino if you're interested. We're always hiring in the restaurants."

"Um, Effie—"

I cut her off. "Effie will be fine. I will handle this for her."

"Will she reopen?"

I stared at the smoldering ruins, knowing I was about to make Effie hate me even more than she already did after last night.

"No."

In the car, I looked at Aldo. He was calm, returning my gaze. "They know."

"Yes."

"That was retaliation—at least the start."

He nodded.

"They'll come after me next. Try to get to her."

"No. They're frightened of you. They will make contact, though. They'll want compensation."

I leaned my head back. "Yes."

"I upped security at the estate and the hotel. They are scouring the building and parking areas. Everyone is on high alert."

"Effie…" I trailed off. "Fuck, I have no idea how to tell her. She'll hate me more than ever."

"What happened last night, Roman?"

"It got heated. Things…happened."

"Is she okay?"

"Yes. But she is angry."

"There is a fine line between love and hate."

I barked out a laugh. "I know which side of the line I'm on, Aldo. And after I tell her that her home and business are gone, that line will never be crossed again."

"Have you told her about the Santini brothers yet? How they found her?"

"No."

"Maybe it's time you tell her the whole story. Let the chips fall where they may."

I stared out the window. I already knew how they would fall.

Into dust, never to be whole again.

Effie was in the chair in the bedroom, her Kindle open on her lap. She wasn't reading, though, but staring out the window. I studied her from the door. She looked as exhausted as I felt. Last night had flipped something in her, and I was about to add to it. I only hoped she could handle it.

I walked in and sat on the bed, facing her.

She tilted her head, studying me. She must have seen something in my expression, and she closed the device, leaning forward. "Roman, what is it?" Her eyes widened, and she reached out to clutch my arm. "Is it Nonna V?"

I was surprised she touched me, and I took full advantage of it and covered her hand in mine. On some level, I was pleased over her concern for Nonna, but it didn't surprise me that she put aside her own feelings to reach out and care. "No, Nonna is fine. But I have bad news."

Her hand tightened. "Tell me."

"Bagels and Bites burned down this morning."

She blinked. "I'm sorry, what?"

"Your building burned down. I'm sorry, Effie, there is nothing left."

"But how—why? How did you know?"

"Aldo got a call from the police. Margi had given my name, and when they couldn't reach me, they called him. We went to the scene right away." I gripped her hand. "It's all gone, Effie."

I watched the news sink in. Myriad emotions played across her face. I saw that inner core of strength inside her tighten and come alive.

"Was anyone hurt?" she asked, a tremor in her voice.

"No. Margi worked ahead yesterday, so no one was there."

"Thank God for that," she whispered. "It's all gone? My apartment too?"

"Yes."

"Oh God. What do I do?"

"You have your insurance information?"

"Yes, it's all in the files you brought over."

"I'll help you with all that."

She stood. "I want to go there. Now."

"No, Effie. The place is crawling with firefighters and police."

"I have to see it."

"There is nothing to see. You don't want to look at a smoking ruin."

Suddenly, her anger flared. "Stop telling me what I want, Roman. How to feel. What to do. I know you rescued me, but stop it. You don't own me."

"You think because I rescued you, I think that?"

"I have no idea what you think."

"What I think is you're not going anywhere."

She pushed past me and headed to the bathroom. She slammed the door, and part of me was grateful for her anger—even if it was directed at me. It showed her resilience. Her strength. She was going to need that.

I went to my desk, waiting for her. She couldn't stay in there forever.

She came out, her face pale, her eyes damp but calm.

"I want to go to the spa. I need a massage."

I was surprised but pleased. "I'm sure that you do."

"Maybe a facial."

"You can have any service you want." I picked up the phone. "I'll arrange it and take you down."

"I can go down on my own," she informed me haughtily.

"You need a passcode to do that."

"It's 6984," she replied.

"Vi gave it to you?" I asked, angry.

"I watched her punch it in. I'm not stupid."

I drew in a deep breath. "It only works on that elevator."

She crossed her arms. "I am well aware of that. I also know any other floor would have your men stationed at the door. I'm quite sure I'm safe getting a massage."

I called the spa, angry. I instructed the manager that Effie was coming down and to give her anything she wanted. I met her baleful gaze as I spoke. "Make sure you get her lunch."

Effie rolled her eyes and headed for the door, stopping. "I have no money."

At my frown, she shook her head. "Tips."

I pulled out some twenties and handed them to her, then followed her to the elevator. I let her punch in the code, planning on changing it later. She was eerily calm and collected. The door opened, and I swept my arm out. "Enjoy."

"I will."

I followed her down the hall, and she opened the door that led to the private entrance of the spa. She turned and looked at me, annoyed. "I can find my own way."

I lifted my eyebrows and didn't move. She huffed and walked into the spa, and I heard some greetings being called out. I waited until she spoke, asking about a massage and a mask for her face. Then I turned and went to the elevator, the urge to go sit in the spa strong. She would be angry if I did that. Furious. She needed some time to comprehend what I had told her and to consider her future. And she didn't want me around while she did.

I hadn't told her the whole truth. I'd never mentioned the Santini brothers, retribution, or why they were even more dangerous now than before. She would ask more questions, and once she knew how this entire fucked-up situation started, she would never again look at me without hatred in her eyes.

I wasn't prepared to handle that yet.

But it would happen. Of that, I had no doubt.

I returned to the suite, planning on working until she returned. But I was restless. Unsettled.

Effie was in my building. Safe. She was getting some pampering. Giving herself time to think and come to terms with what had happened.

I reached for her file and found her insurance information easily. She was extremely organized and detail-oriented. I called and left a message for her insurance adjuster, stating I was representing her. I left my number for him to return my call.

After a few more minutes, I called Aldo.

"Put a man outside the spa and one at the elevator."

"Will do."

I flipped through some pages in the files on her building. I scanned her mortgage documents, pleased that at least the property value had gone up since she bought it and she would have a cushion. Little comfort to her right now, but it would be one day.

My phone rang, and I hit speaker.

"Costas."

"She's gone."

I stood slowly. "What?"

"Carl was outside the spa and thought he'd let them know he was there. Tammy said Effie changed her mind and decided to go for a walk. She left out the front door that led to the mall before we got there."

I shut my eyes. The mall door led to the main entrance, which led to the street. I had never ordered the people in the spa not to let her go. They'd have no idea.

Effie knew that. She'd asked me for money, and I'd given her over a hundred bucks. I should have known she wasn't going to pamper herself in order to feel better. She didn't do shit like that.

She'd played me.

And now she was out on the streets alone, unprotected, and upset.

"Get my car."

"Already waiting."

I smashed down the phone.

I didn't have to guess where she went. I already knew.

I threw myself into the back seat, not surprised to find Aldo there.

"Temper," he warned.

"Fuck you," I hissed. "She is out there, no idea of the price on her head. If they see her before I get there, I'll never find her again."

"We will. They won't be looking there today."

"They fucking better not be."

CHAPTER 18
ROMAN

I worked myself into a frenzy on the short drive. I jumped from the car before it even stopped moving. Scanning, looking. Desperate. My heart hammered in my chest, my rapid pulse echoing in my ears. There was no sign of Effie.

And then I spotted her. Huddled. Alone. Sitting on a decrepit bench across the street, firefighters and police still around. She was staring at the yellow caution tape surrounding the spot where her little diner used to stand. She was a hunched mass of pain, and the sight of her despair killed my anger. Relief flooded my body, and I was shaking as I strode toward her, grateful she was there and unharmed.

I dropped to the bench beside her. She startled, so intent on her lost diner she hadn't even noticed me. It would have been so easy for the Santinis' men to have taken her. She wouldn't have put up a fight. Terror filled me simply at the thought.

"Don't…" she began.

I held up my hand. "I won't. I should have brought you. I'm sorry."

She looked surprised, then turned her gaze back across the street. "There is nothing," she whispered. "All of it's gone."

"You can buy it all again, Effie. I checked your insurance. The value of your property. You can rebuild."

She shook her head, her voice a choked sob. "Not the building," she said.

"What then?"

"My photo albums. A few boxes of my mom's. They were all I had of her, and now they are all gone."

I turned, daring to touch her cheek. She looked so fragile right now. Vulnerable. "No, Effie."

"What do you mean, no?"

"When you reacted so badly the other day, I knew you could never go back and live there. I sent my men, and they removed all your things. Everything is in storage at the hotel. Safe and sound."

"Wh-what?" she stuttered.

"Your memories are safe, Little Tiger. Nothing is lost that you loved."

Her beautiful eyes filled with tears that coursed down her cheeks, but she didn't make a sound.

"Do you want to stay, or can I take you back now?" I asked.

She shook her head, trying to stand, but she was shaking so badly, she could barely stay on her feet. I swung her into my arms and carried her to the car. Aldo had the door open, waiting for us, and I slid in, holding her tight. She was weeping without making a noise.

Something about this woman and her silent tears dug deep into my soul. I felt her pain. I wanted to take it away, but I knew I couldn't. All I could do was try to help her. Ease her through this new trauma.

And God help me, I wanted to.

She looked up, the red rims of her eyes making me ache.

"Thank you," she whispered.

I pressed a kiss to her head, and she tucked her face against my chest.

I met Aldo's gaze, seeing only empathy. I nodded in understanding.

I finally got it.

Feelings.

Whoa, whoa, whoa.

Fucking feelings.

I took Effie to the storage locker in the basement of the hotel, showing her the boxes of her possessions.

"I didn't move the furniture. I planned to, but we hadn't done it yet. Except that chair," I indicated the one in the corner with a couple of boxes on it. "It fit into the truck."

"That is the one piece of furniture I would have saved if I were given a choice. Thank you." Effie touched a stack of boxes. "Thank you for doing this for me."

I offered her a small smile, unsure what to do. I wanted to drag her into my arms. Beg her to talk to me and tell me what she was thinking behind those lovely eyes. In a short time span, her entire world had crumbled and disappeared. She'd been attacked, kidnapped, subjected to me and my intense world, and now everything she had worked for was gone. Yet she was standing, weakened, but not falling. She was grace under pressure, as Nonna would say. I admired her. Respected her strength.

I also longed for her. I wanted her to depend on me. I wanted her to seek the shelter of my embrace. Look at me the way she had the night I'd made her mine.

I wasn't sure that would ever happen again.

"Roman?" she asked.

I realized she had been saying something, and I had missed it.

"I am sorry, Little Tiger. What did you say?"

"I want to go upstairs."

"Of course. Anytime you need something from down here, one of my men will bring you. In the meantime, it is all safe."

In the elevator, she was quiet. She let me loop my arm around her waist, not pulling away. In my suite, she looked lost.

"I will order some food and tea."

"I'm not hungry."

"You need to eat. You have a lot to face, and you need your strength."

I headed to my desk, and she spoke.

"You didn't hurt me."

I turned. "What?"

"The other night. The desk. You didn't hurt me."

I walked toward her. "You were angry with me."

"No. You did exactly what I told you to do. I was shocked."

"Shocked?"

"I saw the marks on your back from my nails. The bite marks on your neck and lip. I cursed you and said things while"—she swallowed nervously—"while we were together. I didn't know I could do that. Or that sex like that would be so…" She trailed off.

"Incredible?" I asked.

She nodded, and I ran my finger down her cheek. "I was caught up in the moment, Effie. We were a tornado of passion. Fueled by lust and anger. It happens. It was rough and real."

"Why were you so angry, Roman?"

I paused, then drew in a long breath. I owed it to her, to be honest.

"Because some of the things you were saying, that Nonna was nagging me about, rang true, Effie." I stepped closer. "Because you aren't my prisoner. You are more than a plaything. More than I expected and I didn't like it."

"So what do we do?"

"I have no idea."

"Which pisses you off even more?" she asked with a slight smile.

"Yes. But none of that matters. What matters is making sure you're okay. I'll help you with all the paperwork and dealing with the insurance company. But you have to stay where you are safe, Effie."

She met my eyes. "Was it a gas leak?"

I shook my head. "No."

"You should have told me that."

"I know."

"Are they still after me?"

"They won't get to you here. I will figure out how to stop them."

She nodded. "Okay."

She began to go past me, and I shot my arms out, dragging her close. She didn't fight me, letting me hold her.

Yet, it felt as if she were a million miles away.

And I wasn't sure how to get her back.

The call I had been expecting came in the afternoon as Aldo and I went through some numbers and planning for the new building in Ottawa. Vi had Effie downstairs in the spa, having insisted she needed some girl time and spoiling. I agreed to allow it. I had men posted outside the spa so I knew she would be safe. There was no chance of her running again.

Since I had brought her back, she had been quiet, reflective, but calm. I had helped her with the insurance adjuster, and everything was moving forward. She was withdrawn, and there had been no change in our physical relationship, but she did sleep beside me at night. Invariably, I woke up with her on my chest and a raging hard-on. Neither of us tried to do anything about it.

My phone rang, and I glanced at the number. "It's them," I announced.

Aldo nodded, and I hit speaker.

"Costas."

"We need to talk."

I sat back, simply the sound of Timothy Santini's voice making me angry.

"Is that so?"

"You took something of great value to us. It cost us a lot of money, time, and frustration. There is a price to be paid for that." He paused. "You disrupted our business for no reason. There was nothing for you there."

"I see. So you burned down a diner to show your displeasure?"

"Retribution has to start somewhere," Gregory rumbled from the background.

"Let me remind you of something. You are not allowed to conduct any of your filthy business in this city, province, or country. You broke those terms."

"We were not there."

"Your men were. Your scum were in my territory."

"It was only temporary."

"You know what else is temporary, Timothy? My fucking patience," I snarled.

"What occurred was no business of yours. You broke the terms as well. You killed our men. We are demanding satisfaction. We want the package back."

I shut my eyes, knowing what I was about to do would forever change my life. Forever change the path for Effie.

"Did you know I became engaged recently, Gregory?"

Aldo began to shake his head, but I kept talking.

Gregory made a spitting sound. "Like I care."

"You should. The *package* you want back...is my fiancée."

There was stunned silence.

"So, I believe it is *I* who wants satisfaction," I said slowly.

There were frantic mutterings. Some cursing.

"We must meet. Neutral ground."

"The convention hall," I agreed. "Room C as usual. Ten o'clock."

I hung up.

Aldo looked at me. "What have you done?"

"Stopped a war."

"And created another huge problem. She is a target now, Roman."

"She already was. As soon as this shit happened, she became a target. If I didn't take her, she'd be in some god-awful place having horrendous things done to her, if not dead by now. I've been protecting her since the moment I figured out what Marianne had done. When the building was torched, I knew I would have to continue to protect her."

"We could send her somewhere. Make her disappear. One of your strongholds where she'd live a quiet life."

"She isn't leaving here."

"You care about her. Admit it."

"I care enough to want to make up for causing this."

"You're lying to yourself."

"Enough."

He shook his head. "How are you going to play this?"

"I have a plan. We need to bring their money, plus be ready for whatever they ask."

He narrowed his eyes. "And once the word is out—and it will be—how will you explain this to your brother? Your nonna?"

"Luca will understand. Nonna, well, I suppose she gets her wish. I'll take Effie there, and I'll add more security to the estate. They'll both be safe."

"You're going to marry her?"

I shrugged. "I might as well. I have no desire for a wife, but it will send a message. And Nonna will be happy."

He regarded me. "And Effie?" he asked quietly.

"She'll accept it."

He stood and looked at me. "Vi has become very fond of Effie. And she thinks that your relationship would actually work. She thinks Effie suits you. And, oddly enough, that you suit Effie. She says Effie is too good for this world and she needs someone like you to protect that goodness. But don't destroy her, Roman. Don't compound this by keeping her a prisoner the rest of her life. You're better than that. If you're going to marry her, give her what she deserves. What you deserve."

"Which is?"

"Honesty. A home. Children. Build a relationship with her. Have a real life, Roman. Give her love."

"I don't believe in love."

He shook his head. "Then you're a fool."

It was raining when we arrived at the convention hall. It was an agreed-upon neutral place if I had to deal with another group within my town. This time of night, the building was vacant. But I was Roman Costas, and no building was closed to me.

"They've arrived already," Aldo informed me.

I nodded. "Let them wait, the fucking bastards."

"You really want to set the tone of the meeting with open disrespect?"

I met his gaze, mine steely and determined. "They need to remember who they're dealing with." I paused. "Maybe you do as well."

He held up his hands and left the vehicle, turning his back to the car.

I knew I should feel badly for saying that, but I was barely holding on. The thought of being in the same room as the Santini brothers made my skin crawl. I leaned forward and picked up the bottle of scotch and took a deep swallow, shuddering as the liquid burned its way down my throat. I straightened my shoulders and rapped on the window.

The door opened, and I stepped out into the drizzly, cool evening.

"I have your back, Roman," Aldo murmured.

I turned and faced him. "I know."

We walked into the building, my men in front and back. Two more stood outside the door to Room C. "They're here, boss."

"Good. Look sharp. Shoot and ask later. You understand?"

They nodded, and I opened the door and walked in, my shoulders back and a scowl on my face.

Gregory and Timothy Santini stood as I walked in. We acknowledged one another with a tilt of our heads. I sat down, and they followed suit. Aldo stood to my side.

I looked between them. You could tell they were brothers. Older than me by ten years or more, they had lived a hard, violent life, and it showed. They had broken noses, scarred faces and hands. Both were shorter men, heavyset. Ugly. I imagined the only way they got women was to kidnap and force them. Then again, some women liked ugly men. They felt superior.

A sewer rat was superior to these two.

"It seems we have a problem," I began.

Gregory held up his hand. As the elder brother, he often handled negotiations. I had been surprised when Timothy led the call earlier. He usually followed his brother.

"We did not know she belonged to you. We never would have touched her."

"But you did. I left her that morning, happy in her little diner, and by that night, she was gone. When I found her, she was beaten, bruised, and terrified. And now, you burned down her dream."

I tamped down my rage. "An innocent woman is bad enough. *You touched my fiancée. You hurt her.* I could kill you for that right now."

"Her sister—"

I slammed my hand on the table and stood, yelling. "Her sister—*that bitch*—is not the issue. The issue is you came to my city and kidnapped a woman. My territory, which is off-limits to you. For that transgression alone, I could kill you and not be held accountable. The fact that you kidnapped and hurt my fiancée gives me the right to destroy you. Raze and burn everything you hold dear, make you watch and kill you, and then—and only then—would I be satisfied."

Aldo put a hand on my shoulder, and I sat down. The Santinis shifted in their seats.

I put my hands flat on the table and exhaled. "But today is your lucky day."

"Tell us your terms."

I glanced at Aldo, and he tossed the bag on the table. Timothy pulled it toward him, opening it and looking confused.

"Your money. I'm returning it. Unless Marianne skimmed off the top."

"We gave her a hundred grand."

I barked a dry laugh. "She took thirty." I snapped my fingers. "Wire it to them. Now."

Aldo pulled out his phone, tapping on the screen. "Done."

The brothers exchanged a look, clearly perplexed.

"You are out nothing but a couple of useless men. Who sang the second they saw my gun, so no loss there for you. We are even on the money. I owe you nothing. Now the debt is yours."

"What do you want?" Gregory asked.

"You stay on that side of the river in the US. You never come back here. You never take another woman from my territory. Or my brother's. I find out you have been here, you have broken this olive branch, hellfire will rain down on you. On everything you touch. I will wipe you out, and there will be nowhere you can run. You have no idea the length of my reach."

"Why?" they asked at the same time.

"My fiancée detests violence. I am doing this to honor her. She has suffered enough." I paused. "There is one stipulation."

"What?"

From my pocket, I withdrew a small rectangular box. I opened it and laid it on the table. "I cannot trust you to keep your word. You have given it before, and yet here we sit. You will allow us to embed these trackers in you. As long as you stay on your side of the border, they remain inactive. The minute you cross into my territory, I will know."

"And if we refuse?"

"You will be leaving here in a body bag. And the people I have in position will move in and take everything you built. By tomorrow, the world will be rid of your memory and control."

I sat back, crossing my legs. "Your decision."

"You want us to believe you will not use this to track and kill us?"

"My word is not in question here. I have never broken it. I don't care what you do as long as you stay away. And you will not use others to do your dirty work. You are done here. For good."

"And there will be no further revenge?"

"To you? No."

"To whom, then?"

My voice became cold. "Marianne must pay."

"Her sister will allow this?" Gregory asked skeptically. "Women are softer."

"Her sister will do as I say."

His eyebrows rose at my harsh tone. Then he nodded. "We agree."

One of my men came forward and implanted the devices. I refused to touch either man, and I knew

Aldo felt the same. I would make sure Henry got a reward for doing so.

"How did you connect me with her?" I asked, curious.

"Our men saw you at her shop after the fire. It didn't take much guessing."

I thought about the fact that Effie had gone there on her own later that day. It was only divine intervention that stopped them from taking her from me. I drew in a long breath, keeping my temper.

"Your business in Canada is over," I announced. "Do not return. Ever."

They stood, and I held up my hand. "I have a bonus for you."

"And that is?"

"Marianne. She took a flight to Vegas. I'm looking for her. If you find her, there will be no retribution for ending her life. In fact, I would consider it a debt fully paid, especially if she suffers."

Gregory narrowed his eyes. "You are a cold man, Roman Costas."

I shrugged. Marianne had ceased to be a person to me the moment she chose to set this plan in motion. She meant nothing to me, and she deserved to be punished. Effie would be horrified, but if it happened elsewhere, she wouldn't hold me accountable. The bottom line was, I wasn't going to give Marianne another chance to hurt Effie. She would try, I knew it as clearly as I knew the Santini brothers would find a way to break this deal.

And when they did, they, too, would die.

"Remember that," I instructed them.

Without another word, I left the room.

CHAPTER 19
ROMAN

I stopped in the hotel, showering in the gym. I always kept a set of fresh clothes there for when I worked out. I refused to go to my suite with the lingering scent of the Santinis anywhere on my person. Simply being in the same room as them made me feel filthy.

Aldo didn't say a word to me, but I knew he was thinking about what had occurred as much as I was. I also knew he would cover the hotel and casino for me. I wasn't safe to be near anyone right now.

I let myself into the suite, not surprised to find Effie asleep. I sat and watched her for a short time, allowing the calmness she always afforded me to wash over me. I was desperate to touch her, but I refrained. Unless she asked, I wouldn't.

Back in the office, I left the lights off, wanting the darkness. I poured a good measure of scotch into my glass, staring out the window at the Falls. The lights on the water showed the power of the flow, even with the darkness shrouding it. Up close, the thunder of the water was incredible. High up in the building, enclosed in glass, all I saw was the spectacle.

I sat down at my desk, switching on a lamp. I opened the drawer, taking out the small box Nonna had slipped into my pocket. I stared at the dusty, faded box for a moment, then flipped open the lid. Inside, the ring glowed with a life of its own. A cushion cut diamond glittered in the light, the deep color of the emeralds flanking the stone an unusual shade of green.

Like Nonna's eyes.

My mother's eyes.

My eyes.

This had been my great-grandmother's engagement ring. It was passed to Nonna. She had offered it to Luca since I insisted I would never marry, but Luca declined, saying he wanted something more modern. In private, he told me it was only right it go to me.

"You are her favorite," he said, stating the fact simply. "And you have the green eyes." He clasped my shoulder. "One day, you will find the right one, Roman. I know it."

I doubted that, but what he said was true. Although she treated us fairly, Nonna and I had always been extremely close. I looked like my mother, favoring her coloring. It drew Nonna to me the same way it pushed my father from me. I was too painful to be around. He never got over my mother's death, and once she was gone, our interactions were sparse and usually fraught with tension. He concentrated on Luca, grooming him to take over, only bringing me in when our mother passed and he deemed me ready. But he was never satisfied with me. I often wondered how he would feel knowing that Luca went against most of what he stood for. Nonna insisted it was our mother in us.

I didn't disagree.

I stared at the ring, slipping it from its mooring. I held it up to the light, imagining how it would look on Effie's finger. How I would feel seeing it.

If she would hate it.

Hate me.

With a low curse, I put it back in its box and poured more scotch. I switched off the light and sat on the sofa, thousands of thoughts swirling in my head.

I couldn't take it back. I had claimed Effie, and within twenty-four hours, the word would be out.

No one would dare touch her or risk my wrath and revenge. And the Santinis would be only too happy to share what had already occurred.

There was no choice in the matter. She had to stay with me. Married to me, in many ways, she would be untouchable. I owed her that debt for putting us on this course. I would marry her, and she could live with Nonna at the estate. We could find common ground. Maybe have a baby or two to please Nonna. Effie could live a good life. She wouldn't have to work, worry about money, or anything else. I would take care of her. Give her everything she wanted.

Except for love.

She was one of those girls. She wanted to be loved. Cherished. She deserved it, but it wasn't something I could give her. I was incapable.

I loved Nonna. Luca. Even Aldo and Vi in my own way. But it wasn't fully, with utter abandonment, the way Effie wanted to be loved. I cared, looked after, and fixed. That was what I did.

My mood grew darker the more I thought about it. I cursed Marianne Warner. I cursed my own stupid mouth. My lack of a soul.

I startled at the sound of Effie's voice. She appeared in front of me, bringing with her that lovely scent that drifted in the air around her. "Roman?" she asked, her voice low and sleepy. "Are you all right?"

"Go back to bed, Effie."

"Why are you sitting in the dark?"

I barked a laugh. "People like me love the dark."

She sat on the coffee table in front of me. "People like you?"

I drained my glass of scotch. "People like me," I repeated.

She switched on the light beside me, making me utter a curse and cover my eyes. She said nothing for a moment, then to my shock, slid down on her knees between my splayed legs. She ran her hands over my thighs in what I knew she meant to be a soothing manner. My body tightened at her touch, the lust I felt for her roaring through my entire being.

"Roman," she murmured. "What is it? Tell me what you need."

I met her gaze. Goddamn it, I swore I could see her soul in the luminous depths. Her sweetness and beauty of her very being showed in her eyes. No one looked at me the way she did.

She stared back at me with nothing but concern and worry in her expression. The blue was vivid in her pale face, the dark of her hair setting off her creamy skin. She wore another shirt of mine. It was too large, and the neckline was stretched, hanging off one shoulder. I drank in the expanse of skin showing. Our eyes locked and held, and before I could think, I leaned down, cupping her face. Her eyes widened, but she didn't pull away. I bent close, our lips almost touching.

"What do I need, Little Tiger? I need the one thing I can't have."

"Which is?"

"*You*. I fucking need you."

"And you hate that."

"Yes. But it's true. I fucking need you more than I need to breathe." I brushed my mouth over her trembling lips. "Tell me I can have you. Don't deny me," I begged, my voice strained, my body tense and anxious. I never begged. But for her, I would.

"Yes," she whispered.

I yanked her into my arms.

She was mine.

EFFIE

I woke up to an odd noise, and I looked around, confused. The door to the bedroom was open, but the office down the hall was dark. Then I heard it again. The sound of glass moving. Roman was in his office. I glanced at the clock, surprised to see it was only just past midnight. He usually wasn't back until later.

I slid from the bed and padded down the hall, stopping at the entryway to the office. The room was dim, but there was enough light from the windows that I could see Roman sitting on the sofa. A bottle of scotch was on the table in front of him. He was hunched over, the glass hanging loosely from his hands. His head was down, and his forearms rested on his thighs. His body screamed exhaustion and tension. Always aware, he didn't even notice I was there.

I stood in front of him.

"Roman?" I asked quietly. "Are you all right?"

He didn't look up. "Go back to bed, Effie."

"Why are you sitting in the dark?"

He barked a laugh. "People like me love the dark."

I pushed the bottle over and sat on the coffee table in front of him. "People like you?"

He drained the glass of scotch. "People like me," he repeated, his voice emotionless.

I switched on the light beside him, and Roman cursed and covered his eyes for a moment, then sat back with a sigh. I studied him. He had left earlier wearing a suit. Now he was in a T-shirt and sweats, his hair damp. He'd obviously had a couple of glasses of scotch, if not more. His expression was tormented, his body tense. I wasn't sure what to do or say, surprised at how intense the need to comfort him was. I slid down onto my knees between his splayed legs and ran my hands over his thighs, wanting him to know I was here.

"Roman," I murmured. "What is it? Tell me what you need."

He met my gaze. Torment didn't begin to cover the expression in his dark green eyes. Fury, agony, distress —they were all there. Plus, a vulnerability I'd never seen before this moment. He was in conflict—at war with an invisible foe I knew nothing about.

Our eyes locked and held, and suddenly he leaned down, cupping my face. His touch was gentle, his thumbs working circles on my skin. He was close enough our lips almost touched. My breathing picked up, and I felt the heat rise between us.

"What do I need, Little Tiger? I need the one thing I can't have," he said, his voice low and gravelly.

"Which is?"

"*You*. I fucking need you."

I swallowed at the desire I heard in his words. "And you hate that."

"Yes. But it's true. I fucking need you more than I need to breathe." He brushed his mouth over mine. "Tell me I can have you. Don't deny me," he pleaded, a tone to his voice one I hadn't expected from him. It tore at my soul, and I couldn't deny him.

"Yes," I whispered.

In an instant, he pulled me to his lap, his mouth covering mine. He kissed me like a desperate man needing oxygen and I was the only lifeline. He held me tight, his hands restless, sliding under the shirt I was wearing, roaming over my back, cupping my ass, pressing me close. His cock was a hard ridge between us. He stood in one fluid movement and carried me down the hall, depositing me on the bed, our mouths never separating.

He pulled back, yanking his shirt over his head and tossing it away. He pushed his sweats down, then in one rough movement, tore the shirt I was wearing up the middle and fisted my underwear, ripping them off my body. He lifted me to the middle of the bed and stared down at me. He breathed deeply, his chest working fast. His hands clenched and unclenched at his sides. His cock jutted out, making me whimper in need.

"So. Fucking. Exquisite."

He crawled up the mattress, and I expected him to attack. To fuck me hard. But once again, Roman Costas surprised me. His mouth gentled, kissing me long and deep, sweeping his tongue in and exploring me. His touches were languid, tender, but no less passionate. He kissed his way down my body, teasing me with his tongue and fingers. He brought me to a shuddering climax with his mouth, then positioned himself over me, our eyes locking as he notched himself inside me.

"Mine," was all he said.

His movements were slow. Teasing. His thrusts powerful, steady, and intense. He played my body like a violin, and he was the conductor, coaxing noises and responses from me I didn't know I was capable of. My orgasm was quick, and I cried out. He only smiled and held himself over me, riding it out.

"That, Little Tiger, is only the start."

ROMAN

I pulled down my shirt sleeves, making sure my cuff links were in place. At the doorway of the closet, I paused, staring at Effie. It was barely seven, and she was asleep, curled up in my bed, her dark hair a mess from my hands, love bites on her neck and shoulders. I knew if the blanket weren't there, I would find them on her breasts and thighs as well. Something about this sweet woman made me want to mark her. I lost myself in unbridled passion whenever our bodies were close.

I'd had her three times in the night. Twice in the bed and once in the shower. Each time had been incredible—unlike any sex I had ever experienced. It was profound on a level I didn't understand and didn't want to delve into at the moment.

I wasn't sure I would like the things I discovered.

I left quietly, not wanting to disturb her. If she woke up and I kissed her, I wouldn't leave this room. We needed a conversation, and I wasn't sure how it would play out. I'd planned on talking to her last night. Instead, I'd made love to her for hours, leaving us both sated and exhausted.

I went to the office downstairs, frowning when I heard voices inside. I found Aldo and Luca there, steaming cups of coffee in their hands.

"Brother," I greeted Luca. "I wasn't expecting you." I glanced at my watch. "Especially this early."

He looked serious. "I didn't expect to hear that my brother now had a fiancée from another associate. It was an unexpected shock."

Aldo stood and left the room. *The coward.*

I sat down, pouring a cup of coffee. "I apologize. I didn't expect the news to travel so quickly."

"Nonna told me she gave you her ring. She obviously saw something."

My patience wasn't the best this morning. "Since the lady herself hasn't been told of the change in our status, I suppose I didn't think to inform you first."

An eyebrow shot up. "The lady hadn't been *told*? You mean asked."

I stood and paced. "You know about Effie. The Santinis connected us. They were watching her shop and saw me there and put two and two together. They demanded retribution. I knew no matter what happened, no matter what I gave them, as soon as I set her free, she was dead. They would snatch her and subject her to atrocities I don't even want to think of. Keeping her is the only option. I am going to marry her and give her the safety of my name. She will live at the estate with Nonna."

He stared, the anger draining from his expression. "Roman. What are you doing?"

"Paying my debt."

"What about a real marriage? What happens when you fall in love?"

I scoffed. "I'm not like you, Luca. I don't believe in romantic love." I held up my hand, stopping him from talking. "I care for Effie. I think we can be content. We are compatible in many ways. Nonna liked her. Vi adores her."

"And you '*care*,'" he said, his tone filled with disbelief.

"Yes."

"What about children?"

I shrugged. "If Effie wants them, I am fine with the idea."

He shook his head. "You are unbelievable."

"She is in this situation because of me. I have no choice because I cannot allow them to touch her. I *will* marry her."

Luca sat down, looking sorrowful. I waved my hand. "Stop. Effie is lovely. You will meet her and like her. I think Justine will as well."

"I want to meet her. Welcome her to the family."

"Fine. I need to speak to her today. Let her know what is happening."

"What if she refuses?"

I blinked. "I beg your pardon?"

"What if she says no? You can't force her, Roman."

"I won't have to force her. She will agree."

"When will you tell Nonna? News will travel, and although Nonna is out of this life, she might hear it, regardless."

"This afternoon, on our way to have dinner with you. Once the ring is on Effie's finger."

He shook his head, saying nothing for a moment.

"So you came all this way to confirm I'm getting married?" I asked suspiciously.

He stood and went to the window, looking down at the gaming floor. Even at this early hour, people were at machines, spending money.

He spun on his heel. "Justine is pregnant."

A real smile broke out on my face. "Congratulations, brother. Nonna will be so pleased. As am I."

He nodded, rubbing his lip. "Justine wants to move closer to her family in Ottawa. She misses her mother especially. And her cousins and friends."

"Understandable. But that would be a lot of traveling for you."

He stood straighter. "I was thinking I could run your casino there. Oversee the final plans, take some things off your plate."

I blinked. "And your place in the organization?" I asked, dreading the answer. I didn't want to step up. I didn't want to take a more active role.

"I would leave it."

"What?" I choked out.

"Neither of us wants it, Roman. You have made millions with your legitimate dealings. Together, we can make millions more. Leave the other behind."

For a minute, I was silent. "Is that done, Luca?"

He laughed. "Things have changed, Roman. We're free to walk away. We make the rules now. The Irish want our piece badly. I'm inclined to let them have it."

"The Irish?" I repeated.

"Our great-grandmother was Irish. Nonna and Mom carry that blood. So do we. You, especially. We have never had trouble with them. They would step in and run it well, I think."

"And you'd just walk away?"

"Well, there would be terms." He studied me. "You could too, Roman. We could both leave this life we never wanted but live because it was forced on us. You'd still be powerful in this territory. You could work with the Irish and maintain your stronghold." He paused. "A fake figurehead."

My mind reeled. I shook my head. "Luca, this would take incredibly thorough, lengthy planning. Agreements. So much change."

"Change is good." He gripped the back of his chair. "I want a different life, Roman. I want to know my kids. Love them. I do not want them to have this legacy. I don't want to be a part of it anymore. If you don't support me in this, then you can have it all."

I stood. "Let's not jump to conclusions. We need to sit and plan this all out. Talk about it. Bring Aldo in on the conversation."

He nodded. "Yes. But first, you have another conversation that has to happen."

"Yes."

He looked at me. "Think before you speak to her, Roman. Women need to hear the words. To feel reassured that they are loved."

"And if I don't love her?"

He lifted his eyebrows. "I think you need to think long and hard about that denial."

"I have the utmost respect for her. I enjoy her company. We suit physically. Isn't that enough?"

He shrugged as he walked toward the door. "You tell me."

CHAPTER 20
ROMAN

E ffie was curled up in the chair in the bedroom. She liked to sit there, looking out the window when she wasn't reading. She was a quiet soul, and she never complained to me about staying in the suite. In fact, she rarely complained.

I stopped in the doorway, looking at her. She peeked up, offering me a sweet smile. I strode toward her, stopping as I looked at the tray beside her. Tea and toast. With honey. Little crumbs were on the plate, making me smile. The mouse feasting had happened again. I leaned down, bracing my arms on the chair. I observed her silently. She looked rested, calm. She was incredibly lovely. I liked to look at her.

She met my gaze for a moment then dropped her eyes. When she lifted them again, her cheeks were flushed, and she shifted a little. I knew she was thinking about last night. The way I'd made her cry out. Clutch the sheets. Come so hard she'd grasped me, whimpering and repeating my name as she orgasmed time after time. I couldn't stop thinking about it either.

I bent and kissed her. I slipped my tongue into her mouth, tasting the tea. The sweetness of the honey. The sweetness that was simply Effie. By the time I drew back, my cock was twitching, and she was breathing faster. I pressed my forehead to hers.

"Little Tiger."

She laughed. "Roman."

I sat across from her. She furrowed her brow. "What is it?"

"How do you know there is anything the matter?"

"You get a small tic in your jaw. You clench your fists."

I wondered if anyone else had ever noticed those small tells.

I wasn't one to beat around the bush. "I had a call. The men who took you figured out the connection between us, Effie. They demanded your return."

Blood drained from her face, leaving her white. She began to shake, the tremors so hard her body almost spasmed.

I dropped to my knees in front of her, stroking her arms and internally cursing myself. I should have been a little more circumspect with my words. "Hush. Calm yourself. It will never happen."

I waited until she drew in some deep breaths.

"I met with them. Returned the money Marianne took from them and canceled the debt."

"So, that's it?" she asked, her voice hopeful. "I can go?"

"Go where, Effie?" I asked, curious. Her building was gone. She had nowhere to go.

Did she really think I would let her walk away?

"I'll find a place."

I shook my head. "They are not honorable men. They blew up your diner in retribution. If I allow you to leave, they will come after you."

"They admitted blowing up my place?"

"Yes. I don't trust them. I never have. You are still not safe. You never will be." I gathered her cold hands in mine. "Don't ask me to let you go."

"So, I stay here the rest of my life? Hiding in this room?"

"No." I drew in a deep breath. "I continued with the story that you are my fiancée. Except now, it must be real."

"What?"

"You have to marry me, Effie. As my wife, you will be protected. You can live at the estate with Nonna and be safe."

"Live with your nonna?" She frowned. "As your fake wife?"

"There will be nothing fake about it. You will be my wife in every sense of the word."

She was quiet for a moment, pushing at my hands. She stood and paced the room. "So, you expect me to marry you, hide on the estate, be a little on the side when you're in the mood, while you, what, live here, screw whatever or whoever you want? You expect me to be a good little wife and keep my mouth shut? Grow old with nothing and no one? Maybe I would rather die quickly."

I stared at her, shocked at her words. I recalled Luca's advice and knew I had to fix this.

"No, Effie. I realize I worded that wrong. *We* will live at the estate. Together. As husband and wife. You will have the protection of my name. My men will watch over you when I am not there. I will adjust my schedule and be home more. We can travel. Have children if you want." I took her hands back in mine. "You will never have to work again, Effie. Never have to worry about a mortgage or your safety." She looked down, and I slid a finger under her chin. "You must feel this attraction between us, Effie. It is almost a living thing. I need you like I have never needed a woman. You calm me. Center me."

"You paid those men all the money Marianne took?"

"Yes, I canceled that debt and then some."

"So now I owe you."

I shook my head. I owed her more than she would ever know. "I am not asking you to marry me because you owe me." I cupped her face. "I cannot stand the thought of you out there alone. Without me. I want to protect you. Care for you. I want you to care for me. Calm me with your body and your lovely voice. Laugh with me and remind me not to be so serious all the time."

She whispered the one word I couldn't give her. "Love."

"I can't promise you that. This is what I am capable of. Caring for you. Protecting you. I vow to build a life with you. Be faithful to you. I will take my vows seriously." I captured her lips, kissing her. "And that, Effie. That spark between us. It is what connects us."

She was silent.

"Marry me."

"Do I have a choice?"

"Yes. You can stay here in the hotel. Live here. Be escorted by my men when you leave. But I will not see you again. I will carry on with my life and you will have yours, but it will be limited. As my wife, you will have everything."

"Except love."

"Men like me don't love."

She shook her head slowly. "You really believe that."

"I know it. I offer you my name, my fidelity, my protection, and my bank account. It is all I have."

Effie frowned, tears in her eyes. But she didn't cry. She extracted her hands and walked away, stopping to face me.

"I disagree. I think you have so much more to offer. And what you can't see is worth more than your bank account and everything else put together."

The bathroom door clicked shut behind her.

EFFIE

I stared in the mirror, studying my reflection.

How could I look the same when my whole world, the life I knew, was changing? From the moment Roman Costas stepped into my diner, nothing had been the same. Everything I knew was gone. Any semblance of the life I'd had disappeared.

Now my choice was to marry the man.

So that I could stay alive.

I hung my head, cursing Marianne. Where she was, what she was doing, I had no idea. No doubt she forgot about me the moment those thugs dropped me in the trunk. She went on her merry way, once again shirking responsibilities and not caring who she was leaving behind or what she had done. She'd been like that her whole life, but not even I suspected her capable of doing what she had done to me.

Marrying Roman Costas. I had vaguely recognized his name when he introduced himself. I knew he was important. Powerful. His presence indicated he was scary.

How I had ended up here, I still didn't understand. But I would forever be grateful to him for saving me.

Grateful enough to accept his marriage proposal? Or, really, his demand.

I wasn't sure Roman was used to asking for anything. He was too much of a control freak. He took. He ordered. He commanded, and he got what he wanted.

I lifted my head and met my own gaze. He said he wanted me.

I thought of his declarations that he didn't love. I disagreed. I didn't have much experience with men, but the way he looked at me sometimes said more than simply caring. I pulled at the neckline on my shirt, exposing the tiny marks he'd left behind. Love bites, sucking kisses to my skin. Those weren't from a man only interested in protecting me.

Were they?

He loved his nonna. That was undeniable. He spoke of his brother with affection. His new sister-in-law. Even Aldo and Vi. Surely a man who felt fondness for that many people was capable of romantic love?

He certainly enjoyed the physical aspects of our relationship. He admitted to needing me in a way he'd never needed another person. He said I calmed him.

That had to mean something?

My own feelings for him were complex and unsettling. I had never wanted another man. Never needed to feel anyone's touch the way I craved his. Despite the fact that he was a dangerous man, he made me feel safe and protected. I knew, without a doubt, he would never hurt me. He went out of his way to make me comfortable. I loved how he teased me when we were alone. When he could just be Roman. Part of me wondered if he felt that way with anyone else. He wasn't the powerful mob man with me. The business tycoon. The lethal enemy. The brother who had to be strong. The grandson who had to be vigilant. The friend who couldn't give all of himself to the relationship because he couldn't show any weakness. With me, he was simply Roman.

I tossed my hair and pinched some color back into my cheeks. I could do that for him. Be that soft spot I thought he needed, even if he didn't or couldn't see it.

Together, we could find our path and make this work. Build a life on what we offered each other—something the rest of the world knew nothing about.

I shut my eyes and nodded, my decision made.

I could do this.

Roman was at his desk, staring at something in his hand. He looked up as I came in, and for a moment, we regarded each other in silence. He stood, rounding the desk and leaning on the wood. He held out his hand, and I let him take mine and pull me close.

"It has to be this way, Little Tiger. There is no other solution."

"I know."

"So you will marry me?"

"Yes."

He touched my cheek. "Good girl. I will arrange it all."

I frowned then nodded.

"What?" he asked.

"I don't get a say at all?"

"You can have anything you want, you only have to ask."

"I would just like something pretty about it to remember. Some flowers or something," I replied.

He frowned. "I will make sure of it." Then he pressed a box into my hand. "We can start with this."

I traced my finger over the faded velvet, almost afraid of what was inside. I peered up to see Roman watching me, a smile on his lips. "Never what I expect," he murmured and took the box from my hands. "Why are you shaking?" he asked.

"Because what is in here will change everything."

"Oh, Little Tiger, everything already has." Then he opened the box.

I gasped at the beautiful ring, the brilliant diamond catching the sunlight, the beautiful green of the emeralds setting off the unique setting.

"My great-grandmother wore this ring. She was Irish, and my great-grandfather made this to match her eyes. My nonna wore it as well. My mother wore it on occasion, although my father insisted on buying her a different wedding ring. It goes to the child with the green eyes. Or if there are none, the firstborn." He slipped the ring onto my finger, the metal feeling cold and heavy on my skin. "A perfect fit."

I stared down at the stunning piece of jewelry. I had never in my wildest dreams thought I would wear a piece so beautiful.

"Roman," I breathed out. "It's—" I shook my head, at a loss for words.

"It marks you as mine, Effie. Taken." He bent and kissed my mouth, his lips lingering. "And soon, the whole world will know."

I nodded, unable to take my eyes off the ring. He laughed low in his chest. "Do you like it?" he asked, sounding playful and boyish.

"Very much."

"We need to go see Nonna this afternoon. And we're having dinner with Luca and Justine tonight. I will make arrangements." He stepped back. "I have to go. Be ready in two hours. Wear one of the dresses I bought you."

I had no words to say. No questions to ask. I was too busy processing everything, and my brain was on overload.

Roman cupped my cheek. "Are you all right, Effie? You've gone pale again."

"I'm fine. It's"—I paused—"it's a lot to take in."

"I'll be right beside you."

Recalling my thoughts earlier, I straightened my shoulders. "Yes, I'm fine."

He smiled and tugged me into his arms, kissing me until I was breathless and dizzy. He shook his head as he pulled back. "You're more than fine, Effie. You are breathtakingly perfect."

Then he left me alone.

CHAPTER 21
ROMAN

Two hours later, I entered the suite, not surprised to find Effie waiting for me. She was always punctual. I stopped, smiling at her.

She wore a pink dress. Lacy, frilly, diaphanous. Girly and feminine, it suited her, the hem falling below her knees, the short sleeves covering the last of the bruising. She had her hair loose, a long dark swath of silk over her shoulders. Her makeup was light—just enough to hide the faded marks but show off her luminous eyes.

I lifted her hand to my mouth, kissing the ring that resided there now. "Beautiful," I murmured. "Thank you."

She blushed, running a hand down the skirt in what I had come to recognize as a nervous gesture with her.

310   MELANIE MORELAND

"All will be well."

She nodded, and I crooked my arm. "Let's go see Nonna."

She let me lead her to the elevator. In the car, she was quiet, and I racked my brain for something to distract her.

"I saw Margi and Anne earlier."

Effie frowned. "Where?"

"At the hotel. They were applying for jobs. I made sure they both got one. Bill, too. Your weekend staff were hired as servers at the deli restaurant by the casino entrance. That worked best with their schedules. Margi and Anne will be working in the main dining room. Bill is in the kitchen. So your staff are all employed."

She looked surprised.

"What?"

"You think of everything."

I shrugged, then pulled out a set of papers from my inside pocket. "I need you to sign these."

She took them, peering at the pages. I chuckled.

"It's a marriage license, Effie. Nothing else. Make sure I have all the information correct."

She scanned them, glancing up but not saying anything. She took the pen I offered her and signed her name. "I'm not even going to ask how you got all my information."

I took the papers back and returned them to my pocket. "Best not to."

"Am I allowed to know when the nuptials will be held?" she asked, lifting her eyebrow in a silent challenge.

"A week Friday."

She looked shocked. "But a license takes three weeks."

"Not when you're me. I'll have it this week. We're only waiting until next week so my event coordinator didn't quit on the spot when I informed her I wanted the Cascade room and to move whoever was in it."

Judith's face had been amusing.

"I beg your pardon, Mr. Costas?"

"Cancel whoever is in the room and move them."

"To where?"

I waved my hand. "Another hotel. I'll cover all the costs. I want the room for something else."

"What, may I ask?"

"I'm getting married. My fiancée wants pretty, and there isn't a prettier room in the city than the Cascade room."

She exchanged a glance with the chef I had brought in for the meeting. I kept talking.

"Chef Renaldi, she loves your pasta. I want the menu simple, elegant, but it needs pasta. And she nibbles. Charcuterie. Antipasto. Lots of seafood. Whatever else is on the books that night gets relegated to your other chefs. You are on this."

I swung my gaze back to Judith. "We'll be married by the windows. I need flowers. Round tables and chairs. The best linen. A dance floor. Everything. No expense spared."

"How many?"

"It will be small. Less than a hundred, maybe even fifty." I met her distressed gaze. "Can you handle this?"

She glanced down at her tablet she carried everywhere with her. "I'll call the Embassy. I know Fredric was moaning about a cancellation. The convention using the Cascade room might be open to moving their event with some, ah, incentives."

"Give it to them. Tell them the room is suddenly unavailable. It's beyond your control. Offer them all free nights here another time. Pad the event coordinator's budget. Whatever you have to do. But I am using that room. I don't care if I lose business. There is plenty to be had."

We had a wait list for all our event spaces.

I stood. "Make the arrangements, and we will meet again tomorrow. I need plans, menus, everything by then."

A smile tugged at my lips as I recalled their shocked faces and silence. I planned to surprise Effie—she asked for pretty, and pretty I would give her.

Effie looked dazed. Almost as stunned as Judith. I smiled at her, teasing.

"I get what I want, Effie."

"Obviously," she said dryly, glancing down at her hand.

Chuckling, I lifted her hand to my mouth again, nuzzling the skin. I was strangely relaxed about the whole wedding thing. Almost…happy. I wanted it to be a nice day for her—I wanted to do lots of nice things for her.

We pulled up to the driveway of the estate, and Effie looked nervous again as the guards opened the gates and we headed to the house.

She had no reason to be nervous. Nonna would be beside herself with happiness. How Luca would react later was the mystery, but we would handle this one family member at a time.

Nonna looked surprised and pleased to see us. She cupped my face, kissing my cheeks as always, then did the same to Effie. "To what do I owe such an unexpected pleasure?"

"We have news," I said, making sure to inject a lightness to my tone.

"Do share."

Silently I held up Effie's hand so the ring caught the light. For a moment, Nonna was transfixed, staring at the ring, then a wide smile broke out on her face.

"Roman, my boy! I knew it!"

She threw her arms around me in a rare display of emotion. Then she hugged Effie, standing back and gazing at us. I was shocked to see tears glistening in her eyes. I had never once seen Nonna cry. She shook her head. "You have made me so happy. I knew you were the one for him," she said to Effie. "I could see it."

She wiped at her eyes quickly. "Pardon this silly old woman. I will get champagne. Excuse me."

She turned and hurried away, and I stared after her. Effie glanced up at me. "What is it?"

"She cried. I have never seen her cry."

"She thinks you're happy."

I heard the trace of sadness in Effie's voice. I looped my arm around her waist, pressing a kiss to her head. "I am, Little Tiger."

"Really?"

"Yes. Now let's go join Nonna."

We sat in the sunshine, sipping champagne. I told Nonna the wedding was the following Friday, and she looked at me askance.

"Roman. How?" Her eyes widened. "Why?"

"Because I don't want to wait. Nothing else," I said firmly. "I want to marry Effie and move us here. She'll be happier."

Nonna looked delighted. "I will love that." She narrowed her eyes. "You will be here more?"

"Yes. I promised Effie I will."

"Good. You need a life."

I laughed at her reprimand. I stood, taking Effie's hand, and we went inside. We went to my wing, and I indicated the rooms. "Look around. Change what you want, but not my office."

"Oh. Ah, I think I'll get used to the space first."

I nodded. "It is rather masculine. Try not to go overboard on the girly stuff."

She smiled. "Maybe just a little softening."

I wrapped my arms around her waist, drawing her back to my chest. "I can hardly wait to have you in that bed, Effie. Make it smell like you. Like us."

"With your nonna down the hall," she murmured, teasing.

I chuckled, nipping her neck. "The other side of my —*our*—very large house. And she takes her hearing aids out at night. You can scream as loud as you want, she won't hear you." I kissed the soft skin. "And if she did, she'd ignore it, knowing we were trying to make her grandbabies."

She turned in my arms. "Roman, are you—"

I cut her off. "Yes, Little Tiger. No more questions or doubts. We are getting married."

I took her hand and went down the hall. "You can have this room. Make it into whatever you want. A reading place. A room where you can be alone. It has a great view."

She walked to the window. "It is lovely."

I went behind her, resting my chin on her shoulder. The vineyards looked endless from here. The dense trees on the two sides of the property offered privacy. The sun glinted off the water in the pool to the one side. "Peaceful," I agreed.

"Can I plant some vegetables?"

"Yes. There is a garden Nonna likes to work in. You can add what you like." I watched the trees sway in the light breeze. "This will be your home, Effie. You will be the mistress of this house. It is yours to do with what you like." I paused. "This is Nonna's home as well."

"I would never disrespect her."

"I know," I replied. "And she will step aside on any decisions."

"She won't have to. We can work together."

Something warm dripped into my chest. Her words were soft, her voice sweet. There was nothing but truth in her words. I spun her, kissing her. When we pulled apart, I rested my forehead to hers. "I can't wait to marry you. To call you Effie Costas. My wife."

Her smile made me feel ten feet tall.

Luca was reserved but polite when I introduced him to Effie. Justine was more exuberant, chatting to Effie like an old friend. We sat at my table in Maple II, away from prying eyes.

Aside from my brother's, that is.

Effie had become decidedly more nervous as we approached the city, her grip on my hand tightening as the hotel came into view. I hadn't offered her any words of comfort other than to keep my hand clasped with hers and squeeze her fingers. I had no idea how my brother would act, but if he was out of line, I would step in.

By the time the appetizers were done, he seemed warmer toward her. Cordial.

"How did Nonna react to the news?" he asked me quietly, watching his wife and my fiancée interact.

"She cried."

He gaped at me. "Nonna never cries."

"She did. She recovered quickly, but there were tears. Then she gave me shit about only having a short time to find a dress and make sure the house was"—I lifted my fingers in quotation marks—"'in order' for Effie. As if it wasn't already pristine."

"You made her happy, Roman."

"She likes Effie."

"I do too."

I lifted an eyebrow. "Such praise, brother. So quickly."

He pursed his lips, dipping his chin. "You are different with her. Whether you see it or not, you are. She suits you."

"Vi says the same thing."

He chuckled. "Vi is a smart woman. I assume she will stand for Effie. Aldo for you?"

"I planned to ask you."

He smiled. "I will escort Nonna and sit with her and my wife. Have Aldo by your side. He belongs there."

"You do as well."

"I am always beside you, Roman. I have your back as well. Let me sit with my wife and Nonna."

"Are you worried about trouble?"

He smiled so the women didn't wonder what we were discussing. "I always am. How many will be there?"

"Very few. Only some trusted allies. This is private, much like yours was. Effie has only a few close friends to invite. Most of the room will be my list. I plan to keep it small without upsetting anyone."

"Good plan."

Luca lifted his glass. "To Roman and Effie. May they be as happy as Justine and I. *Salute*."

We clinked glasses, Justine only taking a small sip. I knew they weren't publicly sharing the news of her pregnancy yet as it was early. I winked at her knowingly, and she smiled as she tilted her head toward Effie and winked back her approval.

I met Effie's lovely eyes, something in me relaxing. She was with me, and that was where she would stay. And soon, the world would know.

Whatever the fallout of that was, we would handle it together.

In the car, Effie turned her head from looking out the window. "Is Justine pregnant?"

"Why would you ask?"

"She didn't drink her wine, had no shellfish, and she looked a little tired. Luca was very protective of her."

"He always is, but yes, she is. He told me this morning."

"How lovely."

I didn't like the sadness in her voice. I took her hand. "We can have children, Effie. If that is something you desire, you only have to tell me."

She smiled and nodded, but she still looked sad. I took her chin in my hand. "What?"

"I need to see how things, ah, go before deciding something like that. We should get to know each other a little better first. Maybe settle into a life with each other first before adding the stress of a baby."

I didn't blame her for being cautious. Still, I wanted her to know I wasn't against a child. "Babies are usually considered a miracle. A gift."

She smiled. "That wasn't what Marianne thought about me."

"Forget about that woman. She will never come near you again. If she even tries—" I stopped speaking, my hands curling into involuntary fists.

"What would you do?" Effie asked, her eyes wide.

"Kill her."

"Roman, you don't—"

I cut her off. "She will never so much as breathe the same air as you, Effie. Ever. What she did was unforgivable. Heinous. She deserves whatever fate has in store for her. I will not help her—ever. And nor will you."

"You would kill her to protect me?"

"Yes. I would do whatever it took to protect you."

I was surprised when she turned and flung her arms around my neck. She kissed me with a passion that stirred the constant embers that burned inside me when she was close. I yanked her tight, kissing her back.

"Thank you," she whispered.

I dragged her onto my lap and made sure the privacy screen was in place. She moved over me, grinding on my erection. I dragged my mouth to her ear. "You have to be quiet, Little Tiger. Can you do that?"

She whimpered, and I covered her mouth, holding the sound down. I had a feeling we were about to get louder.

EFFIE

I sipped my coffee, running a hand through my hair. Roman had woken me before he left, telling me that Vi would be here at nine and to be ready. He didn't say for what, and I knew better than to ask him. I showered and got ready after he left, pleased to see my bruises were almost gone now. The dark ones on my legs and stomach were yellowing and fading, the ones on my face and arms easily covered. Roman still scowled when he saw them and was infinitely tender when he kissed over them. Actions that gave me hope for our marriage. For us. I knew I was already partially in love with him. Despite his hot and cold, despite his violent side, he had claimed a part of me no one else ever had—or ever would. I worried over him, wanted to make his life better. Easier. I loved the look on his face when he would watch me. He had one facial expression when he left the suite—stoic. Stern. Intense. But when he was with me, he was funny, tender, intense in an altogether different way. And when he made love to me, fucked me, whatever he did to me, it was unbelievable. He never hurt me, even when he was rougher, but the orgasms were incredible. He was a giving, controlling lover. He was also an amazing teacher, showing me how to enjoy my body, enjoy his. His eyes darkened when I explored him. His grunts of pleasure, whispered words of praise, and constant dirty talk were all music to my ears. He made me feel desired. Sexy. Something I had never felt until he entered my life.

And despite how it was happening, or even the why, we were getting married. I echoed his whispered words of wanting Friday to come soon. I wanted to hear him call me his wife. To be Mrs. Effie Costas. To finally belong somewhere.

When I was growing up with Marianne, she always made me feel like an interloper, even in my own home. Our mother tried her best not to let it happen, but Marianne always needed the attention on herself, and it was easier to fade into the background and let her have the limelight, the first choice in everything. The big bedroom, the toy, the color of swimsuit Mom was purchasing for us. If I lingered too long over a pretty blouse or a pair of shoes, those were the ones she had to have. I learned early on in life not to let her know what I wanted. It was tiring.

With Roman, there was no competition. He hated her. I was number one. He promised me his fidelity, and I had no cause to doubt him.

When he informed me he would kill her if he found her, I should have been horrified. Begged for her life. Yet I remained silent. He was right. If she came near me again, it would only be to hurt. I was done trying. I would no longer protect her. After what she had done, she didn't deserve it.

Vi knocked, and I let her in. She immediately grabbed my hand, effusive over the ring. "Aldo said it was spectacular, but wow!"

I smiled. "Overwhelming."

She eyed me. "You don't look like the blushing bride. Do I need to kick some mobster ass?"

I laughed, knowing if I said yes, she would spar with Roman without a problem. Tell him off without mincing words. But I shook my head. "Just all unexpected."

She nodded, pouring a cup of coffee. "Love is grand."

"Oh, he doesn't love me. He is just protecting me."

She looked amused. "Is that what he told you?"

"Yes."

"Okay, then. I'll have lots of fun proving him wrong." She looked at me over the rim of her cup. "The sex is wild with him, isn't it?"

I choked as I tried to swallow. "Pardon me?"

"Aldo is a tiger in the sack. Or against the wall. The sofa. Anywhere. The man knows how to use that huge cock of his. His fingers and tongue are a close second. I imagine Roman is equally as talented. He's got that dirty-boy look under his polished exterior. Am I right?"

I felt myself blush. "I'm not sure I should be discussing that with you."

She laughed. "You said all I need to know."

There was a knock, and she grinned. "Ah, they're here."

"Who's here?"

She opened the door, revealing Gerry wheeling a tall rack filled with covered garment bags. He smiled at me. "These were all I could get today. If none of them suit, more will arrive tomorrow."

"For what?"

He grinned as he lifted a bag off the rack, unveiling a beautiful gown.

"Your wedding."

CHAPTER 22
ROMAN

I finished with my manager, walking through the lobby. Everything was in order. Perfect. Exactly the way I demanded. The right people doing their jobs made my life easier in many aspects.

I stopped when I spotted Gerry in the boutique, and I went in. "Gerry?"

"Boss man," he greeted me.

"Why are you down here? You are supposed to be upstairs with Effie and Vi helping her pick a dress. She didn't like any of them?"

Gerry laughed, indicating a rack of dresses. "Your lady picked a dress in five minutes. It fit her perfectly, aside from the length. The seamstress has it and will have it back tomorrow." He looked delighted. "No fuss, your fiancée. I held it up, she said yes."

I frowned. "I thought this could take days. Hundreds of gowns."

"For some. I asked her to describe the perfect dress. I pulled one from the rack, and we were done. Now I hope you plan on letting her choose her flowers."

"I can arrange that."

"Then we're all set. And by the way, green is the color for the day."

"All right," I responded.

"It suits her dress choice."

I hesitated. "Was she happy, Gerry?"

He laid his hand on my arm. "I believe so. Overcome a little. She wasn't expecting it. She thought she would wear one of the dresses you bought her last week. Not really high-maintenance, is she?"

"No, she's not."

I headed to the planning office, looking forward to when I could use my office upstairs again. I knew I could, but I didn't want Effie feeling more trapped than she already was.

Aldo was there, looking tired.

"You were here last night again?"

He nodded. "A few problems on the floor." He held up his hand. "I took care of them." He took a sip of coffee. "How did the dinner go?"

"Good. Luca likes her."

"We all like her."

"Thank you for covering. I know you've pulled a lot of extra nights. Once the wedding is over, we'll figure out a schedule that keeps our spouses happy."

"Vi understands. She, as well as I, recalls when I was gone a lot because of our situation. You covered all the nights for me then. I'm returning the favor."

I cleared my throat. "Would you stand beside me next week, Aldo?"

He looked confused. "What about Luca?"

"I spoke with him. He agrees it should be you." I smiled, thinking of what Luca said. "I haven't told Effie yet, but Luca is going to walk her down the aisle. He feels she should have that."

"I would be honored to stand with you." He paused. "You looked pretty serious yesterday after your talk with Luca. Anything the matter? Aside from the unexpected fiancée thing?"

I told Aldo what Luca had said yesterday. He listened, his surprise showing.

"He wants to walk away?"

I nodded. "He is right. The business is ours now. We make the rules, not my father. Not an organization. Each family is responsible for their own future. Others have left. Handed over the reins and walked away." I took a drink of coffee. "Neither of us wanted what my father had. We hated his ways of doing things. Violence was his first response. Not"—I smirked—"that I objected to it. But there are other ways."

Aldo nodded. "So Luca would run Ottawa."

I met his eyes. "I was thinking I would keep this place. You could have Toronto. I know you love the big city. So does Vi."

He looked incredulous. "You'd give me Maple II to run?"

I drew in a deep breath. "I'd give you Maple II outright."

"Roman—"

"There would be fees."

"Of course."

"But it would be your vision. Yours to do as you want. Same as with Luca. I would have a stake in the business. A monthly draw."

He shook his head. "But here?"

"I would figure it out. All of this will take time if we go forward."

"I don't know if I can leave you, Roman."

I smiled at the man I trusted with my life. "You aren't leaving me. You'd be down the road. That one runs without me there twenty-four seven. This one can as well. I'll hire the right people. Without the illegal stuff to worry about, it won't be as...hands on."

He looked thoughtful. "We'll talk more. Think it over. Carefully."

"After the wedding," I agreed.

I returned to the suite, not surprised to find Effie in her favorite spot. I was beginning to wonder if I needed to have the chair moved to the estate with her.

Unable to resist, I bent and kissed her. I liked how her mouth felt underneath mine. As usual, that feeling of completion welled inside me now that she was close.

I sat across from her, studying her face. Her eyes were tranquil and warm. She smiled at me. "Thank you for today," she said, sounding shy. "The dress, the flowers. I didn't expect any of it." She reached out, touching a blossom beside her.

I returned her smile. I had sent Judith up to have her discuss the types of flowers Effie wanted for the wedding. Once she had done so, I met with our on-site florist and sent up an arrangement for Effie after recalling her saying she had never received flowers. I kept the card simple, signing it,

I CAN'T WAIT UNTIL FRIDAY.
YOURS, ROMAN.

Audrey informed me that Effie had been surprised and pleased with her flowers. Watching her touch them, I decided to make sure flowers were sent to her regularly at the estate.

"You were very quick with your dress selection."

Effie nodded. "It was as if Gerry already knew what I would love." She paused. "It's not really traditional."

I laughed. "Neither are we. Whatever you picked, you will be lovely."

"Vi picked her dress too."

"I understand green is the color of the day." I winked at her. "I would have gone violet-blue if I were choosing."

She blushed, the color highlighting her prettiness. "You gave me a choice." She held up her hand. "I wanted to complement my ring."

I leaned close, running a finger down her warm cheek. "Nonna will love that. Thank you."

Our eyes locked for a moment, and I bathed in the sweetness of her gaze. She had no idea how she bolstered me with her presence. I wasn't sure how it happened. I cupped her cheek, and she turned, pressing a kiss to my palm. Once again, she disarmed me with her affectionate gestures.

I pulled my hand away, feeling the warmth of her mouth on it.

"Do you have the names of the people you want to invite?"

She handed me a list. "Just a few."

I scanned it and nodded. There were less than a dozen names, and five of them now worked for me. "Invites will go out tomorrow. Hand-delivered."

"You said it will be small?"

"I am inviting some important people in my world. Not to do so would be considered disrespectful. I would rather it only be us and those we are closest to, but for now, I need to do this. But I am keeping the numbers very small, yes. Just over fifty."

She looked wistful. "I wish my mom could be there. I'll have no family."

I took her hand. "My family will be yours, Little Tiger. You will not be alone again. I will keep you safe." I paused. "I swear I will try to be a good husband to you."

"I know."

"You're not thinking of Marianne, are you?" I asked.

"No. Not at all. She is not someone I consider family anymore. You don't do what she, ah, tried to do to family. To anyone."

I cleared my throat. "Luca would like to walk you down the aisle if you are agreeable to that."

She blinked. "Really?"

"Yes. If you want. We thought it might be intimidating for you to walk into a room of strangers."

She dropped her head, shaking it slightly as a smile curled her lips.

"What?"

"You keep telling me you're cold. That you can't love. You insist you will 'try' to be a good husband, yet I feel the doubt you have. I already know you'll be a good husband, Roman. You're a good man."

I laughed dryly. "I've killed people, Effie. I'll kill again, I'm sure."

"For fun?"

"To protect those I love. To ensure their safety. To keep my businesses free from them."

She was quiet, then shrugged. "Morally gray, then. But it doesn't make you evil. You do what you have to in order to survive. In my mind, you are still a good man."

"Would you think that if you knew I was actively pursuing your sister to eliminate her?"

She stood. "I ceased having a sister a long time ago. I only realized it a few weeks ago. The sister I hoped to have never existed."

And with those words, she walked away.

The night before our wedding, I lay in the large bed of my suite, wondering why I had given in to Nonna. She had arrived early that day and, among all her other decrees, announced that Effie would be staying with her tonight.

"It is tradition," she insisted.

"Nothing about this wedding is traditional," I replied dryly.

"I am aware, but it is how it should be."

And three hours ago, she had taken Effie with her, closing the door between the two rooms. I had no desire for a bachelor party or any of the other silly traditions some couples liked. There was no rehearsal dinner, no practice ceremony. We had dinner in the restaurant as a family, and I worked afterward, making sure all was well with the hotel and casino. Then I came upstairs and had a drink, trying not to sulk about the fact that Effie would be down the hall and not beside me later. Why it bothered me so much, I had no idea, so I pretended all was fine and sent her away with a smile and a kiss on the cheek under Nonna's watchful eye. I ignored the teasing from Luca and Aldo until I kicked them out and headed to the gym, before returning to the suite and showering.

Except, I couldn't sleep. Without Effie beside me, I found it impossible to relax. I knew she was only a short distance away. There were men outside in the hall, and she was perfectly safe.

But I wasn't beside her.

I tossed and turned and eventually gave up, swinging my legs over the mattress and running my hand through my hair in agitation. With a low growl, I stood and headed through the closet and into Nonna's suite. Effie was on the bed in the guest room, curled up with a book, not asleep either. She looked up at me, shaking her head. I strode forward, scooping her into my arms and turning, carrying her back to my suite.

"What are you doing?" she whispered. "Nonna says you can't see me after midnight until the ceremony."

"It's eleven fifty-five," I replied. "I'll shut my eyes for the rest of the night. But this is utter nonsense. You're sleeping with me."

I deposited her on the bed, sliding in beside her and pulling her back to my chest. My entire body relaxed at her closeness. "This is where you belong."

"Nonna won't be happy."

I pressed a kiss to her neck. "I'll have you back early. She won't even know."

She snuggled back with a happy sigh. "I prefer it here too."

"Good. This is where you'll be the rest of your life. Now go to sleep."

"Good night, Roman."

"Good night, Little Tiger."

I carefully slipped a sleeping Effie onto the bed in the guest room in Nonna's suite. The one Nonna thought Effie had been using until I informed her otherwise.

I stood beside the bed, gazing down at the woman I would marry later that day. With her dark hair spread around her and her hand tucked under her chin, she looked lovely. Still innocent. Even though she was no longer a virgin, she would remain that way. It was part of who she was. Sweet and kind. Loving. Despite everything her sister had done to her during her life, the loss of her mother, the struggles she'd gone through with her business and relying only on herself, she remained so.

I should feel guilty bringing her into my world. Chaining her to me because of my own desires. I could send her to live elsewhere, free from worry. A new name, a new place, no connection to me. But the thought of doing so did something to me, and I couldn't. Somehow I needed her in my life. I needed that sweetness. Her affection. I craved her body as much as I craved her smile.

So I was keeping her.

I placed a small box on the pillow beside her and bent, pressing a kiss to her forehead. I left the room, pulling the door shut behind me. I stopped when I saw Nonna sitting on the sofa, staring at me knowingly. A pot of coffee was in front of her. She always made her own, disliking room service even though she was treated like royalty here. I sat across from her, knowing better than to try to avoid the conversation we were about to have. She handed me a coffee, and I took it, taking a sip of the dark French press.

"You could not wait one night?" she asked.

I was honest. "No. I rest better beside her."

She nodded. "I assumed that would happen." She sat back. "She is good for you, Roman."

"I am glad you approve, Nonna."

"I think she will be the catalyst for change that is needed." She took a sip of coffee. "If you allow that change."

"Did Luca talk to you?"

She nodded. "I am thrilled about all his news." She set down her cup. "Your mother hated what your father did, but she loved him. He was a good husband and father until she died. It was as if the goodness she brought out in him died with her. I hated how he treated you boys, as if you were things to mold and order around. How he pitted you against each other. Your mother had always hoped you would have different paths. Perhaps now, you can." She drew in a deep breath. "I want you to live. To love. To have what your grandfather and I had." She grasped my hand. "Open yourself up to Effie, Roman. Show her the man you are. Give her the life she deserves. The one you deserve. Whether you stay in this life or create another, put her first. Put yourself first."

I met her eyes. She knew there was more to the story of Effie and me than I had told her. But she trusted me enough to stay quiet. To know I was doing what I had to do.

"I am thinking about it all, Nonna. And I put Effie and her safety first."

She sat back. "That is good."

I stood, bending to kiss her cheek. "I will see you later."

I began to leave when she spoke again.

"Roman, *piccolino,*" she murmured.

I turned.

"Try to put your heart first. You will find great rewards when you do."

I had no words to respond.

CHAPTER 23
ROMAN

I tugged on my sleeves, tense and agitated. My body was tight with nerves, and I told myself it was because of the faces in the room in front of me. Heads of families, business associates, legal and otherwise, important people in my world. Some more important than I was, others less. I reminded myself they were all here on my turf, but it didn't quell the jackhammers in my stomach. I glanced around, keeping my expression aloof and stern, meeting the eyes of a few people and nodding. I offered a warmer expression to Effie's few friends, who all looked a little out of their depth in the room, but I was glad she had some familiar faces in the small crowd.

Beside me, Aldo chuckled, pressing his hand on my shoulder. "You might want to smile. You're getting married, not facing a firing squad."

I inhaled, letting it out slowly, and I loosened my shoulders. I took in the room, the flowers and candles everywhere. The lovely tables spread out and the large dance floor for later. The sun was high in the sky, and by the time the ceremony and dinner were done, the room would be glowing with candlelight and music. Six o'clock had taken forever to come. It was as if there was nothing I could do to speed up time. The hotel and casino ran like clockwork today with no problems to distract me. The paperwork that seemed to be endless was caught up. I was ready to explode when Aldo arrived, and we headed to the gym to work off my excess energy. I couldn't even sneak in a visit to Effie since she was in another suite getting ready, and Nonna had firmly denied me any more access.

I hoped Effie liked the room. I'd told Judith to give her anything she asked. I made all the arrangements I needed to and left the details to them. I didn't care about the colors or the flowers as long as Effie was happy. It was the least I could do since I hadn't really given her a choice about marrying me.

The music changed, and Luca appeared at the end of the aisle, Nonna on his arm. She wore a pale mint-colored dress, and she looked happy as he escorted her to her seat in the front row. She stopped before sitting down, and I went to her, kissing her cheeks. She cupped my face and smiled, whispering words of love to me. Once she was seated beside Justine, whom

Luca had sat a few moments prior, he looked at me with a wide grin. "Wait until you see your bride," he murmured.

A moment later, Vi walked down the aisle, self-assured and lovely. Her green dress hugged her curves, and she threw a saucy wink at Aldo as she went past. "Later, big boy," she intoned, making him chuckle. She looked at me. "Brace yourself," she warned, waggling her eyebrows.

I squared my shoulders, folding my hands in front of me and focusing my attention to the end of the aisle. Nothing prepared me for the vision of my bride.

She looked tiny compared to Luca. And she was gorgeous. Her gown was lace, with long sleeves, and the bodice fitted to her torso, modest yet so incredibly sexy, it set my blood on fire. The skirt flared out from her waist, the lace flowing over a tidal wave of deep green silk. As she walked, the green caught the light, swirling with the lace. It was stunning. The emerald earrings I had left on her pillow glinted. My ring was on her finger. She wore her hair up away from her face, some curls escaping around her ears and throat. Tiny pearls and glittering beads were woven into the intricate hairstyle. Her makeup was light and flawless, illuminating her incredible eyes.

I had never seen anything so beautiful in my life.

Effie smiled serenely as she walked down the aisle, one hand clutching Luca's arm, the other her bouquet. But I saw the fear in her eyes, the sadness they held. She was nervous in this room of strangers, trying desperately to hide that emotion. I saw it and I hated it. I never wanted her fearful or sad. I wanted her glowing and happy—especially on this day.

Luca stopped a short distance from me, and I stepped forward, taking her proffered hand that trembled in my grip. I drew her to me, waiting as Luca kissed her cheek and took his seat. We faced each other, and before the minister could speak, I held up my hand, ignoring protocol and everyone's curious stares.

"Give me a moment."

No one dared to protest. I cupped Effie's face, feeling how cool her skin was under my touch.

"Roman?" she whispered.

I leaned close, my lips to her ear. "You are exquisite. Thank you for the dress. For you." Then I kissed her softly, feeling her smile against my lips. I heard Nonna chuckle, and behind me, Aldo snickered.

"You're getting ahead of the game, Roman. Reel it in, boy."

I winked at Effie. "I have you now. Are you ready?"

She nodded, some color in her cheeks now. "Yes."

I stepped back and nodded at the minister. "Make it quick."

Luca barked out a laugh, and many joined in. Effie handed her flowers to Vi, and we linked hands. She looked at me, her eyes no longer scared or sad.

Perfect.

EFFIE

My nerves kicked in as I heard the music, and I began to shake. I peeked out, seeing a room filled with strangers. Solemn faces, some looking bored, others curious. The few people I knew looked uncomfortable, and I had a feeling they would leave once dinner was done.

My heart sank.

What was I doing? Marrying a man who would only admit to feeling an obligation toward me. I felt more for him, but he insisted he was incapable.

Did he mean with me? Or with anyone?

He should marry someone he loved. Be happy. Not resign himself to marriage with me because of some debt he felt he owed. Why he didn't feel that way, I didn't understand. He'd rescued me from Marianne's horrendous plan. He didn't owe me. It was the other way around.

Luca returned from escorting Nonna to her seat. Vi turned to smile at me. "Showtime," she whispered and squeezed my hand. "Are you okay?"

I nodded, unable to speak.

"You look beautiful. Remember, Roman is waiting for you. Everything is going to be fine."

Then she turned and began walking, the green dress she wore complementing her coloring. She held her head high, looking polished and confident.

Luca held out his arm. "Ready?"

I swallowed, sadness rushing through me. I couldn't change my mind. I couldn't leave Roman at the altar. I would marry him and offer to let him go even though the mere thought of that made me even sadder. I slipped my hand over Luca's waiting arm and nodded. It seemed to be the only thing I was capable of doing right now.

We paused at the end of the aisle, waiting for Vi to get to the front. People were on their feet, staring, many of them no doubt finding me lacking. A ripple of fear coursed through me. I knew how dangerous these people were, simply from their presence. I gripped

Luca's arm tighter, and he patted my hand in understanding. "Focus on Roman," he said quietly as we began to walk.

I sought out Roman's gaze. He stood tall and proud at the front, waiting for me. Dressed in a dark suit, his tie a deep green to match my underskirt, he was incredibly handsome. He was watching me with his usual intensity, his hands folded in front of him. He had a smile on his lips, subtle, but present. His expression was hard to determine, although he swept his gaze over me head to toe, then did it again, seemingly transfixed. Then his brow furrowed, and he stepped forward before I expected, taking my hand Luca offered him and pulling me toward him. When he held up his hand, telling the minister to give him a moment, I was shocked and unsure. He cupped my face, the intimacy of his touch, of the way he surrounded me, protective and determined, I was no longer lost as he spoke.

His whispered words calmed me. His touch soothed me. He met my gaze, and I saw the certainty in his eyes. His query of "Are you ready?" and his unexpected wink gave me the strength to say yes.

Then I stepped forward with him and became his wife.

The next few hours were a blur. Photos, introductions, some well-wishes and far more formal congratulations were said. As if sensing my fear, Roman never once left my side unless I was next to Aldo and Luca, who seemed to have formed a guard around Nonna, Justine, and me. And the brief moments I was without Roman, his gaze never left me.

The meal was spectacular, everyone commenting on the feast. I was hard-pressed to eat anything, my nerves still high, and what I did swallow was like ashes in my mouth. More than once, Roman leaned over, pressing a cube of cheese or a morsel of some other delicacy into my mouth.

"Eat, Little Tiger," he whispered. "I want to dance with my wife, so you need your strength."

I managed to eat enough to satisfy him. I was glad we had no head table. Instead, we sat with his family at one of the round tables so we weren't on display. As it was, I felt the constant glances, some curious, some unfriendly, a very few genuinely kind. I was like a fish out of water, and I wished I was at the table with my guests as an observer, not the main attraction.

Once dinner was done and the cake cut, the music began. Roman stood and thanked people for coming, his voice projecting throughout the room. He was calm and looked at ease as he informed the crowd we would be leaving shortly for our honeymoon, but he expected them to stay and enjoy the bar and the casino if they so desired. "House accounts have been set up for each of you. Aldo will ensure your enjoyment," he announced.

Amid the applause, he held out his hand and pulled me onto the dance floor as a lovely song began to play. He held me close, leading me around the floor.

"Honeymoon?" I asked quietly.

"You didn't expect one?" he responded, sounding amused.

"I didn't."

"Well, it was meant as a surprise. It is only a couple of days. We'll take a longer one in the fall."

"I have nothing packed."

"Vi did it for you. You have nothing to worry about." He frowned. "I think you're worrying about enough as it is."

"I'm sorry?" I questioned.

He looked down at me. "Why did your eyes look so sad coming down the aisle, Little Tiger? I know you were nervous, but there was more. Was the thought of marrying me so terrible?"

I was surprised by his words. That he had seen my fear and my sadness. I was also shocked he was asking me here and now, but as I looked around, I realized to anyone looking, all they saw was a couple whispering to each other on their wedding day. Roman held me tight, his hand spread wide across my back. He was leaning close, his voice low, concerned.

I decided to be honest. "I was sad. For you."

"For me?" He frowned. "I don't understand."

I sighed. "Because you feel you had to marry me, Roman. I hate the thought that you are giving up a part of your life you shouldn't because of some misguided guilt."

He blinked, shook his head, and swept me around so we were close to the corner. He stopped dancing, cupping my face, his body protecting me, once again throwing us into our own world. "Listen to me, my wife, and listen well. We are married because I chose to marry you. Not out of guilt. Not out of some obligation. Because I wanted to. We are going to make a life together that suits us both. Do you hear me?"

He traced circles on my skin with his thumbs. "I'm certain I'm not what you had in mind for a husband. I never planned on getting married. But we suit each other, Effie. You calm me. Focus me. I am obsessed with you on so many levels. I want you. Constantly. Never second-guess that. I am exactly where I want to be. Understand?"

I tried to take in his words. Calm. Focused. Obsessed. Exactly where he wanted to be.

A small flicker of hope ignited inside me. Maybe he felt more than he had let on. He had planned all this. Ensured the day he could have kept fast and simple was pretty and filled with music, flowers, and even a touch of romance. The earrings on my pillow, the way he stopped everything to reassure me, his closeness. All of it had to mean something, right?

I met his questioning gaze. His patient, worried gaze. He wanted me to be happy.

"I understand."

He lowered his face to mine and kissed me deeply. Passionately. His mouth was possessive and claiming. It obliterated anything and everything else. He pulled me close, letting me feel his desire. His obsession.

I was breathless when he pulled back, resting his forehead on mine. "What say you now, wife?"

I stared up at him, his green eyes dark with hunger. Passion.

"Take me on my honeymoon, husband."

He smiled, satisfied. "Done."

I stared out the window at the cascade of lights below me. I had never seen so many people, so many lights. I was in awe.

Roman came up to the window, his profile a dark shadow behind me. He leaned his hand on the glass, resting his chin on my shoulder. His warm breath tickled my skin. "Incredible, isn't it?"

"It is," I breathed.

"I'm sorry it's not more exciting."

"No," I protested. "I've never been to New York. Or on a private plane. And I have never stepped foot in a penthouse, never mind stayed in one."

He chuckled. "We'll visit a few places here"—he pressed lingering kisses to my neck that made me shiver—"and we'll go somewhere warmer in the fall."

"What places?"

"Wherever you want, Effie. But I need some alone time with you as well." The kisses turned wetter, his tongue stroking my skin, his teeth nibbling. "Lots of alone time with my wife."

The desire in his voice was evident. Not long after our dance, he had tucked me to his side, and we had slipped away. After a brief ride to an airstrip, we boarded a private plane, and it flew us to New York. I looked around at the opulent interior, the cream-and-black leather seats wide and comfortable. He had sat back, one leg bent across his knee as he studied me.

"You are so beautiful," he said.

I flushed at his words. "I feel rather overdressed," I replied, smoothing a hand over the long lace skirt.

"No, I want to take that dress off you later."

My flush deepened.

"We left so fast," I said, trying to change the subject. "You won't get into, ah, trouble?"

He rubbed his jaw slowly, the movement sexy. "No. All the men in the room understood exactly why we left. You were a siren in that space, Effie. Sexy, classy, beautiful, and still so innocent. I doubt a man there wouldn't have given his riches to have you. I wasn't going to give any of them a chance to so much as touch you."

"How much have you had to drink?" I asked, startled, although his words thrilled me. His tone of voice was low, possessive, almost guttural.

He threw back his head in laughter. "And that—your complete lack of knowledge of how utterly captivating you are. That is the sexiest thing about you."

I rolled my eyes. "No more scotch."

He leaned forward, resting his elbows on his thighs. "You doubt me, Effie? I saw the looks. The desire in the men's eyes, the jealousy in the women's."

"Not everyone looked at me that way."

"No. But a lot did. And they don't get the chance to come close to you. Ever. No one will ever bother you or hurt you. I will not allow it."

"Roman," I said, my voice sounding breathless.

He held out his hand. "Come to me, wife."

I did, and he pulled me to his lap, my gown spread out like a snow-covered lawn. I straddled him, feeling his cock hard and pressed between us. He pulled me to his mouth, kissing me deeply. I whimpered at the possessive feel of his lips.

And then the captain made his announcement that we were departing, and the flight attendant appeared, a smile playing on her lips. "I must ask you to take your seat and buckle up," she said.

Roman stood and set me in the seat across from him, buckling me in himself. He kissed me again. "Until later," he promised.

From the dark look in his eyes, I knew later was now.

He turned me in his arms, covering my mouth with his. I wrapped my arms around his neck, and he lifted me, carrying me down the hall to the bedroom. He kept kissing me as he undid the row of buttons on the back of my dress, taking his time and slowly unhooking them one by one. I pushed on his shoulders, and he shrugged off his jacket, then stepped back, tugging on my sleeves. "Show me what that dress is hiding."

I let the dress fall, a pile of green and white at my feet. The corset and barely there lace underwear caught his attention, and he traced a finger over the lingerie, his breathing becoming deeper. He helped me step away from my gown and stood back, twirling his finger, indicating I should do the same. I laughed as I spun, the look on his face intensifying.

"I have the sexiest wife on the planet," he mused.

"The dizziest, as well," I quipped.

He yanked off his tie, pulling his shirt over his head, then dropped to his knees in front of me.

"Once I'm finished with you, Effie, you won't know up from down." He took my hand, placing it on his head. "Hold on to me. Don't let go."

He tore away my underwear and lifted my leg over his shoulder. "And I want to hear you, wife."

I gave him exactly what he wanted.

CHAPTER 24
ROMAN

Effie slept beside me, her dark hair spread across the pillow. Elbow bent, I rested my head on my hand, watching her. I never dreamed the fire that raged behind those lovely eyes of hers and her shy, sweet nature. She was an amazing lover, eager to learn, ready and willing to please. I loved watching her gain confidence, tell me what she liked, what she loved. There was little she disliked, except being held down and being frightened in the dark. It brought back too many memories for her.

I traced my finger along her arm, pleased to see the skin clear of bruises. She had a small scar along her hairline only she could see. I could feel it under my finger when I would stroke her head, and it would forever remind me of how we came to be.

I hated the thought of leaving today, going back to Canada. But I knew it had to be done. I liked having her to myself. Showing her New York. We played tourist briefly, but I was thrilled to discover she would rather be alone with me than out staring at architecture or the Statue of Liberty. She'd mentioned always wanting to skate at Rockefeller Center, and I promised her we would return over the holidays and do that. I would get her a room where she could see all the sights easily, including the tree she found so fascinating.

She sighed, moving a little, her hand reaching out. I grasped it, kissing the delicate fingers, loving how the ring looked on her hand. The diamond band I had added completed the package, marking her as firmly taken. The platinum ring on my finger stated the same thing, and I enjoyed the weight of it. To my surprise, I found I liked being married.

Or perhaps it was because I was married to Effie.

I genuinely liked her. Our conversations were varied. She was witty and clever. At times hilarious. Other times silly. She made me want to be silly with her and make her laugh. We were surprisingly compatible in many ways.

Especially sexually.

I never dreamed I'd find the thought of being monogamous so agreeable. I couldn't be bothered to look at another woman. Effie was everything I needed. Being faithful suited me.

Effie suited me.

She stirred and woke, her luminous eyes finding mine.

"Good morning, wife."

She stretched, the action causing the sheet to fall away and her breast to be exposed. The rosy nipple was taut, still chafed from my mouth a few hours ago when I woke Effie and took her in the dim morning light.

She smiled, tugging up the sheet. "Down, boy."

I laughed and bent, kissing her. "There is no down with you."

She huffed in fake frustration. "I won't be able to walk on to the plane later."

"I'll carry you."

"The people in the hotel must think I can't walk."

I often swept her into my arms and carried her across the lobby if I was feeling the need to get her alone. Which happened every time we were out of the hotel and she was dressed for any length of time.

Like lunch.

She was smaller, her legs not covering the ground as quickly as mine. It was easier and faster to carry her.

That way, I could kiss her in the elevator without much trouble either.

"The people in the hotel, as you refer to them, are paid not to comment."

She traced her fingers along my jaw, her touch alone making my blood rush faster. "Such power."

I tilted my head, leaning into her hand. "My power doesn't impress you. Nor does my wealth. I have to strive to get your attention."

She shook her head. "You have my attention. All of it, Roman. Because of what beats here." She rested her hand on my heart. "Not the number in your bank account or who you can control."

"Why do you insist on seeing me in such a positive light? I am not what you think I am."

"You're not what you think you are either."

I furrowed my brow. "I don't understand."

"Do you think Aldo is a bad man?"

"I think he's one of the best men I know. Despite things he does in the world we live in. He is loyal and true. He loves those he considers family. He would die for them. That means a lot in this life."

"I know you're not a saint, Roman. I know your world contains more shades of gray than I can understand. You've been honest about that. Vi says the same about

Aldo. But if you can think of him as a good man, why can't you give yourself the same grace? You're loyal, you love your family, you are good to your employees." She paused. "You married me to protect me. In my world, that means a lot."

"Marrying you has not been a hardship, Effie. Despite how we came to be, we suit very well. I look forward to our life together." I cupped her cheek. "You are my wife. My family. I will protect you. Care for you."

I saw the shutters come down over her eyes. I knew she wanted the whole thing. Love. Romance. I shook my head. "I do have affection for you, Effie. I care. I quite adore you, in fact. More than anyone else. It is all I have to give you. Respect, passion, my fidelity. Can that be enough for you?"

She pulled herself up, moving away from my caress. "Of course. You were very clear on that, and I am very lucky."

"Effie—"

She shook her head, climbing from the bed. "It's fine, Roman. I understand. And I am happy to be your wife. I will do my best to please you."

She slipped into the bathroom, and I dropped my head into my hands in frustration. I wasn't lying. I had great affection for her. The thought of something bad happening to her was abhorrent to me. I had to keep her safe. But I was incapable of the kind of romantic love she wanted. The kind Aldo and Vi had. That Luca and Justine shared.

I pulled myself up to the headboard, resting my hand on my bent knee. I didn't want to lie to her, and I didn't want her thinking that one day I would change. She had to learn to accept my limitations.

I flung back the covers and headed to the bathroom, where I could hear the shower. I was going to show her my affection in the only way I knew how.

And she was going to enjoy it.

Another fact I discovered about Effie was her enormous capacity for letting things go. By the time we left the shower and for the rest of the day, she was simply Effie. Charming, sweet, and sexy. She never mentioned our conversation and didn't pout or try to bring it up again. She just moved forward. She was quiet when we left New York, her eyes sad as the plane lifted off the tarmac. She watched from the seat across from me, her elbow on the armrest, her chin propped up on her hand.

"We'll be back, Little Tiger," I assured her.

"I look forward to it."

It seemed as if I was the one who couldn't let things go. "Yet you look sad again. Like this morning."

She shook her head, offering me a smile. "It is just that I am returning to a world I don't know, Roman. I'm feeling a little trepidation."

I ran a hand over my face. Of course she was nervous. I should have figured that out without her telling me.

I reached out my hand. "Come here, Effie."

She unclasped her seat belt, and I pulled her to my lap.

"Sheila will not be happy I'm not buckled in."

I wrapped her up in my arms. "I've got you."

She rested her head on my shoulder.

"Effie, your life will be different—but better, I promise. You can putter around the house, help in the gardens, visit with Nonna. See Vi. Go shopping. Money is not an object. You don't have to be up at some ungodly hour anymore and working until you're exhausted."

"But I was useful. I had a goal, things I accomplished every day," she admitted. "I loved Bagels and Bites. It was all mine."

"You can't ask me to let you do that again."

"I have to ask you for everything?"

I sighed and pressed a kiss to her head. "Until all the danger has passed, the estate is the safest place for you. If you want to go shopping or leave, you will have protection. I will not risk you. Not after everything I have done to ensure your safety."

She stiffened, and I tightened my grip. "I don't mean that. I am not talking about marrying you. I do not regret that in the least. Just give me this for a while, Effie."

"So we could discuss my reopening my diner at another time?"

I shut my eyes at the pleading in her voice.

I let out a dry chuckle. "Why is it that every other woman I ever met would jump all over the chance to never have to lift a finger again, yet you, my wife, are trying to find a way to go back to a life of drudgery?"

"It was hard at times," she replied. "But it was the life I knew."

I pressed her head to my shoulder, resting my chin on her fragrant hair. "Please try this new life before you reject it, Effie. For me."

She was quiet for a moment before replying. "I will."

"If one day you want, we can discuss opening a Bagels and Bites in the hotel," I offered. "But in the future."

"Oh," she replied, beaming at me. "I love that idea."

"But for now…"

She nodded. "I'll stay at the estate."

"Nonna is thrilled with the idea of your being there. Of my being around more. And it will be your home. Change it and make it yours. However it suits you."

"But not your office or Nonna's suite."

"I might let you do something to my office, but yes, Nonna's suite is to her taste."

"I was thinking some lace curtains would be lovely in your office. Add a touch of whimsy."

"I will whimsy you if you add lace in that room," I growled, grinning when she laughed.

"Noted."

I slid a finger under her chin and bent down, kissing her. "Thank you. I promise you, Effie. Life will be good with me."

She smiled and leaned her head back to my shoulder, her gaze once again drifting to the window.

I hated that her eyes still held a trace of sadness.

And I hated that I hated that fact.

I left early for the casino, arriving and heading up to the suite. It felt odd to be there now without Effie. Her scent was still in the room, and I inhaled it into my lungs, the perfume making me feel better somehow. My closet looked empty without her things in it, and I had to remind myself they were all at the estate now. She wasn't gone; she was at home. My home.

Our home.

The words felt strange, yet oddly right. Effie was my wife. She was at home waiting for me.

I shook my head at my peculiar thoughts and turned my mind to business.

I had only been away a short time, but I had a lot of messages and emails to catch up on. I walked the floor, spoke to managers, and was pleased at how well things had gone while I was out of town.

When I returned to the suite, Aldo was there. He shook my hand with a grin. "You look good, Roman."

I sat down, reaching for the coffeepot. "I feel good. It was short, but we enjoyed the trip."

"Effie well?"

"Of course."

"So it was a good honeymoon."

"I've had no experience with other honeymoons, but I would say it was a success."

He nodded, looking away. He sat forward, leaning his elbows on his thighs. He had an odd look on his face, and I frowned.

"What?"

"Gregory Santini was in touch."

Instantly, I was tense. "And?"

"His message was brief. *The package has been recovered and disposed of.*"

I sat back. "They found Marianne."

He nodded.

"And they killed her."

"Tim did, from the little I got from Gregory. He didn't want to talk over the phone, and I didn't want to meet him."

I nodded. "Good plan." I turned my chair, staring out the window. I wasn't upset about Marianne's death. In fact, the dark side of me hoped she suffered. I did have concerns about telling Effie, though. I had to admit, I was worried about my wife.

"Why?" Aldo asked.

I turned back, realizing I had spoken out loud.

"Because she's her sister? Even after what she did?" he asked.

"That, and she is still, ah, emotional over the wedding and everything."

"Everything?"

I found myself telling Aldo the whole conversation Effie and I'd had. He furrowed his brow. "You told her you had affection for her?" He looked displeased. "Like one would a pet."

"No, she knows it is different."

"Does she?"

"Of course," I snapped, regretting my decision to confide in him. "I care for her. She is my wife, and I will make her a priority. I'm changing my life, shortening my hours, staying at the house. I even agreed to have a baby with her if that was what she wanted. What more does everyone want?"

Aldo laughed, the sound dry. "Something you are not willing to give, obviously."

"Something I can't give. I do not *have it* to give."

Aldo stood. "If you say so. I'm going to work on the staff budget. We need to work out the schedule for the next while, so when you're ready, buzz me."

He left, and I had the distinct impression he was angry with me.

I didn't understand why everyone seemed so upset by my honesty. The only one who seemed to accept it was Effie.

I shook my head and dismissed Aldo's ire. I had to figure out how to tell my wife her sister was dead.

I hoped she wouldn't get overly emotional. As far as I was concerned, the world was better off without Marianne.

But as pointed out to me by the man who had arranged to kill her, women were softer. And I knew Effie's capacity for forgiveness.

I had no idea what to expect.

I waited until after dinner. I made a special effort to get home early. I was surprised to realize how often Effie drifted into my thoughts. I wondered what she was doing. If she was feeling all right. If the house felt strange to her. I worried that she would feel overwhelmed. Then I wondered when I had started worrying so much over someone other than Nonna. And I couldn't figure out the niggling feeling of almost missing Effie. I never missed anyone.

I'd sent Effie flowers that she'd placed on the center hall console. I admired them when I walked in, and I was kissed warmly for my efforts. I enjoyed dinner on the patio with Nonna and Effie. Nonna had made Effie her favorite risotto, and I poured glasses of the white wine she had liked so much at lunch last time.

After dinner, Nonna excused herself and went to bed. I worked a bit in my office then went to our room, not surprised to find Effie reading on the love seat. She enjoyed the quiet pastime.

I stripped to my boxers and got ready for bed, then sat in front of her on the coffee table. She looked up from her Kindle, closing the cover and meeting my eyes.

"What is it, Roman? You've been on edge since you came home."

Those words surprised me. I thought I had hidden it well.

"You noticed," I mused.

"I notice everything."

I drew in a deep breath, wondering why this was so difficult. I took her hands in mine, stroking the knuckles.

"I got some news today."

"Bad news?"

I decided to be blunt. "It's Marianne, Little Tiger. She's dead."

Effie blinked. "Dead?"

"The men she tried to make the deal with…they caught up with her."

"And killed her."

"Yes."

"How?"

The question startled me. "What?"

"How did they kill her?"

"Good God, Effie." I ran a hand through my hair. "I didn't ask."

"Oh."

I waited for the hysterics. Something. Instead, she was quiet. "Do I report her as missing or something?"

"If you want."

"I can't exactly call someone and say she was murdered, can I?" she asked. "I guess with Mom gone, and only me, there is no one else, so it doesn't really matter."

I studied her carefully. "Effie, are you all right?"

"Yes. Well, I'm confused, but I'm fine. Maybe feeling guilty."

"Why are you feeling guilty?"

She met my gaze straight on. "Because I think I should feel something sad. Be upset. She was my sister. Or half sister. But all I feel is relief. She can't hurt me anymore."

"No one can hurt you, Little Tiger. I would stop anyone trying."

She nodded. "That's it, then." She opened her Kindle. "Or was there more?"

I blinked. "That's all I know."

"Okay."

I furrowed my brow. Knowing her sweet nature and tender heart, I was confused by her reaction. I had expected…something. Tears, at the very least. Recriminations, something.

"Are you tired?" I asked.

She shook her head. "I was this afternoon. I took a little nap."

I met her gaze, lifting my eyebrows. "Maybe you want to come to bed anyway."

She began to shake her head, then her lips lifted in a grin. "Oh."

I stood, holding out my hand. "I missed you today, Little Tiger."

"You did?"

I pulled her from the chair. "I did. The suite seemed empty without you." I paused. "I felt empty too."

She slipped her arms around my neck. "Let me see if I can help you with that, husband."

I lowered my head. "Perfect, *wife*."

I woke, my hand searching for Effie. Instead of her warm little body against me, all I felt was cool sheets. I sat up, gazing around the dark room and listening in the silence. The bathroom door was open, and she wasn't there. She wasn't curled up on the love seat either. An unusual sense of panic hit me, and I got out of bed, pulling on my robe. I noticed the curtains moving in the breeze, and I pushed them back, looking around the back of the house. I spotted Effie, a small shadow by the pool, her silhouette outlined in the moonlight. I opened the patio door and crossed the lawn toward her. As I drew closer, I heard her quiet crying, and my heart cracked. Without a word, I sat behind her, pulling her back into my chest and wrapping my arms around her. She startled, then quickly wiped at her face. "I didn't mean to disturb your rest," she whispered.

"I would rather you wake me up than sit here alone in the dark, Effie," I said quietly. "You don't have to hide your grief from me."

"You hated her."

"And you loved her."

"I loved the image I had of her. She was never the sister I wanted her to be. I hoped she would be. But she was part of my life. A life I no longer have anything of. Everything I knew, I loved, is gone."

Something in her voice broke me, and I held her closer. "You have me. Nonna. Aldo and Vi. A different life, yes, but I promise you, one that won't contain so much struggle."

"I know. It's just..." She trailed off, a long, shuddering sigh escaping her lips.

I pressed a kiss to her head. "I know, Little Tiger. I know. Let it out."

Instead of more tears, she leaned back into me. "It's so peaceful out here."

"It is. I often sit and listen to the wind. Look at the stars."

"What do you think about?"

I pondered her question and decided to be honest. "Sometimes I would think about walking away. Concentrating on the wine and estate. Letting Luca have it all. Or I would be planning the future in my head. Other times, I wouldn't think at all. The dark and the quiet gave me a place to not think." I tightened my arms. "Those were the good nights."

She traced a pattern on my hands. "Would you?"

"Would I what?"

"Walk away?"

"I don't know."

She didn't comment. There were no platitudes about doing better or finding a different path. She simply hummed. "You'll figure it out."

We sat quietly, our legs in the water, the silence surrounding us. I felt her tension drain away, and I lowered my head to her ear. "Ready to come back to bed?"

"Yes."

I stood and helped her up, scooping her into my arms.

"I can walk."

"But you don't have to."

In our room, I pushed her robe off her shoulders and held up the comforter. "In."

I dropped my robe to the floor and slid in next to her. "Stay this time," I ordered. "If you need me, I'm right here."

"I like that."

Her words made me smile. "Me too."

CHAPTER 25
ROMAN

Over the next couple of weeks, I found being a husband extremely easy. Or perhaps it was who I married that made it easy. Effie was a constant delight, surprising me at every turn. I found myself thinking of her all the time. Planning ways to make her smile. I texted her during the hours I was gone. Called to check in. Sent flowers. I took her and Nonna out to dinner. I brought her here to the casino to stay a couple of nights when I was taking the overnight shift. I snuck upstairs to fuck her, leaving the room regretfully, shocked at how much I wanted to stay with her.

She loved to cook and bake, and Nonna enjoyed having her company. The two of them became close quickly, and Nonna smiled all the time. They gardened and strolled the vineyards. Had lunch with Vi. Went shopping one day, well guarded and protected, but I worried the entire time. Effie bought a few things but nothing big. I had given her a credit card with her new name and opened a bank account, depositing a large chunk of cash in it. When I checked the balance, wondering if I needed to replenish it, I was amused at her purchases. Some candy, a sock shop where it appeared she'd invested in half a dozen fuzzy pairs of socks, and a menswear place. When I arrived home that night, she waited in our room, wearing nothing but the silk tie she had picked out for me. She let me bind her to the bed, and she blushed the next day when I wore the tie, declaring it my favorite. Effie was an enthusiastic lover, wanting to learn, eager to please. I loved watching her discover her sexuality, and the caveman in me liked knowing I was the only man to ever know her. That I would be the only one to ever have the pleasure of her body.

Aldo cleared his throat, bringing me out of my musings. "Sorry," I muttered.

"Should I ask what has you staring out the window? Or whom?" he asked with a smirk.

I shook my head. I didn't want to talk about it with him. With anyone. I hadn't expected to feel this way about Effie. I hadn't expected to feel anything aside from the lust that raged through me whenever she was close. But I couldn't get her out of my mind. My day wasn't complete until she was close. There was no denying I missed her when I was away from her.

I was beginning to think I was obsessed with my little tiger.

"I think you are."

I shut my eyes. I had spoken out loud again. It kept happening when I was thinking of Effie.

"It's all right, Roman. I'm obsessed with Vi. Luca is with Justine. That's what happens when you're in love."

I was about to deny his words, but I stopped. On some level, I admitted I had feelings for Effie. More than I expected. What exactly they were, I wasn't ready to discuss, so I remained silent.

He grinned, glancing at the file open on his lap. "This is very detailed."

I flipped open a copy of what he was looking at. "It would have to be if we hand over the reins. Have you talked to Vi?"

He nodded. "She is torn. She loves the city, but she has grown inordinately fond of Effie. She hates the thought of not seeing her every few days."

I waved my hand. "We'll arrange a car anytime she wants." I paused. "Or I was thinking of getting a chopper. Fast trip between the estate and downtown."

He nodded. "Great investment for time saving."

"Yep. Less than thirty minutes door-to-door. The casino has a helipad now."

"She'd love that."

My phone rang, and I glanced at the number and frowned. "Nonna?" I asked. "What is it?"

"When are you coming home?"

"I work late tonight."

"Something is wrong with Effie."

I was on my feet without thinking. "Is she ill?" I asked.

"No. She was busy all day unpacking some boxes in your room. I found her outside, white and shaken. She said she was fine, but she looked anything but. She said she was tired and didn't want dinner. Something is wrong, Roman."

I glanced at Aldo, who nodded. "I'm on my way."

"Good."

EFFIE

I stared at the small pile of boxes. I wanted a certain sweater, and I knew it had been on the back of my chair. I hoped Roman's men had packed it. It was dreary today and chillier than it had been, and I decided it was a good day to sort out a few boxes.

The past while had been unexpectedly tranquil. I loved the estate. Nonna and I got along so well, and she bent over backward to ensure I understood I was the mistress of the house, not her. But I only laughed when she would defer to me, and I insisted she knew better. We gardened and walked through the lovely vineyards every day. We cooked and baked. Vi came over, and we sat on the patio and laughed, sipping wine or coffee. I had never known such a decadent lifestyle. Not having to work. Roman had given me a credit card, black and elegant, and told me to use it freely. He had also handed me a debit and bank card, giving me the passwords to both. *"I put money in for you. Tell me when you need more,"* he had instructed.

I had gone online with the new laptop he had gifted me and looked at the account, staring at the screen and the fifty-thousand-dollar balance. I was sure that was more money than I could spend in a year. The day we went shopping, I used the debit card and bought a few little things I needed. My only big expense was a tie I thought he would like. He was fascinated with my eye color, and I saw a beautiful violet-blue tie with a black pattern woven into it and bought it for him.

He loved it.

What he did with it still made me blush.

As much as I loved it here, my husband was an enigma to me. Roman insisted he was incapable of romantic love, yet he displayed every trait of falling for me. Flowers and gifts showed up all the time. He texted and called. Teased me. Kissed and touched me every chance he got. Brought me to the casino some evenings, simply to see me. Made love to me. But when I tried to discuss feelings with him, he shut down. I decided to leave it. He reminded me of a stray dog we'd found once in the backyard. Terrified and skinny, he wouldn't come close, but he didn't leave either. It took us weeks of patience to get him to trust us. More for him to be comfortable with being close. Marianne had written him off, furious he didn't instantly love her. I sat on the grass day after day, offering him scraps, until one day he came to me. He was my companion until he died, and he never liked Marianne, choosing to ignore her. She, in turn, hated him. He was the only thing I ever had I didn't have to share.

I had to wait for Roman to come to me. Nagging him would do no good except to push him away. I had to be patient. I was certain I would be well rewarded when he was ready.

I sighed as I lifted the lid to the first box. I was still conflicted over Marianne's death. Glad to know she could no longer hurt me or steal what I worked so hard to have, yet sad to think she had died violently, never really knowing happiness. She was always too busy vying to be the center of attention instead of enjoying the fact that she usually was. She always hated it if she thought someone paid more notice to me or even our mom than to her. I never understood it.

The bottom line was that Roman was right. He had said she was jealous of me and would never love me the way I wanted her to.

I stifled the voice that told me neither would he.

Because I already knew I was in love with him. It was complicated and messy. I knew he would never return my love, but I had his affection. His ring. His vow. His eternal protection.

I would be satisfied with that.

I had no choice. For now.

The box was filled with books, and I fitted the lid back, carrying it down the hall to the room Roman told me to make over as mine. I planned on some shelves for all my books. When I could afford it, I went to book shows, met my favorite authors, and had my books signed. Often, I had to pick them up at used bookstores, but with the added signature, it made them so special to me. This box contained Stephanie Rose and Carrie Elks books—two of my favorite authors.

I opened another box, pleased to discover my sweater. I gasped in delight at seeing my old cell phone and charger they had tossed into the box. Roman had given me a brand-new fancy one, but this one had some pictures and phone numbers I could transfer over. I plugged it into an outlet and went back to unpacking a few more boxes.

I paused after a while, surprised to see I had been at it a couple of hours. I had carried a few boxes down the hall, put some of my old clothes into the massive closet, and started a box for charity.

I sat down and sipped at some cold water. Roman's—well, our—closet held a small fridge constantly stocked with water, and I was grateful for it.

My phone was charged, and I noticed my voice mail was full. I sat down and listened to it. Most were from Margi and Anne when I went missing, worried and concerned. I had seen them last week, and we'd had coffee one day when Roman took me to the casino. They thought it was so romantic he didn't want to be without me. I didn't try to explain to them, preferring that they chose to think Roman had swept me off my feet.

The last message, though, had me on my feet in horror.

I dropped my phone to the floor, backing away as if the phone would bite me.

The message continued to play, the voice droning on in that familiar, nasal tone that always made me tense.

"So, dear sister, I heard the funniest rumor," Marianne spat out. "The news is that you married Roman Costas today. I was certain I had heard wrong. I mean, what would a strong, powerful man like him want with a loser like you?"

There was a pause.

"Did he tell you, Effie? Did he tell you what he did?"

ROMAN

I was out of the car before it had even stopped in the driveway. I headed inside, Nonna greeting me.

"Where is she?"

She shook her head, wringing her hands. "She went outside for a walk. Over an hour ago, Roman."

"But it's cold. Raining. Why would she go outside?"

"She refused to listen to me." Nonna grabbed my elbow. "She was so white, almost in shock. Something spooked her, but she refused to say anything. You must find her." She indicated the back of the house. "She is out there."

I took off running, everything in me tight and distraught. What could have happened that upset Effie so much? Outside, I headed toward the vineyards, almost stumbling when I saw her. Standing in between a row of vines, not moving, the rain pelting down, harder now than only a minute ago. I raced toward her, shouting her name. She turned, seeing me, pure fear skittering across her face. She began to run, slipping on the grass, falling and getting up, going as quickly as she could.

I roared in frustration, not understanding.

Why was she running?

What the fuck had happened?

Why was my wife so scared of me?

I caught up to her faster than she expected. I grasped her arm, spinning her around.

"Don't," she pleaded. "Don't hurt me."

I stepped back, shocked. "Effie," I pleaded. "I would never hurt you."

"Why," she sobbed. "Why would you do it?"

I had no idea what she was talking about. But she was wet, shivering, and overwrought. I bent and scooped her into my arms, not letting her go even when she struggled. I headed straight to our room, setting her on her feet in the bathroom. She hung her head, the way her shoulders bowed making me think of the night I had dragged her out of that awful basement.

Not even waiting until the water warmed, I pulled her into the shower. I didn't give a shit if my shoes and suit were ruined. I let the cold water spray on my back until it heated then I turned, letting the warmth saturate her clothing. I waited until I felt her shivers stop before stripping her of her clothing, then doing the same to mine. I kicked the wet material to the side of the shower. She never looked up, and her fists remained clenched. When I knew she was warm, I shut off the water and wrapped a towel around her. I dried her off then myself. I draped my robe around her, wanting her to have the material to nestle into. I led her to our room and pushed her gently into a chair and poured a hefty glass of brandy. She sipped the fiery liquid, grimacing. I tossed it back, set the empty glass on the table and took her trembling hands in mine.

"Tell me. Tell me exactly what happened."

She glanced over, and I saw an old cell phone. I picked it up, and she took it from my hands, connecting to voice mail. The tremors returned full force as she set the phone on the table, and a voice I never wanted to hear again spoke.

"So, dear sister, I heard the funniest rumor," Marianne said, sounding as if she'd smoked a hundred cigarettes earlier. "The news is that you married Roman Costas today. I was certain I had heard wrong. I mean what would a strong, powerful man like him want with a loser like you?"

There was a pause.

"Did he tell you, Effie? Did he tell you what he did?"

I shut my eyes at her words, knowing what was coming next.

"He gave me the idea to sell you. To settle my debt. Contact the Santini brothers, he said. So, I did. If he married you, no doubt he plans on doing the same thing once he's tired of you. I bet he got a kick out of taking your cherry. And now the bastard has set them on my tail. He probably has a life insurance policy out on you. I bet he's fucking you real good, isn't he? Pretending he cares? I heard he's a user and a player, so don't get too comfortable. I hope he hurts you badly. You've always been such a thorn in my side. I hated you then, and I hate you now. I hope—"

I couldn't listen to any more of her vicious vitriol. I grabbed the phone, throwing it at the wall, feeling intense satisfaction as it exploded and she was silenced. For good.

Then I turned to Effie. The fear in her eyes broke me.

She believed her. Her fucking horror of a sister knew exactly how to beat Effie down with a few words. Her already shaken confidence was crushed under the weight of Marianne's lies.

"I didn't. I swear. She is twisting what happened."

"She—"

"No." I shook my head. "I was angry when she suggested giving you to me for a bit of 'fun.' Furious that she would do something so hideous. I lost my temper, and yes, I told her to peddle her offer elsewhere. I had no idea she would, Effie. I have no clue how she found the Santini brothers and made her deal. If I'd had any inkling she'd do such a thing, I would have gone and found you right away. Yes, when I figured it out, I did everything to find you because I felt guilty. Horrified that my anger and outburst had caused you pain. Especially once I met you. Saw the sweetness you carried with you. I knew it would be crushed, and I couldn't take it. But it changed. I swear to you, it all changed."

She began to shake her head, and I framed her face with my hands, refusing to let her look away. I needed her to see my eyes. To know what I was saying was true.

"Once I got to know you, it became paramount to protect you. But that's not why I married you, Effie. I rescued you because I had to." I drew in a deep breath. "I fell in love with you because I had no choice. My heart wanted you."

Her eyes widened.

The moment Nonna had called, everything changed. The thought that Effie was ill or hurt broke down any resistance. I knew I loved her. All my denials and stupid ideas of not being able to love were blown away.

Because it was Effie. My Effie. My wife.

And I wasn't letting her go until she accepted that fact.

Accepted me.

"I love you," I repeated. "Everything about you. I'm so tired of fighting it. Trying to resist, when all I want is to be with you. To love you."

Tears poured down her cheeks. "She—"

"No," I said again. "She lied. She did it to hurt you. Everything she did was to hurt you. I am not lying. You are never leaving me. I would die before I let anything happen to you, my little tiger. Believe me."

She whimpered, and I leaned closer. "Look into my eyes, Effie. See the truth. I am yours. I have been since the day you told me to leave your shop. I was just too stubborn to see it." I pressed my mouth to her trembling lips. "See it now, please, baby. See me."

Our gazes locked and held. She was unsure and worried. Still scared. But I saw the way she struggled, wanting to believe. Hoping.

"You love me," I murmured, leaning my forehead to hers. "I know you do. You have loved me and been patient. I'll do the same, Effie. I'll wait."

Then I gathered her in my arms, holding her close.

I was never letting her go.

CHAPTER 26
EFFIE

I woke surrounded by warmth. I was cocooned in Roman's robe and wrapped in his arms. His entire body was pressed against me, keeping away the bad dreams and the cold. Outside, the rain continued, the heavy drops ricocheting off the glass. I knew he was awake from his breathing and the tightness in his grip. I stared at the window, the events of last night replaying in my head. The call. Marianne's voice. The horrid words she said. My utter panic. In a flash, I relived every moment of that awful night I'd been taken. The men and their rough hands and cold expressions. Marianne's delight in seeing my terror. The glee on her face when she tripped me.

The blackness that surrounded me when I woke up. My despair, knowing Marianne had done this and my life was over. The constant terror every time one of the men would come down the stairs. The pain they inflicted.

And then Roman appeared.

My life and my world would never be the same.

And last night, he told me he loved me. He stared into my eyes, nothing but truth and love blazing at me. That look of fierce tenderness I had glimpsed at times was fully trained on me. His voice was drenched in desperation. Begging me to believe him. Trust *his* words, not hers.

Marianne who had done nothing but lie and hurt me.

Roman who had rescued me, cared for me, and gave me only truth when I asked.

I believed him.

But I couldn't say the words back.

It was as if the events of the last weeks had caught up to me. I was speechless, rendered almost numb by everything I had gone through. The good and the bad.

And every single one of them was tied back to Roman.

I sighed and struggled to get up. Roman pulled me back to him. "Where are you going?"

"To the bathroom," I replied, my voice sounding scratchy and raw to my ears.

He released me, and I felt his reluctance when he did.

In the bathroom, I looked in the mirror. My hair was a mess, and I was pale. I washed my face, brushed my teeth, then sat on the vanity chair, trying to brush out the tangles. Roman came in without knocking, frowning when he saw me.

Wordlessly, he took the brush from my hand and stood behind me, carefully removing the tangles and snarls, never once causing me discomfort. He didn't talk or ask me any questions. When he finished, he set down the brush and turned on the shower. He held out his hand, I let him untie the robe, and we stepped into the shower, glancing at our wet clothing still in the corner from last night. I knew I needed to remove them, but at the moment, I couldn't be bothered to do so. I grabbed a hair clip and bundled my hair into a bun on the top of my head as he shampooed and began washing himself. I watched him as I did the same. The casual way he handled his own body. His powerful muscles that stretched and jumped as he moved. He had a few scars, which only seemed to make him more beautiful to me. I found him captivating.

He rinsed his face, pushing his hair away, and opened his eyes, meeting mine. I was unable to look away. He looked at me, his expression and touch tender as he reached out, stroking the skin on my cheek.

"Are you all right, Little Tiger?"

"I'm fine."

He smiled, shaking his head. He kissed me softly. "Liar."

"I will be."

He took the soap from my hands, running it over my shoulders. "I know. I'll make sure of it."

At the table, Nonna studied me. "You are still pale. What is the matter? Roman, what have you done?"

Roman chuckled, shaking his head as he sipped his coffee. "The husband is always at fault. Good thing Aldo warned me."

"I'm fine. Roman didn't do anything wrong."

Nonna made a funny noise in the back of her throat.

Roman slid his hand over mine, squeezing my fingers. "Effie had an unexpected call last night, Nonna. From the grave, so to speak. It shook her."

Nonna frowned. "Your sister?" she guessed.

"Yes. She had left me a voice mail a few days before her, ah, accident. I heard it last night."

All Nonna knew about Marianne was that she had died in an accident and that we weren't close. Roman had omitted any details about her involvement with the two of us getting together. Nonna hadn't asked many questions since Roman told her I didn't want to talk about Marianne.

"How terribly shocking." Then she turned to Roman. "You are here for breakfast, so you are gone this evening?"

He shook his head. "No, I am staying here for the next few days. I want to be close to Effie."

"No," I burst out.

They turned to me, shock on their faces at my outburst.

"I mean, I'm fine. Really. Nonna and I were going to work in the garden if the rain lets up and make bagels later. Tomorrow, Vi is coming for lunch. I have plans on Friday. Don't disrupt your schedule to babysit me."

"I'm not babysitting. You've had a big shock. I want to look after my wife," he said quietly, studying me. "Do you not want me around, Effie?"

Nonna stood, taking her plate to the kitchen. I knew she was giving us some privacy. Roman crossed his arms on the table, studying me. "You don't believe me," he said. "You don't believe that I love you."

"I simply need some time to sort everything through in my head," I admitted. "Last night—hearing her voice… It brought back a lot of painful memories."

"You believed her."

"I didn't know what to believe."

He rested his chin on his steepled fingers. "Believe this. I fought against loving you because I was sure I had no idea how to love. Not the kind of love you deserved. But last night when I was rushing here, when I thought you were hurt, I knew I was exactly the man you deserved because no one could possibly love you more. I will protect you with my last breath. I want to spoil you. Laugh with you. Love you." He drew in a long breath. "I want to build a life with you, Effie. Tell me what you need me to do, and I will do it. But don't ask me to stay away from you. That is one thing I cannot do any longer."

I blinked at his words. They were heartfelt. Real. I felt his love as he gazed at me.

"I don't want you to stay away from me."

He relaxed. "Good."

"I just want to be normal. I need a little time, Roman. Just a little time."

He studied me, then nodded. "Fine. I'll go today, but I will be home tonight. Aldo and I are trying to stay away a few nights in a row and see how our managers step up."

He wiped his mouth and stood, then surprised me and bent low, pulling my head to his and kissing me. "You love me, I know it," he murmured. "You've shown it in a thousand ways, and now I'm going to show you."

He left me with the feel of his mouth on mine and his touch on my skin.

It was early when I woke up, once again surrounded by Roman. It was that way every day waking up with him, but the past couple of nights, he'd been extra close to me. I shifted, rolling over so we were facing each other. He was still asleep, his face relaxed and the tension gone from around his mouth and eyes. I traced the contours of his face, ran my finger down the bridge of his straight nose and lightly ran my fingertip over his full lips. I glanced up, stopping when I saw his green eyes open, sleepy and warm. An indulgent smile pulled on his lips.

"Don't stop, Effie. I love it when you touch me."

"You do?" I asked.

He propped his head on his hand, his elbow pressing into the mattress. "Yes. I should have known immediately how different you were. I liked your touch. Now I crave it. I hate being away from you."

"Oh," I whispered.

"I think about you when we're not together. I wonder what you're doing. If you're thinking about me."

"I do."

He smiled, tracing his finger along my jaw. "My Effie," he murmured. "However we started, I am so grateful to have you."

He slowly bent his head, giving me a chance to say no. But I didn't want to say no. I wanted to feel his mouth on mine. To taste him. We needed to reconnect. To move as one, locked in an intimacy as old as time. To feel that link.

I needed him.

His mouth covered my lips, his body shifting so he was over me, pressing me into the plush fabric, claiming me. His heat branded me. His warmth soaked into my skin. His tongue mated with mine, and he groaned low in his throat.

"Every time," he rasped. "Every time with you is so fucking erotic. You make me crazy."

"Make love to me, Roman. Show me."

Seconds later, I was under him, his large body blanketing my smaller one. His mouth worked me, teasing, exploring, his tongue mating with mine in long, sensuous passes. He slid his fingers up my arms, entwining our clasped hands over my head as he deepened the kiss, this one somehow different from any other kiss we'd shared before. I felt his emotion, his love and need in the caress. It was intimate, hot, and intense.

He moved over me, kissing and tasting me everywhere. The crooks of my elbows, my wrists, and shoulders. Across my collarbone and down to my navel as he played with my nipples, his fingers plucking and teasing. He kissed the arch of my foot, tracing lazy pathways up my leg to my inner thigh, only to start again with the other leg.

I was a mass of quivering limbs, shaking moans, and pleading whispers by the time he finished his explorations and settled between my legs. When his mouth closed around my clit, I arched high off the bed, keening his name. My orgasm was fast and hard, and he licked me through it, groaning and praising me in his low, raspy voice. I had barely come down when he notched himself inside me and began to move. His mouth covered mine, and I tasted myself on him, whimpering as he filled me. We moved like the ocean early in the morning when the tide leisurely drifted in. Easy, deep, and slow, our bodies in perfect synchronization. He whispered my name, his mouth against my ear, his arms holding me close.

"Please, Roman," I begged, tightening my legs around him.

He moved faster, deeper, hitting me exactly where I needed. Stars exploded behind my eyes as another orgasm washed over me, and I clutched him tighter. He gripped me, his hips pivoting then stilling as we crested, locked together, not a whisper of air between us.

His mouth was gentle as he kissed me.

"My little tiger," he whispered. "I love you."

I felt his sincerity. I buried my face into his neck, feeling the same emotion.

And still, I couldn't say it back.

The sky was still overcast, which matched my mood on Friday morning. Roman stepped into the bedroom, tugging down the sleeves of his pure-white shirt. I admired his suit, the deep green setting off his eyes. His tie and shoes were black, and the color combination was striking.

"You look handsome," I said with a smile.

He sat in the spot across from me, lifting his coffee cup. He took a sip, eyeing me over the rim of the cup. "You look ravished," he replied, then winked. "I like it when my wife looks that way." Then he frowned. "You also look sad. Your eyes are dim."

I shrugged and swallowed. It amazed me how he noticed my emotions by the color of my eyes. "Today is the anniversary of my mom's death," I confessed. "It still hits me hard."

He took my hand. "You should have said something. I'll stay home."

"No, it's fine, Roman. I'm going to get flowers and go to the grave later. I-I want to do that on my own."

"Alex will go with you." His tone brooked no argument. "And he will drive."

I was getting used to Alex following and taking me everywhere, so I nodded in agreement.

"I would like to accompany you and pay my respects," Roman murmured.

"I go every few months. Maybe next time? Today is just…" I wasn't sure how to explain it. "It is personal for me, Roman."

He studied me and nodded. "I understand."

"I might have coffee with Vi afterward."

"Good. She will make you smile." He sat back. "I'll take you out for dinner tonight. Overlooking the Falls. We'll stay at the hotel."

"That would be lovely."

"I was thinking maybe we could take Nonna to Luca's this weekend. Have a family dinner. He and I need to do some more talking, and Nonna would love to see Justine."

"She will miss him when he moves."

"She will. But she knows he has to make his wife happy. Justine is very close with her family, and she misses them a lot. With a baby on the way and Luca stepping back, it makes sense. Nonna can visit, and they will come here. And she has you now." He finished his coffee. "She is incredibly fond of you, Effie."

He stood, bending down and cupping my face to kiss me. "As am I."

His mouth was tender, his words sincere. I gripped his wrists, enjoying the feel of his mouth on mine. "I know," I whispered. "Roman—"

He cut me off with another kiss. "When you're ready, Little Tiger." He kissed me again. "Let me know when you are leaving. And if you change your mind, I will come with you."

"Thank you."

He pressed a kiss to my forehead and left, with one last look over his shoulder. As the door shut behind him, my shoulders dropped. He told me he loved me every chance he got. He showed me in his touches, his care. And I knew I loved him. He knew I loved him.

Why couldn't I say it?

I poured another coffee and pulled my feet up under me. I heard the distant rumble of the car leaving the front of the house, and I knew Roman was gone. It tugged on my heart a little. Part of me wanted him to come to the cemetery with me. To have his strength beside me when I stood at my mother's grave. I went often and laid flowers, but today felt different. Darker, more severe, and poignant. I wondered if my mom knew Marianne was dead. If she knew why. I wanted to tell her myself, alone. Part of me believed that she would know I was there and she would forgive me for any part I had in Marianne's death. I knew how deeply Roman hated Marianne, which was why I had to do it alone. I wasn't sure he would understand. He saw things in very black-and-white terms, and I didn't know if he believed the ones we lost could see or hear us. I did, so I needed to do this by myself.

I waited until after lunch and the rain had stopped. I wore a pair of sturdy shoes, jeans, and a light coat against the chill of the day.

Alex drove me, and I stopped at a florist and got a bunch of lovely flowers that contained all my mom's favorites. My hands shook as we rolled to a stop in the graveyard. Alex opened my door, and I stepped out onto the damp gravel. "I'd like to go alone."

He hesitated. "I have strict orders to keep you in my sight at all times. I'll stay a respectful distance away, Mrs. Costas."

I wasn't surprised. Roman took my protection very seriously, even though I thought he could let up, given that Marianne was gone. Maybe once he relaxed a little, he would.

Alex followed me and stood near the small hill by my mother's grave. He scouted the area, but the cemetery was quiet, only a few others visiting lost loved ones. A couple was mourning over a fresh grave a short distance away, the man bent over the weeping woman's head. I sent a short thought of healing toward them as I walked on the rain-soaked grass to my mom's headstone. The etched heart and her name were dewy with the weather that had been plaguing us the past few days. I knelt and laid the flowers, brushing away the dirt around the headstone. "Hi, Mom," I mumbled, my throat feeling tight. "I'm sorry

I haven't been by in a while. Life's been kinda crazy. I miss you."

I stayed that way for a few moments, letting the silence surround me. Some heavy drops fell from the tree limb above me, hitting the headstone and my head. I shook my head to get rid of the wet. "You already know, I guess. I'm sorry. I know you loved her —at least as much as she let anyone love her."

There was an odd sound, and I saw Alex rushing toward me. I began to stand, confused when he stumbled but kept coming. "Down!" he yelled. "Get—"

He was almost to me, his gun drawn, when he fell. Stunned, I rushed toward him, dropping to my knees to check his vitals. I stopped in shock at the figure that appeared by the small hill.

I blinked to make sure I was seeing what I thought I was seeing.

"Marianne?"

ROMAN

I was restless at my desk, unable to concentrate. I paced the room, stared out the window, but found no pleasure in the view this morning. The swirling water and thunderous power of the Falls only enhanced my tension instead of dispelling it. It had been that way all morning.

I glanced at my watch. Effie would be departing for the cemetery shortly. Despite her affirmation she wanted to be alone, I was thinking of heading that way and being there when she was done. Perhaps she would need me.

God, how I wanted her to need me.

Frustrated, I headed to the other office, intent on studying the latest architectural ideas for the new casino, but the plans and details held no appeal. Aldo walked in, looking surprised to see me.

"Roman."

"Hey," I greeted him, flipping through the drawings.

"You don't like those?" he asked. "I thought some of the ideas were incredible. I also thought a few of them could be modified for some renos you want done here."

"Hmm," I replied.

"Or maybe those zebras in tutus greeting the guests would be a better idea."

"Perhaps," I said, then shook my head. "Wait, what?"

Aldo laughed. "I was wondering if you were listening. Where are you today, Roman?"

I sat down, rubbing my eyes. "Lost somewhere between hell and forever."

He sat down. "Effie?" he guessed. "Things are still unsettled?"

"The only thing that is settled is that I'm in love with my wife. I'm certain she feels the same. She shows it in everything she does, but she has yet to say the words." I barked a laugh. "I'm obsessed with every little thing she does. Says. Feels. Wants. I worry about her every second. *Me*. The man who didn't care about anything or anyone. I deserve her hesitancy."

"You always cared, Roman. You were just selective in your level of caring."

"Well, Effie has blown that shit out of the water."

"I agree, she loves you. So does Vi. But Effie has been through a lot of trauma lately. Give her time to find her feet. Keep being patient." He paused, taking a sip of his coffee. "As much as that is killing you."

I nodded, flipping the pen in my hand in agitation.

"Where is she?" Aldo asked. "Vi said she might see her later but was unsure if the plans were certain."

I explained about the date and that Effie was at the cemetery.

"I wanted to go with her, but she wanted to be alone." I huffed a breath. "I was wondering about going anyway. Alex sent a text they had left. I was thinking about being there when she was done. Giving her the privacy she wanted but staying close if she needed me."

"I think that is a great idea. Show her you'll be there for her. That she can rely on you."

I frowned. "Do you think that is part of the problem? She doesn't know I'd do anything for her?"

Aldo shrugged. "I'm sure she is trying to figure it all out. Go. I'll cover the floor. Wait for her. Take her somewhere lovely and buy her lunch. Hold her hand. Be there for her if she cries. As strong as Vi is, she needs that sometimes." He smiled fondly. "I like being the one there for her."

I stood. "Good idea."

I stopped by the computer room and in minutes knew where the plot was located in the cemetery. Downstairs, I got flowers for Effie. I would give them to her after she was done.

In the car, that restlessness continued. The day felt ominous. It had to be the continuing weather. The dark, gloomy skies were beginning to get to me. That had to be it.

My phone rang and I hit speaker. "Aldo."

"Roman," he said, his voice panicked. "Fuck, where are you?"

His voice made me anxious. Aldo never panicked. "We're almost to the cemetery. What the fuck is wrong?"

"Gregory Santini called. Fucking Timothy lied. He's hooked up with Marianne. She got to him. *She isn't dead*, Roman. She's here in Niagara Falls. Timothy is with her—his tracker went off. Gregory was calling us to warn you."

"Speed up!" I yelled at my driver. "I need to get there now!"

"I'm on my way with men, Roman."

I hung up. By the time he got there, this would be over.

Ralph stepped on the gas, the car lurching forward so quickly I was flung back in my seat. I grabbed the gun always with me in the car and checked the chamber. I called Alex, roaring in frustration when the call went unanswered. I tried Effie's number, only to have it go to voice mail.

I shut my eyes, tamping down my panic. If Marianne got to Effie before I could stop her, I had no idea what would happen. I needed to get to my wife. To save her.

If I didn't—

I couldn't finish that thought.

I would. I would rescue my wife, and this time when Marianne was dead, she would stay that way.

I would make sure of it.

EFFIE

I was stunned. Marianne walked toward me, her face drawn up in a sneer. "Not happy to see me, little sister?" she asked, sarcasm evident in her voice.

"You-you're dead."

"Ah, the rumors of my death are greatly exaggerated." She grinned, the action making her look evil. "I should know. I started the rumors."

"Why?" I asked.

She laughed, the sound making me shiver. "To draw you out." She waved the gun in her hand. "I knew you'd be here today."

"I don't understand."

"Of course you don't. You never did." She marched toward me, the gun in her hand aimed directly at me. I stood, backing away from Alex. He was dead, his phone lying on the ground beside him, his blood covering it.

"Effie. The perfect little princess," she ranted. "God, I hated you."

"Why?" I asked again, desperate to keep her talking. Praying someone had heard the shot and would come investigate.

"My life was great until you showed up. Then it was all about the baby. Effie. I had to share my dad with you. You took my new mother away from me. It was only supposed to be me."

Even after everything she had done, I was shocked at the hatred in her voice.

"I always loved you."

She laughed again, coming closer. "You were always an idiot. I've been trying to get rid of you my whole life." She smiled widely. "The incident where your crib railing fell down and you rolled out. That time you fell in the pool and almost drowned. The night that tree limb just missed you. The incident with the poison. I tried so hard, but I always failed. I thought I'd succeeded this time, but you had to fucking get rescued."

"That…that was you? All those accidents?" I sputtered. I had always thought I was just unlucky. Marianne had been responsible all those times?

"But you saved me."

Marianne sneered. "Made me look good."

My God, she wasn't simply a narcissist: she was psychotic. Deranged.

She tossed her hair. "There is no rescuing for you this time, little sister."

"If you kill me, Roman will hunt you down."

She laughed. "I have my own protection now. Roman will join you soon enough."

I shook my head in disbelief. Roman was too protected. She kept talking, her voice furious and high-pitched. Her eyes were wild, her gaze jumping around.

"How you got him to marry you, I have no idea. It should have been me. He should have seen what I could do for him."

"He married me because he loves me."

Her eyes narrowed. "Then he'll pay to get you back. I'm not going to kill you. I'm going to take you, and Roman is going to pay big to get you back. I want his money." Her smile grew. "He just won't get back the same little princess I took from him. By then, it'll be too late." She chortled in twisted glee. "For both of you."

My stomach lurched, and I covered my mouth with my hand. "I can get you money, Marianne. Roman has lots. Tell me what you want, and I'll get it. But don't touch me. Please."

"Like I believe you."

I heard the screech of tires and some shouting. Noises I was certain were muffled gunshots. I turned my head, positive it was Roman's voice I heard. I gasped as Marianne rushed forward, grabbing me by the hair and yanking me toward her.

Roman appeared, racing over the hill, seeing us. He held up his hands as he approached. "Let her go."

Marianne laughed, the sound crazed. "Not happening." She aimed her gun at him. "Don't come any closer."

I screamed as Roman kept coming, and Marianne shot at him. His body jolted, his arms flying upright, and he stopped, looking down at his shoulder. Blood soaked the material of his suit. But he kept walking.

He met my wild, panicked gaze. "It's going to be fine, Effie."

He stopped a short distance away.

"Tell me what you want, and let her go," he demanded.

Marianne shook her head, and I smelled her odor. She was high. Dirty. She reeked of weed and alcohol. And she was frantic. She tightened her grip on my hair.

Roman tried to get her attention. "Timothy is dead, Marianne. I killed him, so your backup is gone. You have two choices. I kill you, or I give you what you want and you give me what I want."

I felt the cold barrel of her gun pressed into my neck. "You think you want my worthless sister?" she goaded him. "She can't be that good in bed."

"I'll give you five million. You name the account, and it'll be transferred now. You let her go and leave us alone. You can live a good life with five million."

Marianne scoffed. "Why should I let her be happy?"

Roman looked distressed. "She won't be. She doesn't even love me. But I love her. Give her back to me. Ten million."

I felt Marianne's excitement. Ten million dollars. She would live the life she always wanted and would cease to care about me.

Until she ran out of money.

"No," I protested, struggling against her. "Roman, no!"

He shook his head, listing slightly. He was losing blood. Too much blood. It soaked through his jacket sleeve and dripped from his hand. I had to get to him.

"I love you," he insisted. "She can have it all."

"I'm not worth it!"

"Yes," he insisted. "You are."

Marianne's temper broke, and she dug her gun deeply into my neck. "You can't have her. She doesn't deserve it!"

Roman rushed forward, stumbling, trying to stay upright. Trying to get to me. Every instinct kicked in, and I lifted my foot, stomping on Marianne's instep. She cried out, and I spun, pushing her away. I raced toward Roman, pointing the gun I had taken from Alex's lifeless body and shooting it over my shoulder, not knowing where the bullets would land. I felt a sharp pain graze across my leg and another along my head, but I ignored it. I heard Marianne's cry of agony as I dropped to my knees, cradling Roman's head.

"No," I sobbed. "Roman, please. Stay with me. I do love you. I love you so much. I need you. *Please.*"

Marianne lurched to her feet, spitting in rage. Blood ran down her arm where one of the bullets had pierced her skin. She lifted her gun, aiming it right at me, but before I could do anything, another gunshot rang out. A small hole materialized in her head, and the look on her face was one of shock.

Then she dropped.

Aldo appeared, running fast, his gun drawn. He looked determined. Furious. Like an avenging angel set on murder.

Roman's eyes fluttered, and he lifted his hand, the blood from his injury coating his skin.

"Now you're safe."

"Stay with me. I love you," I pleaded.

He tried to smile, but it was more of a grimace. "That's all I need."

And he passed out.

CHAPTER 27
ROMAN

I woke up with a gasp, my first coherent thought of my wife.

"Effie."

Aldo loomed over me, his face concerned. "She's fine, Roman." He indicated the side of the bed I was in. "She's asleep, finally."

I looked over, the movement making me grimace. Effie was in a chair pulled beside the bed. She was asleep as Aldo said, her skin pale. Gauze was wrapped around her arm, and there was a bandage on her head from the gunshot inflicted on her by Marianne.

"She hasn't left your side, Roman. She refused to go anywhere. I had to force her to get treated."

I drank her in. She was alive. Hurt, but alive. The threats to her had been eliminated.

My gaze swung back to Aldo. "Status."

He knew what I needed.

"Marianne is dead. Timothy is dead. Gregory is shitting himself, terrified of your retribution over this."

"How did this happen?"

He shut his eyes. "Jesus, Roman. What a clusterfuck. Do you know what I felt, racing to that cemetery? Seeing you lying there bleeding out, with Effie hovering over you like an angel, bleeding herself? And that psycho bitch aiming her gun, determined to kill you both?"

"You got her first."

"Right between the eyes."

"Thank you."

He nodded, and I cleared my throat. He grabbed a glass, lifting it to my mouth, and I drank the cool water greedily. Then he sat. "I thought we'd lost you. Shit, I should get the doctor."

My body ached like a bitch and my head pounded, but I was determined. "No. Tell me everything first."

"According to Gregory, Marianne somehow seduced Timothy. Turned him against Gregory. Gregory said when he spoke to Timothy, he ranted at him about being used and he should be in control. He'd been acting odd, and Gregory figured out what was going on. Confronted Timothy. Found Marianne with him. They argued, and Timothy threatened Gregory, knocked him out. When he came to, he called me."

"And you found us."

"Yes."

"The site?"

He smiled grimly. "The men cleaned up the area right away. The story of a car repeatedly backfiring was confirmed by the graveyard manager. Who kindly dug a deeper grave than usual where two bodies will never be discovered." A satisfied gleam filled his eyes. "I watched it happen to be certain. Earlier today, a coffin was placed on top, and the family had no clue. A donation was made in the man's name to the Alzheimer's Association. And the cemetery manager has a generous contribution to his retirement fund."

"Alex?"

"His family have been notified and taken care of."

I nodded grimly.

"How long have I been out?"

"Two days. The bitch nicked an artery. You lost a lot of blood, Roman. We got you here as fast as we could, and Dr. Sims started on you right away. Surgery happened immediately. I donated blood, as did Vi.

There was a line of your men willing to do so as well. Effie wanted to, but the doc said no. She was very upset." He frowned. "Another millimeter and I would be attending your funeral, not your bedside."

I sighed, shutting my eyes, already exhausted. "Nonna?" I asked.

"Has been here. So has Luca. He took her home a short while ago. They'll be thrilled to hear you woke up." He smiled. "As will your wife, who refused to leave you."

I turned my head, studying Effie. I didn't like seeing her in a chair. "She needs to be recuperating as well."

"I'll let you pick that fight. She is stubborn and would not leave this room." A grin pulled at his lips. "She even backtalked Nonna."

"My little tiger."

"She is."

"When can I get out of here?"

"You just woke up," Effie's voice interrupted us. I turned my head, meeting her violet-blue gaze. There were circles under her eyes, and she looked upset. She glanced at Aldo. "Which means you should have woken me."

Aldo looked at me with a wink. "I'll go find the doctor now. Give you two a few moments."

He left, and Effie unfurled herself from the chair. Her movements were stiff, and she tried to hide her grimace but failed.

"You should be in bed."

"And you should be quiet and resting. Not interrogating Aldo." She stood and tugged at the blanket. "What do you need?"

I smiled at her. "You."

Instantly, her bravado failed, and her eyes filled with tears. "Oh, Roman," she whispered brokenly. "You have me."

I lifted my arm, pulling her down gently so our faces were close. "I know."

"You do?"

"I heard you, Effie. Before I passed out, while I was out. I kept hearing your voice telling me you loved me. Begging me to stay." I tucked a strand of hair behind her ear. "How could I resist such a sweet plea?"

A sob escaped her lips, and I shook my head. "Hush. I'm fine. I'm right here."

She nodded, tears coursing down her cheeks anyway. I wiped them away. "God, I want to kiss you."

"Why aren't you?"

"I've been out for two days. No doubt I smell horrible, and God knows how my breath—"

She cut me off, pressing her mouth to mine. We kissed gently, our lips moving and sliding, but neither of us deepened the caress. It was a moment of reconnection, of saying hello, of a new, intimate level in our relationship.

She pulled back. "I love you, Roman Costas."

Her words healed every jagged tear of my heart. Brought life to the parts of it I thought were dead. Filled me with a buoyancy I had never experienced. Despite the pain and exhaustion, I felt alive. Truly alive for the first time in my life.

I stroked her cheek. "I love you, Effie Costas."

The door opened, and Dr. Sims and Aldo walked in.

I touched her lips. "To be continued."

EFFIE

The hospital room was finally quiet. Roman was resting, but his face still looked tense. The doctor was pleased he was awake. Aldo was beyond relieved.

Roman had spoken with his nonna and brother, assuring them he was doing well. They planned a visit in the morning. Vi came and took Aldo home, bringing me a change of clothes. She helped me shower since my arm hurt to move too much and I still had a headache. She muttered a lot about my bitch of a sister shooting me, and I didn't argue or defend Marianne.

Roman grumbled about not getting up or being disconnected from all the machines he was on, but Dr. Sims informed him they had removed some of them, and the rest would happen the next day once he was convinced Roman was stable. He was allowed to brush his teeth and have a sponge bath. He complained bitterly to the nurse who did it, informing her his wife would do a far better job. She told him to be quiet and that "his wife" was in no shape to put up with his smart mouth.

He actually listened to her.

He protested about dinner and, while I was showering, spoke to Aldo. Just after Aldo and Vi left, another man appeared, young and eager.

"I brought your food, Mr. Costas," he said and set up the bedside tray. "What else can I do?"

"Did you bring the other items?"

"They're in the car."

"Get them," he ordered, then met my eyes. "Ah, please, Connor,"
he added.

"Sure."

Connor reappeared with two larger bags and set them on the
floor by my chair. He left after making sure Roman didn't want
anything else.

I tried not to laugh when I saw the pillows and soft blankets
Roman had made him deliver.

I opened the food, inhaling the delicious scent, suddenly
famished. I twirled some pasta, shoving it into my mouth,
almost groaning at the taste. Roman chuckled.

"Eat, Effie. It does my heart good to see you eat."

I perched on the edge of his bed, alternating feeding him and
them myself. The pasta was perfection, the chicken piccata
melting in my mouth. We didn't speak, but our eyes met several
times, and the tenderness in Roman's gaze was as thrilling as it
was new.

After I put the dishes back in the insulated bag and
wiped his face and my hands, I curled back up in the
chair, watching him drift into sleep. Dr. Sims said he
would need time to recover from the blood loss and
surgery. The bullet had done some damage that had
to be repaired, and Roman was going to have to be
patient.

But I was looking forward to going home. I was tired
and I hated hospitals, even though this was the nicest

hospital room I had ever seen. It was quiet as well, and the men outside kept us safe, although I knew we were far safer now than we had been before the events at the cemetery.

I kept seeing Marianne's face. Hearing her voice. The way she talked about hating me. How often she'd tried to get rid of me. The pure pleasure on her face as she shot at me.

My arm and head ached, although I was certain Roman was in more pain than I was. He was concerned about me, though, watching me all the time. Wondering what was going through my mind.

I looked over to see his eyes open, a frown on his face. I stood. "Are you in pain, my love?" I asked. "Should I get the nurse?"

"No, I'm fine."

"Don't be brave, Roman. Please."

He touched my cheek. "It's only been a few hours since my last pain pills. I'm still fine. Except you are too far away in that chair."

"I can't get it any closer."

He shifted, lifting his good arm. "Our injuries are on opposite sides, so you can fit here."

"I don't think they'll like that."

"They'll like the new wing I'll add to the hospital to shut them up."

I didn't argue. I didn't want to. I carefully climbed up beside him, fitting into his side. He was careful to slide his arm around me, and I rested my injured one on top of his. He sighed. "So much better."

"Yes," I hummed in agreement.

He pressed a soft kiss to my head. "I never want to be without you again, Effie."

"Me either."

"When we go home, we're going to talk and make plans. Together."

I nestled a little closer to him. "I like the sound of that."

"I'm going to make some changes. More than I planned before." He drew in a long breath, letting it out slowly. "I never want you in danger again."

"She's gone. Aldo said—"

He held me tighter. "She is," he assured me. "He made sure her body was buried. She will never harm you again."

I told him what she had said to me. How she admitted she'd tried to injure me when I was younger. He was quiet until I finished.

"I wondered when you told me about some of your incidents," he admitted.

"She tried to hurt me, then saved me for the attention it got her. I recall people making a fuss over her for being such a great sister. No one paid extra attention to me since I wasn't hurt. She was the star. I never saw it."

"No one did. Someone watched over you all those years," he muttered. "How she didn't kill you... Jesus, how no one saw..." He became quiet. "She was a danger to you for your entire life."

"Not anymore."

"No one will ever harm you, Effie. I will not allow it. You were meant to be mine so I could protect you. And I will always do so."

I let his words soak into my head. Let his warmth soothe me. His determination was clear, his promise real. I was safe with him. I always would be. He would surround me. His love would surround me.

I looked up, meeting his gaze. The fierce tenderness raged in his eyes. His love was on display, and even if I only ever saw that when we were alone, it was enough.

He bent, capturing my mouth. The action made him grimace. That made me grimace too, but we kissed endlessly until he eased away.

"Stop causing trouble, Mrs. Costas. The nurse will come in and threaten us."

"You can handle her, my love."

He chuckled. "Yeah, I can."

And wrapped in his embrace, I slept.

ROMAN

I walked the rows of vines, stopping on occasion to lift a branch, checking on the grapes. I breathed in the rich scent of the soil, the fruit, the evening that surrounded me. For the first time in my life, I knew the sensation of peace.

I had been home from the hospital for a week. A week of rest, time with Nonna and Aldo and Vi. A week of my wife. My Effie.

She brought the peace to my life. With her, I found silence. Acceptance. A rhythm I never knew could exist.

Footsteps behind me made me look over my shoulder. Luca approached, a smile on his face. "Brother."

He hugged me, careful not to press too hard. I shook his shoulder. "Good to see you. How are things?"

We began to stroll. "I have everything arranged. We will meet in two days." He paused. "Are you sure you're all right with this?"

"I am," I replied without hesitation. "I want something different now. We both do. O'Reilly can have it. He's agreed to our terms, and you trust him."

"He has never been anything but up front. And he is forward-thinking. Like us, he wanted to break away from his father's way of doing things. He'll leave the hotels and casinos alone. He will not touch Niagara." We walked in silence for a moment. "But he has a request."

I chuckled dryly. "Of course he does."

"He wants Maple II."

"I'm not surprised. He was my toughest competition when they opened up the possibility of private casinos. He needs a place to clean his dirty money. The casino is the perfect spot."

"I know you've offered it to Aldo…" He trailed off.

"Who has turned it down."

Luca stopped walking. "What?"

I turned and faced him. "We had a long talk the other night. We had a fire outside under the stars. Nonna went to bed. Our wives fell asleep. We talked for hours. Aldo doesn't want the twenty-four seven life running the place would entail. Vi is pregnant. He wants to be part of his child's life. Vi no longer craves the city, and neither does he. He wants to stay on here with me. I gave him fifty percent of the Maple. I'll sell the Toronto one to O'Reilly. But he has to change the name."

"I'm sure he'd be agreeable to that."

"And sign a noncompete clause, not opening near our other businesses. He can open a whole string of his own, just not close to ours."

"Makes sense."

"I hear Santini folded up and ran like the coward he is. His crew is in shambles, and the entire city is out of balance. Tell O'Reilly to step in. Clean it up."

"I'm sure he'd appreciate the vote of confidence." Luca grabbed my elbow. "Roman, are you certain?"

"Luca, I wanted this life less than you did. Even with the changes. I want to be here more with Effie. With Aldo and me splitting responsibilities and going legit, and having the right men with us, we can all have what we want." I smirked. "Besides, with what O'Reilly is gonna pay me for Maple II, I think I can relax financially."

Luca laughed. "The next three generations of our families will never have to work, even before you sell."

"But hopefully, they will. Not hard like Effie or Vi did, but enough to learn the value of what we did. What we struggled to give them." I gripped his shoulder, meeting his gaze. "One day, I want to have a relationship with my kids. A good one. I don't want them to fear me the way we feared our father. I don't want to pit them against each other the way he did us. I want to earn the title of Dad. To have Father's Day and know I am doing the best job I can. I want us to be friends and brothers. Not care who knows that we're fond of each other." I shook his shoulder slightly. "I don't want to kill anymore. I'm tired of blood. Of the worry. The constant game. I just want to live. To love my wife. To be happy."

For a moment, he said nothing. Then he grinned. "Who the hell are you?" He dragged me into a bear hug, somehow managing to hug the right side harder and not hurt me too much. "Welcome to life, little brother. Let's do this."

"Great. Now let me go before you pop a stitch and Effie comes after you. She's tiny, but my little tiger is fierce. She will kick your ass."

He laughed and released me. He held up his hand to fist-bump me. "To life."

I met his fist with mine. "To life."

I found Effie in our bedroom, curled into her favorite spot. She had her head propped up on her hand, and she was looking out the window. I bent and pressed a kiss to her head.

"Luca gone already, my love?" she asked.

I adored it when she called me "my love." Her term of affection never failed to make me smile. "No, he is visiting Nonna in her suite. They are having tea."

"Good talk?"

"Yes. Everything is set." I told her about the upcoming meeting and our more personal conversation.

"You'll be a regular business tycoon."

I smirked. "I doubt I'll ever be that, Effie. But life will be a little more normal, I hope."

"Normal is okay?"

I frowned. "Normal is what I want." I leaned forward. "You eased something in me, Effie. Changed my outlook. My priorities and my needs. I don't feel the urge for violence. I've seen enough. Created enough." I paused. "Make no mistake, anyone who steps in and causes trouble for us, for my family, will be met with extreme consequences, but I think our stepping out of that world will give us that buffer. Luca and I have always been careful to cultivate friendly enemies, not give them cause to want us eliminated. I doubt a man running a hotel and a winery will give them a reason to bother. This was all done with the utmost respect and discretion."

She nodded. "So, life will change."

"It always changes. This time, I think, for the good." I smiled at her. "I look forward to all the good."

Effie tilted her head, studying me. "Life has changed so much the past while."

I chuckled. "All good changes." I paused. "Even the sad ones."

She shook her head. "I am not sad, especially knowing what I know now. It is done. Over." She shrugged. "Perhaps we are even. Her plans brought me to you."

"They did."

"And we survived it all."

I took Effie's hand and kissed it, pressing it to my face. "And we will leave it in the past."

She smiled, but I noticed the slight tremor to her hand. "Effie?" I asked. "What is it?"

"They wouldn't let me give you blood."

"You'd been shot as well. No doubt the doctor was worried over the trauma you'd been through. Too risky."

"That was what I thought at first."

I frowned. "At first?"

"Dr. Sims told me something else."

Worry hit me instantly, and I fell to my knees in front of her. "Effie? Tell me."

"I'm pregnant, Roman."

Her words hit me, rendering me speechless. Realization of what she'd gone through while pregnant tore through me, and my hand went to her stomach. "Are you—"

She covered my hand. "Everything is fine," she soothed. "Me and the baby."

Baby.

My baby. My wife was carrying my child.

Our child.

I was going to be a father. A dad.

Emotion swamped me. Tears filled my eyes as I looked at her. My beautiful wife.

"We'll be parents?"

"Yes. I missed a pill. I forgot——"

I cupped her face, kissing her. Her nose, cheeks, forehead, and sweet lips. I leaned my head on hers, letting her feel my joy. I didn't care about the how. It didn't matter. The only thing that did matter was the fact that we were having a baby.

"Thank you," I breathed out.

She giggled, the sound joyful. "Nonna wanted you to have babies. Now she'll have lots. Me, Vi, Justine."

"She'll burst when we tell her." I sat back on my heels, still holding her face. "When can we tell her?"

"Soon. It's early, Roman." She wiped a tear from my eye. "You're happy?"

"So happy, Little Tiger. The start of our family."

She eyed me speculatively. "We never really discussed this. How many kids do you want?"

I kissed her again. "As many as you'll give me. We have a big house."

She laughed. "This from the man who couldn't love."

"This from the man you taught to love, Effie. Everything I have, everything I am now, is because of you and your love. Your sweetness. You opened up that part of me."

I stood, then bent and scooped her up from the chair. "Let's celebrate."

She grinned, looking mischievous. "Should I ask how?"

I set her on the bed. "The same way we got here."

Then I lifted her shirt and pressed a kiss to her stomach. "Hello, little one. Shut your ears and eyes. Daddy needs to love Mommy."

Effie opened her arms. "They can't hear you yet, Roman."

I grinned. "Good thing. I plan on celebrating a lot."

She smiled against my mouth. "Okay."

The next morning, I couldn't stop smiling. I was up earlier than usual, beating Nonna into the kitchen. I had bacon cooking and coffee brewing. I couldn't handle much else with my healing injuries, but I managed those two tasks.

Nonna was surprised. "Roman. What are you doing in the kitchen?"

I laughed. I rarely ventured in, but this morning, it felt right. Effie had murmured about being hungry earlier when I woke her, loving her back into sleep. I wanted breakfast to be ready when she came out.

"Helping."

She looked around at the mess I had made. "I see."

I shrugged. "Trying."

She patted my cheek. "Good boy."

"Nonna, can you make Effie poached eggs? She loves those."

"Of course."

I puttered, getting juice, making toast, carrying the coffeepot outside to the patio, awkwardly setting the table. Effie came into the kitchen, smiling. "Do I smell bacon?"

Nonna laughed. "I saved it from being burned strips of cardboard."

Effie joined in her amusement and shook her head at me. "Roman."

They were both aware of my cooking limitations. Grilling was my forte. I only grinned. "I made the coffee." It was really the only other thing I could make aside from toast.

We sat at the table. I was famished. I polished off everything they didn't. The entire time, I touched Effie. Her hand. Her leg. I wiped her cheek when she got butter from her toast on it. I kissed her more than once. Nonna watched us, beaming. What happened had scared her terribly. We told her a semi-version of the truth, and she had been horrified that we'd been attacked. That Effie's sister was involved. She spared no sympathy for Marianne's death.

"Good. She cannot hurt you anymore," she murmured to Effie, hugging her hard. "We will not speak of her again."

And that was the end of that.

She had been pleased with the decision Luca and I had made, beaming at us. "My boys. Your mother would be so proud. As am I. Live your life and be at peace. You deserve it." She kissed our cheeks and walked away.

This morning, she was happy, relaxed. I was still on a high from my news and bursting to tell Nonna. But I knew Effie was hesitant since it was early. Still, I couldn't help but slip my hand under the table and place it over Effie's stomach, spreading my fingers wide, knowing our child was there. Effie met my eyes and smiled. I returned her happy expression, then picked up my coffee cup, meeting Nonna's wide gaze.

"What?" I asked.

She looked between us. "Roman," she breathed out. "You—" She stopped speaking, then looked at my wife "Effie, you are with child?"

I glanced at Effie, panicked. I had given it away. But Effie only smiled. "Yes, Nonna. Roman and I are expecting."

Nonna was speechless. Then the most extraordinary thing happened. Tears filled her eyes. They ran down her face, unheeded. I was shocked. Before Effie entered my life, I had never seen Nonna cry. Never once. When I told her we were to be married, she had shown emotion, and tears had glimmered. But this news had unlocked her tears fully. She stood, throwing open her arms. "Roman!"

I stood and held Nonna. She cried for a moment, then pulled back and cupped my face, her joy evident through her tears. "So happy! You will be a father!" She turned and hugged Effie, rocking her like a child, speaking fast in Italian, offering blessings and gratitude. She cupped Effie's face and kissed her forehead. "Such wonderful news."

"It's early, Nonna," I warned. "We aren't sharing the news just yet."

"No, but we must take good care of your little mama. A baby in the house. Oh, I have so much to do!" She turned and hurried away, talking to herself. I sat down and looked at Effie.

"She cried."

Effie nodded, also affected by Nonna's tears.

"I have never seen her cry until this past while. Not when my mother died, not when my father was horrible, never." I linked hands with my wife, staring down at her ring. I looked up, astonished. "But with you… You bring such emotions to us all, Effie. Such joy."

She smiled. "That is a beautiful thing to say, Roman."

"It's true. You are the brightest of lights, and you touch all of us." I brought her hand to my mouth. "Especially me."

"I love you," she whispered.

I leaned close and kissed her.

"I love you, Little Tiger. Always."

EPILOGUE - ROMAN

THREE AND A HALF YEARS LATER

The evening sky was a mixed canvas of yellows, pinks, and purples. The scent of flowers, grapes, and soil permeated the air. I sat at the table, looking across at Nonna. She was holding her favorite girl in the world. My daughter, Gemma Lynn, was snuggled in Nonna's arms, gazing up at her in fascination. Barely a month old, she was rarely out of someone's arms. Her birth had been fraught with peril, and for a short time, it appeared we would never get to have her, but thanks to the miracle of modern medicine and a fabulous doctor, she was with us, happy, healthy, and loved.

On my knees, my son turned to me, his eyes so like his mother's, confused. "Gemmy not talk much."

I laughed and ruffled his hair. "She will, my boy. Then you'll be begging me to tell her to be quiet."

He pursed his lips, which made me grin. He had Effie's eyes, but he was me. Right down to the stubbornness factor. That was what was keeping him up way past his bedtime, because there was going to be a fire tonight. Which meant marshmallows. His favorite thing. He would sit on my lap, and we would slowly spin the stick around until the marshmallow was puffed and golden. And then no matter how many times I told him to go slowly, he would stuff it into his mouth and yelp at the heat, then do it all over again.

Stubborn.

Just like me.

Effie made me a father. Nicholas Robert Costas made me a daddy. His birth unlocked the final piece of my heart. As a child, I had never known the joy of play. Of laughter. Once my mother died, my father ended that. Only when he was out of the house did laughter ring out. Yet underneath the rare times of happiness lay the awareness of how fleeting it was, so I never embraced it.

With Nicholas, it came in abundance. I loved everything to do with him. Feeding, changing, burping. Playing. Watching him grow. Everything he did fascinated me. When Effie told me she was pregnant again, my joy knew no bounds. The love I had for my children was all-consuming, never-ending, and without condition.

More than ever, I was grateful for walking away from the life I'd been forced to live. Told so often I had no choice that I believed it. Until Effie entered my life. Until I realized change *could* happen.

And I embraced it.

My wife came outside, carrying a tray. I began to get up, but she shook her head. "It is not heavy, Roman," she admonished me. "I'm fine. Stop worrying."

She sat down, the tray holding the treats for when the fire was ready. Nicholas eyed the tray, his little fingers already reaching. Effie smiled and handed him a marshmallow, pressing a kiss to his head. "Only one until we roast them."

"'K," he agreed happily, leaning back into my chest. I dropped a fast kiss to his head, running my hand over his dark curls.

"You look tired," I observed, speaking calmly. Whether she wanted it or not, I still worried over my wife. The birth of our daughter had almost cost me her as well. She lost a great deal of blood, and it took her a long time to recover. I wasn't sure she totally had, but she refused to admit her discomfort at times.

"A little," she admitted.

"How about a day in bed tomorrow? Nonna and I have the kids."

"How about we see how I feel?"

Nicholas lifted his marshmallow, pretending to offer me a bite. I, in turn, pretended I would take one, and he tore it away, laughing. I chuckled at his antics, Effie joining me.

"How about you both go out, leave the babies with me," Nonna suggested. "Have a picnic, some alone time."

I looked at Effie, seeing her hesitation along with her excitement at the idea.

"Perfect," I replied. "I'll arrange it. We'll leave after the bambini are down for their afternoon nap."

"Stay the night," Nonna hummed. "I can handle two little ones." She chuckled. "Connor will help."

Connor, the boy who once stole from me, was now a trusted assistant. He loved coming to the house and playing big brother. His sister was happy, still in med school, and making him proud. I paid for all her tuition as a thank-you for a job well done. Connor had a knack for problem-solving, and he handled a lot at the hotel and casino for Aldo and me.

"Good idea." I glanced at Effie. "Okay, Little Tiger? You want to spend some time alone with me?"

She smiled, the light reflecting in her eyes from the lanterns flickering around us. "Yes."

I winked. "Great."

I chuckled to myself as I typed a text to Connor. Alone time for us probably meant a nice early dinner and some snuggles. It was too soon after Gemma's birth, and until I had a vasectomy, I wasn't going to risk my wife. We had two healthy children, and above all else, Effie was safe. That was all that mattered to me. We had our family, and we were content.

Effie was, and would always be, the center of my universe. She brought joy and love to my life. She was the light that lifted the darkness and the person who made me whole.

So any time, be it quiet, loud, sleepy, or sexy, would be perfect with her.

She stood, stopping by my chair to drop a kiss on Nicholas's sticky cheek, then pressing her lips to mine. I cupped the back of her head, keeping her close and kissing her back.

"I love you," I murmured.

She winked. "I know."

Nicholas laughed. "Momma tiss Dada and me."

I kissed his cheek, stealing a bite of gooey marshmallow. I laughed at his affronted face.

"Dada," he admonished, then looked at his marshmallow as if it was now tainted. "New one."

I handed him one, plucking the offending one from his fingers and popping it into my mouth. He sat back with a sigh, nibbling at the soft treat.

Effie returned, taking Gemma from Nonna, then sitting down beside me on the settee. I wrapped my arm around her, not talking but enjoying the rare moment of quiet and togetherness. I had them all in my embrace.

My family.

My world.

Life couldn't be any better.

OUTTAKE - ROMAN

Midafternoon, I pulled up to the house with a frown. There were a lot of cars here, including Aldo's. He had disappeared earlier, saying he had a project to help with, and I hadn't heard from him since. Effie hadn't answered my calls, and Nonna informed me she was "very busy" when I checked with her.

What the hell was going on?

I went inside, instantly smelling the aroma of sugar and baking. I headed to the kitchen, stopping at the sight before me.

Aldo, Nonna, Vi, and two of the guards were at the table, bent over, working on something. Effie, pregnant with our son, was waddling around, talking, and busy with her hands. She was so tiny that at six months, she looked as if she might give birth at any moment. I loved how she looked, round and glowing with our son. I had no idea how she was going to last almost three more months, though the doctor insisted she was fine. But he did tell her to take it easy.

This didn't look like easy to me.

I inhaled again, the scent of cookies hanging thick in the air.

I cleared my throat. Heads snapped up, and Effie stopped what she was doing, looking guilty.

"What is going on?" I asked, crossing my arms. "Effie, I think—*in fact*, I know—the doctor said rest. This doesn't look like rest to me."

I walked in, stopping as I looked at the table. It was covered in cookies. The counters were full of trays of baked cookies, and the island held ones that were, I assumed, complete. I picked up one, recognizing the sunflower shape Effie used to include in her orders. I met her wide gaze, shaking my head. "Explain, Little Tiger."

Aldo stood. "Five-minute break."

Everyone shuffled out of the kitchen, Vi purposely bumping into me. "We got this handled, Warrior. Let us finish."

She was due any day now. I lifted my eyebrow. "Shouldn't you be off giving birth?"

"His daughter refuses to come out," she informed me, side-eyeing Aldo.

"She gets induced in two days," Aldo replied, taking her elbow. "Unless we can get her to come on her own."

"And baking masses of cookies was the plan?"

"It was until you showed up."

Aldo tugged her away, and I looked at Effie. "Is there a reason our kitchen is full of cookies?" I frowned. "Is this more nesting?"

Effie had been doing odd things lately. Changing furniture. Cleaning drawers. Stocking up on towels and blankets as if we were facing Armageddon and she wanted to be warm and clean. Cooking at all hours. The freezer was full, yet she kept going.

She shuffled over and gripped my arm to sit down. As she did, her tummy rolled like a tidal wave, and I put my hand over the swell, bending to kiss the little hand or foot that was restless. "Hello, little man." Our son always moved when he heard me.

I glanced up at my wife with a bemused smile. "What's going on?"

"Bagels and Bites always donated cookies to a fundraiser. Margi phoned to remind me that they had called her and asked if I would still do it this year. I had promised already, so I said yes. I used to donate ten dozen. I had promised twenty this year. I couldn't make and decorate them all myself, so I called in reinforcements."

"But you didn't ask me."

"Um, Roman, you are terrible in the kitchen."

That was true.

"I could have sent help."

She shook her head. "I have my own. You can go back to work," Effie assured me. "We'll be done in a few hours."

"No, I want to help."

"Um…" she said. "Really?"

"Yes. You can show me, and I will do it as well. Then you are going to bed—"

I didn't finish my sentence as Vi came in, interrupting me. "And Aldo can take me home and fuck this baby out of me."

Effie laughed, and I shook my head. "TMI, Vi."

She shrugged. "Effie understands."

Effie nodded in agreement but still looked unsure about my participation in the cookie group.

"Effie," I replied. "I run a multimillion-dollar business I built from the ground up. Surely decorating a cookie can't be that hard. I simply require a little practice." I looked around the table, picking up one. "So, you're baking, they are icing?"

"Yes. All the cookies are baked and cooling now."

I stood, shucking off my jacket. "I think I can handle that. If Aldo and the *men*"—I lifted an eyebrow in admonishment—"can ice a cookie, I am certain I can."

"Oh. Well, it was quiet, and there are still lots of guards around. Joey and Blaine have experience working in a bakery," she replied sheepishly.

Nonna and the men walked in, and I rolled up my sleeves. "Let's get this done."

Effie gave me a cookie and showed me how to ice it. "Like this," she explained. The cookies already had a layer of yellow frosting she and Nonna had put on. Using the bag in her hand, she quickly outlined the petals. She added a finishing little flourish between the petals, tapped a premade center in place and held it up. A pretty little sunflower. "Just keep your hand steady."

I bent over the cookie and copied what she had done. Or attempted to. The icing didn't seem to flow as well for me, so I applied more pressure and a large glop shot out and landed on the cookie. I tried to wipe it off, and it smeared everything. "Dammit," I muttered.

Aldo looked up. "Ease up on the icing bag. You need to concentrate, Roman. Become the flower."

"Become the flower?" I snorted. "Listen to you."

Effie put another cookie in front of me. The edge was broken. "Practice with that," she encouraged, showing me again how to pipe the line.

I concentrated, copying her movements. It went better, and I thought it looked decent. I added the middle and then the flourishes. "Got it!"

Effie looked over my shoulder, patting it. "Um…"

Vi peered at the cookie and began to laugh. "That looks like 'I run a multimillion-dollar business' man has been drinking at his desk before noon."

I compared it to Aldo's, then the others on the completed tray in the middle of the table. Everyone else seemed to be able to do it. Theirs looked fine. Mine looked as if a child had done it—badly.

I took another one, determined. I went slowly, certain this one was perfect.

It wasn't.

And in twenty minutes, I had finished two. Two cookies that could not be used.

Effie looked at my cookies. "Maybe running the hotel is more your forte, my love."

I wanted to agree with her, but I wanted to help her even more. "Show me again."

With a huff, I picked up another one. She put her hand over mine and helped me draw the petals. It was much better. I did the flourish on my own, feeling smug, then added the center. It wasn't perfect, but it was better. I put it on the rack to set and picked up another one. I glanced at Aldo, frowning. He looked way too comfortable, his cookies almost textbook. I bent and concentrated, slowly getting faster and more proficient.

"Looks good," I said triumphantly as Effie gave me a new batch.

Aldo shook his head. "Not as good as mine."

"Wanna make a little bet?"

He rolled his shoulders. "You're on."

"Oh boy," Vi sighed.

"Whoever ices more, wins."

"Looks count, boys," Effie warned us.

I sniffed. "They'll be perfection."

Joey and Blaine got up. "We need to return to the gate."

"Thanks for your help," Effie said with a smile.

"Anytime, Mrs. Costas."

She gave them some cookies as thanks. I tried not to notice most of them were mine. I recognized the art to my flourishes.

Nonna stood. "I am going for a nap. I will help with the final steps later."

I stood and kissed her cheek. She smiled, patting mine, then headed to her suite.

Effie put out the final four dozen and stood back. "Careful, please."

I locked eyes with Aldo. "May the best man win."

Vi snorted. "Hope you have spare cookies. These two and their ridiculous bets."

"You need to leave the room, Effie, so you can judge it fairly."

For a moment, she stared, then she shook her head. "I won't watch."

"Fine."

Vi joined Effie at the counter. "Go," she shouted.

I bent over my task, working as efficiently as I could. Piping the petals, adding the flourish, tapping the center into the middle—or as close to the middle as I seemed to be able to manage.

But Aldo was faster. Cleaner. Far neater.

His looked good. Mine looked as if a drunkard had attempted to ice them and had given up.

Which I was ready to do.

"I fold."

Aldo looked up, shocked. "What?"

I laughed, picking up a cookie. "Picasso. These look like Picasso was in the kitchen. You win."

Effie sat beside me, cupping my cheek, and kissing me. "You have much better talents with your hands," she murmured against my lips.

I grinned. She wanted me all the time. Maybe coming home was an even better idea than I thought.

"Leave," I said to Aldo. "Take your wife home. She wants Anna out. Today. *Do your job*."

Effie laughed, and Vi was already gripping the table to heave out of her chair. Apparently with the right incentive, it could still be accomplished without Aldo lifting her.

She grabbed Aldo's hand, and he laughed, willingly dragged from the kitchen to his fate.

I looked at the cookies sitting everywhere. "What else has to happen?"

"I'll finish icing these. Then I'll package them all once the icing sets."

"Surely to God I can help with that part."

She nodded, picking up a cookie and efficiently finishing it in about a minute.

"I'll grill dinner and load the dishwasher," I offered, slowly finishing another cookie. She did four or five to my one, but it was something. The truth was I liked being beside her.

She glanced up from another cookie, her eyes looking amused. "Okay."

"What?" I asked.

"Could you have foreseen the day you would be sitting in the kitchen with your pregnant wife, icing cookies? Offering to load the dishwasher?"

I picked up the cookie with the broken edge and bit into it. The sweet, dense cookie was rich and soft on my tongue.

"No," I said honestly. "But I wouldn't want a different scenario."

"Really?" She sounded delighted.

"Effie," I began. "I would rather be with you doing anything you wanted to do than be anywhere else in the world. Or with anyone else. Icing cookies, walking in the vineyard, sitting in the sun." I leaned forward and touched her cheek. "Wherever you are is my favorite place to be."

She stopped, mid-cookie. "Oh."

The sound was filled with wonder.

I smiled. "Finish your cookies. Then I'm going to remind you how good I am with my hands, Mrs. Costas. Twice."

"I like the sound of that."

Unable to resist anymore, I bent close and kissed her. "I like you."

I picked up the icing bag, smiling at the pink on her cheeks. I loved being able to make her blush with my simple words and gestures.

My Effie. My wife.

I liked everything about her.

Except maybe these damn cookies.

But for her, I would ice them.

Picasso art or not.

For her, I would do anything.

ACKNOWLEDGMENTS

As usual, a few thanks.

Lisa, thanks for your wise guidance. And embracing my love of misplaced commas. I know you enjoy the challenge.

Beth, thank you for your support and insights. You always make my words better.

Melissa, Trina, and Deb, thank you for your encouragement, laughter, and support.

Sisters Get Lit.erary Services, thank you for your eagle eyes and assistance. So appreciated!

Karen—another one complete. Who knew what would happen that day I asked you to read a little book I had written called The Contract? I had no idea I had began a journey or a friendship that would last a lifetime. I am in constant awe of you. Thank you for everything.

Atlee and girl George—for all the things you do behind the scenes to help Karen and me—thank you so much!

My hype team—you rock and motivate me constantly.

To all the bloggers, readers, and my promo team. Thank you for everything you do. Shouting your love of books—of my work, posting, sharing—your recommendations keep my TBR list full, and the support you have shown me is deeply appreciated.

My reader group, Melanie's Minions—love you all.

MLM—for all you do I cannot say thank you enough. I wish I could hug you all. Maybe one day.

And my Matthew. The man I can't live without—who encourages me daily and loves me in a way that inspires my words. I love you.

ABOUT THE AUTHOR

NYT/WSJ/USAT international bestselling author Melanie Moreland, lives a happy and content life in a quiet area of Ontario with her beloved husband of thirty-plus years and their rescue cat, Amber. Nothing means more to her than her friends and family, and she cherishes every moment spent with them.

While seriously addicted to coffee, and highly challenged with all things computer-related and technical, she relishes baking, cooking, and trying new recipes for people to sample. She loves to throw dinner parties, and enjoys traveling, here and abroad, but finds coming home is always the best part of any trip.

Melanie loves stories, especially paired with a good wine, and enjoys skydiving (free falling over a fleck of dust) extreme snowboarding (falling down stairs) and piloting her own helicopter (tripping over her own feet.) She's learned happily ever afters, even bumpy ones, are all in how you tell the story.

Melanie is represented by Flavia Viotti at Bookcase Literary Agency. For any questions regarding subsidiary or translation rights please contact her at flavia@bookcaseagency.com

- facebook.com/authormoreland
- x.com/morelandmelanie
- instagram.com/morelandmelanie
- bookbub.com/authors/melanie-moreland
- amazon.com/Melanie-Moreland/author/B00GV6LB00
- goodreads.com/Melanie_Moreland
- tiktok.com/@melaniemoreland
- threads.net/@morelandmelanie

ALSO AVAILABLE FROM MORELAND BOOKS

Titles published under M. Moreland

Insta-Spark Collection

It Started with a Kiss

Christmas Sugar

An Instant Connection

An Unexpected Gift

Harvest of Love

An Unexpected Chance

Following Maggie

The Wish List

Titles published under Melanie Moreland

The Contract Series

The Contract (Contract #1)

The Baby Clause (Contract Novella)

The Amendment (Contract #3)

The Addendum (Contract #4)

Vested Interest Series

BAM - The Beginning (Prequel)

Bentley (Vested Interest #1)

Aiden (Vested Interest #2)

Maddox (Vested Interest #3)

Reid (Vested Interest #4)

Van (Vested Interest #5)

Halton (Vested Interest #6)

Sandy (Vested Interest #7)

Vested Interest/ABC Crossover

A Merry Vested Wedding

ABC Corp Series

My Saving Grace (Vested Interest: ABC Corp #1)

Finding Ronan's Heart (Vested Interest: ABC Corp #2)

Loved By Liam (Vested Interest: ABC Corp #3)

Age of Ava (Vested Interest: ABC Corp #4)

Sunshine & Sammy (Vested Interest: ABC Corp #5)

Unscripted With Mila (Vested Interest: ABC Corp #6)

Men of Hidden Justice

The Boss

Second-In-Command

The Commander

The Watcher

The Specialist

Men of the Falls

Aldo

Roman

Reynolds Restorations

Revved to the Maxx

Breaking The Speed Limit

Shifting Gears

Under The Radar

Full Throttle

Full 360

Mission Cove

The Summer of Us

Standalones

Into the Storm

Beneath the Scars

Over the Fence

The Image of You

Changing Roles

Happily Ever After Collection

Heart Strings

My Favorite Kidnapper

Made in United States
Orlando, FL
07 March 2024

44514520R00259